Black President Collection
Season 2, Episodes 1-3

Black President Collection
Season 2, Episodes 1-3

Brenda Hampton
Entertainment

Brenda Hampton Entertainment
P.O. Box 773
Bridgeton, MO 63044

Black President: Season 2, Episodes 1-3
Copyright © 2018 Brenda Hampton

Printed in the United States of America

This is a work of fiction. Any references or similarities to actual events, real people, living or dead, or to real locales are intended to give the novel a sense of reality. Any similarity in other names, characters, places, and incidents is entirely coincidental.

ISBN 13: 978-1986818360
ISBN 10: 1986818365

Black President: Shake Up in the White House
Season 2, Episode 1

President of the United States, Stephen C. Jefferson

"Mr. President," my chief of staff, Andrew, shouted. "There has been an explosion! It occurred at the hotel where the first lady is residing. There have been reports that many people were killed. The whole area is a mess, and I . . . I don't know when we'll be able to—"

Andrew paused as he saw me slowly back away from my son, Joshua. I wanted to just fall to the floor and die. This couldn't be happening right now, and as my heart rate increased, I felt myself about to lose it. All eyes were on me, but before I reacted to the devastating news, I fixed my eyes on the door. There stood Raynetta with scratches, bruises, blood and ashes all over her face and trembling body. Her clothes were ripped, hair was completely disheveled. Tears poured down her face, and as the entire room fell completely silent, we stared at each other without one single blink. Thank God she was alive.

"Stepheeeeeen," Raynetta cried out and rushed into my arms. I held her tight without saying a word. I could feel her heartbeat racing against mine. Relieved to see that she was okay, I closed my eyes to savor the moment.

"I'm glad you're okay." I opened my eyes and could see my mother staring at me. She was still choked up about me seeing my son for the first time. Then again, maybe she was glad to see Raynetta just as much as I was.

"Mr. President," Andrew said, interrupting my thoughts. "What are we going to do about the explosion at the hotel? There is a chance that the first lady was being targeted."

The thought hadn't even crossed my mind. I pulled Raynetta away from me and looked into her weary eyes.

"Go upstairs to the Executive Residence now. Clean yourself up and I'll be there as soon as I can. Whatever you do, do not leave the White House, alright?"

She slowly nodded, and before she left, I asked Secret Service to escort her to the Executive Residence and keep an eye on her.

With Joshua, my mother and Andrew still in the Oval Office with me, I stood with my mind racing a mile a minute. I stroked the fine hair on my chin and unbuttoned the top button on my powered blue crisp shirt that was sticking to my sweaty skin. I could feel sweat beads forming on my forehead. My eyes were watered; this was, indeed, too much. I didn't know what to do about the betrayal of Ina, Joshua's mother, and Levi, the only friend I'd trusted. Nor could I figure out what steps to take with Joshua. He stood in shock after finding out I was his father and appeared frozen while watching me. The news of me, president of the United States, being his father, obviously hadn't sunk in. I knew he wanted answers, but with so much on my mind, I didn't know where to start. I had much to deal with, and the news about the explosion definitely came at the wrong time. After my press secretary, Sam, along with the Director of National Intelligence entered the Oval Office, I had to quickly stabilize this situation and weigh my priorities.

I looked at my mother who stood defensively with her arms folded across her chest. "Handle your business," she said to me. "After all, you are the president. We'll be upstairs in the Yellow Room waiting for you."

I nodded, then addressed Joshua. Seeing him caused the lump in my throat to stay lodged there. I was so happy to see him, yet so sad it had come at a time like this.

"I know this is a lot to process right now," I said to him. "But please go with your grandmother and allow me to take care of a few things. I would like to explain to you why all of this has happened. So please be patient with me."

"I will," he said with a scrunched up face. "But where is my mother? Is she on her way here too?"

"Probably so," my mother said, walking up to him. "But let's go do what your father said. We'll get something to eat and relax upstairs."

Joshua released a deep sigh. He took one last puzzling glance at me, before leaving the Oval Office with my mother. After they left, Andrew invited Vice President Bass to come in, along with my National Security Advisor, Victor Dixon. Based on the information he'd had, he confirmed that the suicide bomber was born in America and resided here. There was no question that this country had made a lot of enemies, and a magnitude of the unfortunate legislation the prior administration had put in place caused the number of enemies in and outside of our country to increase. It appeared the bomber had acted alone, but more information had to be obtained before we could come to a final conclusion regarding his actions.

"He's dead," Victor confirmed. "The FBI is still at his apartment collecting evidence. We should know more soon."

"I hope so," VP Bass said. "This is ridiculous. I don't know what we can really do to stop this kind of craziness from happening. I thought we were already doing enough."

"We can never do enough," Andrew said. "Some idiots will always slip through the cracks. That's a simple fact."

My head was spinning. I was sure that the second I opened my mouth and offered my opinion, VP Bass would have something stupid to say. Right now though, I wasn't in the mood. I needed to make sure Raynetta was okay and I wanted to have a serious conversation with Joshua, before Ina showed up. I had a feeling she wasn't too far behind, and I needed to make some phone calls to stop her and Levi at the airport.

I looked around the spinning room, feeling so out of it. Maybe this was my breaking point. Everyone had one. I had to go sit on the sofa before I fainted. I rubbed my hands over my waves and scratched my head. "I have to make a confession, and it's unfortunate that it has to come at a time like this. I need to step back for a few weeks and get things in order with my family. I'm feeling so overwhelmed. I feel as if I can't function like I need to, until I put a few things to rest. In my absence, VP Bass I would appreciate if you would step in and handle things for me."

Everyone stood stunned while looking at me. They didn't seem to understand why I needed to step away for a while, but when I mentioned some of the specifics relating to Joshua's fake death, everything became clearer.

"Take all the time you need," Andrew said, patting my back. "I'll cover for you, and I'm sure everyone else will too."

VP Bass was the only one who wasn't in conjunction with the plan. "I don't know what you mean when you say cover for him, because I won't cover for anyone. I'm not going to deceive the American people, and if the president can't handle his responsibilities, then maybe he should consider resigning."

I took a deep breath and bit my tongue so I wouldn't have to disrespect her. Maybe I needed to make myself clearer, but I didn't want to do so with everyone else in the room. In a very polite tone, I asked everyone to exit the Oval Office, with the exception of VP Bass.

"Are you sure you don't need me to stay?" Andrew asked. "Just in case things get a little out of hand."

"I predict that things won't get out of hand," I said, smiling as I looked at VP Bass. "The vice president will be more than happy to honor my request, especially since it is her responsibility to pick up the pieces in my brief absence. So, please, do as I asked. We'll speak in greater details about what transpired at the hotel, and I need a meeting set up with the FBI within the hour. In the meantime, Sam, I need you to prepare a statement about today's incident and release it to the public. Let everyone know we're on top of this, and be sure to include my condolences to the individuals who lost family and friends."

Sam nodded while VP Bass pouted. She was ready to bark at me, but she managed to hold it all in until everyone exited the Oval Office.

"Mr. President, I don't care—"

I cleared my throat to cut her off. I invited her to have a seat on the sofa across from me.

"Please," I said. "Take a load off and let me explain again why I need you to step up and do your job."

Like a spoiled brat, she marched over to the sofa and plopped down. Her white skin, cheeks in particular, were rosy red, and the flower-printed dress she wore was too tight for her wide hips and pancake shaped ass. She and I just couldn't get along. Maybe because she was a Republican and I was a Democrat.

She darted her finger at me and spoke in a sharp tone. "I have no problem doing my job, sir, and I always do my job. It's obviously that you're trying to get out of doing yours, without informing the American people. Let me remind you that you took an Oath of Office and you have to play by the rules around here. If you're going to step away for a while, then I suggest you hold a press conference and be truthful about why you can't handle the job you were hired to do."

I stretched my arms on top of the sofa and tapped my shiny loafers on the floor. While gazing at VP Bass's awful pink lipstick that was smudged on her teeth, my look was stern.

"I'm not going to tell the American people anything else about my personal business, and neither are you. If I have to make them aware of *all* my personal business, then we'll have to start putting *all* your personal business out there too. I don't think you want to journey down that path, do you?"

She was quick to answer. "I don't mind if the American people know my business, Mr. President. I live an amazing, wonderful life that is guided by the Heavenly Father. I'm proud to be a conservative woman, and in case you didn't know, my reputation is quite stellar."

I nodded and damn near wanted to throw up from listening to her lies. "The truth is, your reputation is not as stellar as you claim. And as president of the United States, understand that I am privy to a substantial amount of information you may not know about. I can order people to keep their eyes on things for me, and, yes, I can request wiretapping or have your actions recorded without you ever knowing it. That tad bit of information stays between us, and I'm slightly disappointed that you don't know who has the real power around here."

"You may be privy to certain things, but let me inform you that wiretapping and recording people without legal authority is against the law. And if you do so, you will find yourself spending the rest of your presidency behind bars."

I had to laugh; the shit was funny to me. If none of my predecessors hadn't gone to jail for some of the outrageous things they'd done, surely she didn't believe I would go to jail for exposing her for who she really was. I crossed my leg over the other and hurried to wrap this up so I could go tend to my family.

"You're a bigger fool than I thought, but with you in place while I take some time away to get things in order, it won't be the first time a fool will occupy the Oval Office. As you sit at the Resolute desk to do what you're required to do, I want you to know that I always cover my tracks well. You will never be able to trace anything back to me, not even if or when I have to release videos and recordings of you with the dicks of two well-known and very married senators in your mouth. I've been keeping this little information to myself for quite some time, but if you want me to let the American people hear all those," I paused for a moment to chuckle. "Well, those X-rated conversations on your cell phone, I will. That way the American people can see and hear just how conservative and Godly you really are."

With embarrassment washed across her beet-red face, VP Bass sat with her mouth wide open. No words escaped. For the first time she didn't have much else to say. I stood and continued to look at her with a smirk on my face.

"Close your mouth because I have no plans to shove my dick in there too. It won't fit so I don't want to waste your time. See you in two or maybe three weeks. If my time away will be longer, I'll be sure to let you know."

I strutted toward the door and reminded her to turn down the lights on her way out. To no surprise, she didn't respond.

After I left the Oval Office, I made my way upstairs to the Yellow Room. No one was there, but I found my mother and Joshua outside on the Truman Balcony. Joshua was sitting in a chair next to my mother. Two Secret Service agents stood nearby. I didn't want them to eavesdrop on our conversation, so I asked them for some privacy.

"No problem, Mr. President," Lenny said. "We'll be inside if you need us."

After they went inside, I looked at Joshua who still had a look of bewilderment on his face. He moved his head from side-to-side. Tears were trapped in his eyes.

"Can you please come over here and pinch me. I feel like I'm in a dream," he said. "I . . . I'm so confused, and nothing my grandmother has said to me makes sense. Being here doesn't make sense. How can you be my father and I didn't know about you for all these years?"

I made my way over to a chair and sat next to him. Before I said anything to Joshua, I looked at my mother who sat with her fingertips pressed against her forehead. She appeared stressed, and I had rarely seen her beautiful gray hair out of place. Even her designer clothes were wrinkled, and without makeup on, I could see dark spots underneath her eyes. I wanted to get into her shit for what she'd done, but I directed my attention to Joshua instead.

"This is no dream, son, and I'm so sorry that you didn't know about me sooner. There are numerous people who should be held accountable for this tragedy, including your grandmother who not only lied to you, but she lied to me as well."

"I didn't lie to you," my mother snapped and tried to correct me. "I just didn't tell you—"

"Please keep your mouth closed until I'm done speaking to my son. You may not consider it a lie, but I view it as a big lie that has caused irreversible damage. I'm not letting you off the hook, mother, but I do appreciate you for bringing Joshua here. I'm not going to lie to him about all that has happened, and he will know about the role you and Ina played in this. If you don't like what I'm going to say, then I suggest you leave right now. If you decide to stay, please do not interrupt me again."

With an attitude, she whispered something underneath her breath and sat back in the chair to let me know she wasn't going anywhere. I turned to Joshua who remained in a daze.

"The last thing I want to do is come between you and your mother," I said. "But after you hear what I have to say, and you find out the reprehensible things she did for money, I'll let you decide how you wish to move forward in your life. I'm not going to force you to make any adjustments because of me. But I would love to get to know you better and spend as much time with you as I can."

Joshua swallowed hard. He started fidgeting with his hands. "Grandma started to tell me some of the things that happened, but I can't believe my mother would tell everyone I was dead, just for money. There has to be more to this. I'd love to hear from you how we got here."

Revealing as much as I could, I told Joshua certain details from the beginning of my relationship with Ina. About him supposedly being radicalized . . . to his fake funeral. Told him the real reason he was in Mexico . . . to the love I once had for Ina who had gotten pregnant and didn't tell me because, yet again, my mother had offered her money. This time, however, Mr. McNeil offered Ina money that she hoped would enhance her life in a major way. She didn't even think about the damage it would do to Joshua, and even though I mentioned her betrayal, he still wanted to hear it straight from the horse's mouth.

A tear rolled down his face; he smacked it away. "I can't believe she would do something like that. I'm having a hard time believing that you kept this secret, too, Grandma. Please tell me all of this isn't true."

My mother had a hard time admitting she was wrong, but she did. "It is true, Joshua, and I'm so very sorry. If I could go back and do things differently, I would. Lord knows I would, but I can't. I can only apologize to both of you for making one of the biggest mistakes of my life."

Yet again, I didn't know whether to accept my mother's apology or not. She was so manipulative, and, at times, I didn't know if I should believe her. She saw the blank expression on my face, but instead of addressing me, she kept her focus on Joshua. He didn't seem convinced by her words either, so she moved closer to hug him.

"Please don't be upset with me, sweetheart. I love you and I just . . . just made a mistake. Can you forgive me, please?"

Joshua didn't say a word. He wrapped his arms around her. Another tear fell from his eye, and he backed away while looking into her eyes.

"I want to see my mother now. Where is she?" he asked. "You said she would be here."

I touched Joshua's kneecap and squeezed it. "We're going to see her tonight, I promise. All of us will talk, and I expect her to tell you the truth. As I make arrangements for that to happen, I want you to stay right here and work this out with your grandmother. At the end of the day, she loves you and so do I. We both want what's best for you, but there is no question that we all have to come clean in order for us to move forward."

14

Joshua agreed. I reached out to give him a hug, he held me back as well.

"I need to go check on my wife. I'm sure she's been waiting for me, and I apologize for all of this chaos that has . . ."

He backed away from me. "No problem. Go do what you have to do. Just make sure my mother comes here soon."

Ina wouldn't be coming here, but she would definitely see us tonight. I couldn't stop thinking about her and Levi's betrayal, and as I made my way to the master bedroom, I took deep breaths to calm myself. There was a knot in the pit of my stomach. With so much anger inside of me, I predicted that things would soon take a turn for the worse. In no way could I allow them to get away with what they'd done. Before the day was over, there would be hell to pay for sure.

I went into the bedroom and saw Raynetta standing by the window while looking outside. She had on a cotton robe, white house shoes and her long hair was dripping wet. She must've just gotten out of the shower. Her eyes were red, face was pale. She scanned me from head to toe, before rushing into my arms once again. I embraced her as she snuggled against my chest.

"I was so afraid," she said softly. "I didn't know if I was going to make it out of there to see you again. Seeing those dead bodies just did something to me. I've never seen anything so horrific. Everybody thought they were going to die. Lord knows I didn't want to die."

I rubbed Raynetta's back, trying to calm her trembling body. "I know it was scary, and I regret that you were there. You should've never been there, and I'm glad you're okay. I don't know what I would've done if something had happened to you. Please accept my apologies for asking you to leave the White House. It was one of the worst things I could've ever requested."

Raynetta released her arms from around me. She moved back to the edge of the bed and sat down. With curiosity in her eyes, she looked to me for answers.

"What now, Stephen?" she asked. "Where do we go? I saw Joshua and your mother, and I'm so lost because I thought he was dead."

Yet again, I took a moment to explain how and why Joshua was still alive. Raynetta couldn't believe what Ina had done, nor could she believe Levi had betrayed me. The whole time I spoke, she covered her mouth with her hand while sitting in disbelief.

"No, Stephen, no Levi didn't. After all the years he's known you, he resorted to this?"

"Money can make people do some crazy things. When it pertains to millions, you can get a whole lot of people to stab you in the back."

"I get that, but what are you going to do? I know you, Stephen. This is not going to be good."

"It's not, but I don't want to go into details tonight. I need to have a quick meeting with the FBI, and then I need to put certain things to rest with Joshua and Ina. After that, I need to get away from here to process a few things in my head. I'm in no condition to be here right now, and I'm starting to feel like I just . . . just want to hurt somebody. It's best that I step away for a while. After I get my head on straight, I'll come back and the two of us can talk more about this thing we keep referring to as a marriage. I hate to sound harsh about it, but you already know we have some serious problems. I don't know if we can fix this, and to be truthful, I'm getting tired of trying."

Raynetta looked down at the floor and sighed. There was pure silence, before she spoke up.

"I guess what this really means is you're leaving here to go be with Michelle Peoples. I can't believe you're still involved with her, but I guess I shouldn't be surprised."

Just that fast, her assumption set me off and caused me to raise my voice at her. "See, this is what I'm talking about. I tell you I need some space to figure out some things and you automatically assume it has something to do with me wanting to spend time with another woman. The shit I'm dealing with is bigger than Michelle Peoples. If I was going to see her, I would tell you. I'm not, and if it makes you feel any better, Michelle and I are no more. My mother was paying her to pursue me, and I . . ."

Raynetta rolled her eyes and lifted her hand. "Say no more, please. Your mother is such a—a, I don't know what to call her. I will never, ever like that woman. You go ahead and take all the time you need to decide what you think we should do about us. I'm going to do the same, and I'll be doing most of my thinking right here. I don't want to leave, and I feel safe with Secret Service around. Wherever you go, just make sure I can reach you. I need to hear from you, so promise me that you'll call me every day, until you come back. I wish you would let me go with you, but if you prefer to be alone, what can I do?"

"I do prefer that, but I promise not to be gone for long. VP Bass is going to take over in my absence. I will make sure you have access to Secret Service, but please do not stay cooped up in this room. We hide from no one, okay? Go for some walks, stay busy and continue your duties as the first lady. The people in America love you and many of them want to see that you're okay."

"I don't know if I'll feel up to doing anything. And I know I won't be able to get any rest because I have a horrible feeling inside that you're going to do something to Levi and put your life at risk. I know you're upset, but you're not living in St. Louis anymore. That street mentality should have dissipated years ago, Stephen. After all, you are now president of the United States."

"Before I am president, I am a man with feelings. I've been hurt, Raynetta, especially by the people who often claim to have my damn back. With that, I will say no more. I'll give you a call to let you know where I will be. Be sure to have your phone close, so you don't miss my calls."

Disappointment was written all over Raynetta's face, but I wasn't about to change my mind. There was too much going on, and I didn't want her involved. Before I left, I had to make sure Secret Service wouldn't fuck up and let her out of their sight.

"I doubt that I can change your mind, and what else can I do but have my phone on me and wait for you to call? Either that or I'll get a call from someone one day, telling me you're dead because you still haven't learned how to let go when it comes to situations like this. I know you feel betrayed by many people, including me. But doing what you're about to do isn't the answer. If anything, you need to think about the future. About our future, and what's going to happen to Joshua if whatever plan you have backfires on you? I don't think you're thinking clearly right now."

I moved closer to the bed and reached out to lift Raynetta's chin. Her light brown eyes were like magnets and they always tugged at my heart. I moved her hair away from her face that had a bruise on it. My thoughts shifted to the explosion—if I'd told her the details about it, she wouldn't understand. Instead, I leaned in to plant a soft kiss on her lips. She wanted more, and as she leaned back on the bed, I backed away from her. "I can't," was all I said, before making my way to the door and closing it behind me. I heard her call after me, but when my mind was made up about something, it was hard to change it. Levi would pay for what he'd done for sure. I just wasn't sure how I would deal with Ina yet.

President's Mother,
Teresa Jefferson

I didn't know what was taking Stephen so long, but nearly two hours had passed, after he'd left the Truman Balcony. Joshua and I continued our conversation on the upper level in the Solarium. I had given him a brief tour of the White House and tried my best to get on his good side. It seemed like he had forgiven me. I wasn't sure if that would change, once we were face-to-face with Ina. I didn't want to see that heifer again. If she said the wrong thing tonight, I would make her pay for everything. I wasn't even sure how Stephen was going to get in touch with her. She sure as heck wasn't answering her phone. Joshua had already called, at least, four or five times, trying to reach her. I suspected that she and Levi were probably on their way back to the states from Mexico. I wasn't sure about her boyfriend, Theo, especially since I'd had to shoot his dick off. Thoughts of that little incident made me laugh, but when Stephen entered the Solarium and told us it was time to go, this was no laughing matter. I stood, so did Joshua.

"Where are we going?" I questioned. "Did you get in touch with Ina yet?"

"Yes," Stephen said. "She's waiting on us."

With Secret Service leading the way, we all followed. Stephen was whispering back and forth with General Stiles. She was a brave black woman, and I could sense that she was attracted to Stephen by the way she always gazed into his eyes when he spoke to her. She had on camouflage from head to toe with black army boots. Her body was packed with muscles, and her short layered hair was covered with a cap. With beautiful mocha chocolate skin, I would say she was Stephen's type. Then again, who in the hell wasn't? Every woman he'd dated was better than the trophy wife he'd had, but for the sake of his well-being, I was glad Raynetta was okay.

As we continued to walk behind Stephen and General Stiles, I wasn't sure what they were discussing. I figured it had something to do with the explosion at the hotel. It also could've had something to do with Ina and Levi. I was sure Stephen was eager to get this mess over with pertaining to Ina. She was about to get an earful.

After we got into the president's vehicle, The Beast, Stephen looked at Joshua who sat silent while looking out the window at the rain. It was pouring down, but we couldn't hear anything outside of the heavily secured vehicle. A few other Secret Service agents were parked beside us in black Suburbans. They signaled when it was time for The Beast to proceed, and seconds later, we were headed to our destination.

"Did you and your grandmother have an opportunity to talk more?" Stephen asked Joshua.

He looked in Stephen's direction to respond. "Yes, we did. But I need to speak to my mother. She hasn't been answering her phone. I hope she's okay."

"She's fine," Stephen confirmed. "She's at a hotel waiting for us. We should be there soon."

Joshua nodded and kept examining Stephen, as if he'd had a million and one questions for him. "I . . . I still can't believe you're my father," he said. "I kept asking my mother if I could go see my father in jail, if she would show me a picture of him, and I even asked if there was a chance I could speak to him by phone. She kept saying no. Now I know why, but I don't understand how people who say they love you can keep a secret like this for so many years."

Joshua had taken another jab at me. Maybe he hadn't forgiven me like I'd thought. I couldn't really read him, and it didn't help when Stephen started with his insults too.

"It was a very stupid plan," Stephen said to Joshua. "I'm not happy about it either and maybe there is something Ina can say, to both of us, that'll help us understand why she chose to listen to my mother in the first place." Stephen glanced at me, but I turned my head in another direction. "Shame on them both, but what's done is done. We can't go back and undo things, but an explanation for all of this is needed."

Joshua agreed. While him and Stephen made small talk about some of the things they enjoyed doing, I sat in silence and listened. I remained calm during the whole drive, but as soon as we arrived at the hotel and I saw Ina's face, something horrible came over me. With tears streaming down her face, she rushed up to Joshua and embraced him as if he had been away from her for years.

"You need to cut the damn act," I said, walking into the spacious living room area. "There are no cameras here, and if you really cared about Joshua, you never would have hooked up with Levi and fabricated a lie about Joshua being dead."

Ina pulled away from Joshua and directed her attention to me. She smacked away a few fake tears before lashing out. "Go to hell, Teresa! What I did was try to make a better life for me and my son. You wouldn't know anything about that, would you? For as long as I can remember, you've always injected yourself in Stephen's business, tried to run his life and call the shots! If it wasn't for you, I wouldn't have ever kept Joshua and Stephen apart!"

See, I knew this trick was going to blame me for her mess. I rolled up the sleeves on my jacket and removed my diamond watch so I wouldn't lose it when I swung on her. As I stepped forward, so did she. I gritted my teeth as I reached out and tried to snatch that heifer up by her hair. Unfortunately, Stephen grabbed my hand and yelled for me to go have a seat.

"I'm not doing this tonight, Mama," he shouted. "Go sit down, chill out and act like you have some sense. Can you do that for me? If not, Secret Service can escort you out of here."

Mad as hell, I barked back with a tight face. "Secret Service is not going to escort me any damn where. And you need to lower your tone when speaking to me. I'm upset about all of this, and how dare you allow this bitch to blame me for the mess she created!"

"Calm down, Grandma, and stop the name calling," Joshua said with a frown on his face. He looked at me, then at Ina. "Is all of this true? Did you really tell everyone I was dead, when I was in Mexico? Is that why you wanted to move there? And why didn't you tell me the president, Stephen Jefferson, was my father? You told me my father was a criminal in jail. Was the money you received really worth all the lies?"

Ina's mouth opened, but she didn't say anything.

"Speak up, bitch," I said. "We're all waiting to hear how you're going to spin this. If you start with me again, I'm letting you know now we gon' have some problems. You will leave here with one eye, trust me."

Stephen shot me a devious glare so I moseyed over to the sofa and finally sat down. He asked Secret Service and General Stiles to step into the hallway until we got finished talking.

"I'll check on that other thing for you, Mr. President," General Stiles said. "I should know something by the time you're done in here."

"Thank you." Stephen opened the door for them to exit. After they left, he closed the door and looked at Ina who was still standing with her mouth open, looking silly.

"No words can express how disappointed I am in you for doing what you did," Stephen said to her. "You are so lucky that you're still alive, and to be honest, Ina, if you weren't Joshua's mother you would be dead right now. While you may think you don't owe us an explanation, you do. You owe me one, as well as

Joshua. It's not that my opinion about any of this will change, but at least I can get an understanding about why you made a decision to let not only my mother use you, but Mr. McNeil use you too."

Ina swallowed and reached for Joshua's hand. She walked him over to the sofa where they both sat. After she wiped her teary eyes, she looked at Joshua who appeared to be waiting for answers. Stephen remained standing with his arms folded across his chest.

"I made a mistake," she said to Joshua. "I messed up and I thought I was doing the right thing when your grandmother came to me, asking that I not tell Stephen I was pregnant."

I had heard enough. She wasn't going to put this all on me, and since I meant what I'd said about her leaving here with one eye, I snatched off my heel and hurled it right at her damn face. My heel hit the left side of her head, and in total disbelief, she jumped up from her seat. As she rushed toward me, Joshua stood between the two of us.

"Really, Grandma," he said with a mean mug on his face. "You are out of control!"

"You're darn right she is, and she's lucky that shoe didn't hurt," Ina replied.

I was waiting for Stephen to say something, but he didn't say one word. I guess he approved of my move.

"If it didn't hurt," I said. "You would have stayed on that couch and continued with your lies. It's time for you to keep my name out of your mouth, because I already told Joshua why I didn't want Stephen to know he'd had a son. I'll happily tell him again." My eyes shifted to Joshua and I held up my fingers to count down. "One, your mother was unfit. Two, your other grandmother was a crack addict and, three, Ina's father, your grown-ass grandfather, was in St. Louis robbing and carjacking folks. Stephen had gotten away from all that mess. He went to college and I didn't want him involved with such a reckless family like your mother's. He would not be president today had he hung around being her baby's daddy. She didn't have a plan, and she happily took my money, the cars I purchased for her over the years and the house. So don't get this twisted, and do not let her fake tears fool you."

Ina's eyes fired daggers at me. She backed up to take a seat again and so did Joshua. "Is that the best you can do, Teresa? Really? Your run down of what happened changes every month. But when all is said and done, the majority of this is still your fault."

"No, when all is said and done, don't make me pull off my other shoe and drill my foot in that big butt of yours. Keep lying to yourself, okay? I think Joshua and Stephen already know better. They're still waiting on you to take responsibility for this mess and do it now!"

"Just keep at it," Stephen said. "We'll wait until the two of you are done. I'm sure this has been a long time coming."

Ina cut her big round eyes at me and looked at Joshua again. "I do take responsibility for my lies, and all I can say is I'm sorry. I thought money was the answers, and when I got pregnant with you, things weren't looking up for me. I just couldn't give up on my baby, and when your grandmother agreed to help take care of us, I accepted her offer. When Mr. McNeil offered me millions of dollars to say you were involved in a terrorist act, I didn't think it would cause this much harm. I figured I could pretend you were dead and finally move away from St. Louis for good. I wanted us to have a fresh start. Away from everything that was going on in St. Louis, and I could finally rid myself of your grandmother who had been trying to control my life for years." She reached over and stroked the waves in the back of Joshua's head. He looked so much like Stephen, and even with glasses on, Joshua was, indeed, his child. "I was miserable, sweetheart. So miserable and I wanted out. I knew you didn't like living in St.

Louis, and you always planned to move elsewhere, after you graduated, right?"

"Not to Mexico," he said then moved her hand away from his head. "I can understand you being miserable while you were pregnant, but you chose money over me. Did you ever think that I needed to know who my father really was? And what about school, my friends and my reputation? You were okay with people thinking I was a terrorist? Not only can't I go back to St. Louis, but I can never live in the states again without people recognizing my face or accusing me of doing something I didn't do. If I'm supposed to be dead, where am I going to live, mother? Whatever you say, please don't say Mexico because I'm not going there ever again."

"You don't have to. We can go somewhere else. Anywhere you want to go we'll go. I just want a peaceful life, without anyone trying to control it. I want you to be happy and I want you to forgive me for what I've done. I promise to make it all up to you, okay? You can finish school elsewhere and we can start all over."

This trick was trying to drive a wedge between me and my grandson. Not only that, but between him and Stephen as well. He moved closer and spoke up before I did.

"So, now you're going to sit there and talk him into leaving this country with you. What about me, Ina? Your plan is to shut me the hell out, as if me being his father doesn't even matter."

"It does matter," she snapped back. "But I don't know how to fix this, Stephen. It's too late. I can sit here all day apologizing to you and you still will feel the way you do. You'll keep blaming me for all of this, and you will overlook the person who started this crap."

Her eyes shifted to me. Lord knows I wanted to punch her in the face.

"I know who's responsible," Stephen said in my defense. "That person would be you. You made choices that benefited you, and now you're sitting there with your selfish ass, trying to convey to Joshua what you think is best for him. I'm stunned, but none of this should really surprise me one bit."

Ina pounded her leg with her fist. "Stop making me out to be something that I'm not! When you get finished belittling me, I'm still a decent mother. I love my son and I'm going to do what is in his best interest going forward. The only way we can get past this is to move on and start over somewhere else. We need to be far away from here, and that's what I was trying to do when we went to Mexico."

"Bitch, please," I was visibly irritated by her nonsense. "Stop your lying, Ina. You were running around on the beach in a thong, sipping Bahama Mamas with your man and that lying fool Levi. If that's what you call starting over, forget it. Joshua can stay right here in Washington with us. We'll manage to work out this big problem you created, even if we have to change his name." I pivoted in my seat to look at Stephen. "Right, Stephen. Would something like that work?"

"Of course it would. But that's not going to be my choice or yours. Joshua has to decide what's best for him now."

All eyes were on Joshua. He took a deep breath, then stood and shook his head. "I . . . I don't know what to do. I need some fresh air right now. I can't even think straight."

"That's fine," Stephen said. "I'll have Secret Service take you to a park or somewhere else where you can sit back for a while and think about what you want to do. Come back when you're ready and let us know what you decide. Your mother and I need to talk in private anyway. There are some things I would like to say to her that I don't want you to hear."

I surely wanted to hear what Stephen had to say, but he ordered me to leave too. I stood with a twisted face and walked to the door behind Joshua.

"Joshua," Ina said, wiping her fake tears again. "You don't have to go anywhere if you don't want to. You can go out on the balcony to get some fresh air, and as far as I'm concerned, I'm done talking to Stephen and his mother."

The look in Stephen's eyes ripped Ina to shreds, but Joshua saved this situation from getting out of hand. "I'm okay, mother. I just need to get out of here for, at least, an hour. I'll be back."

"We'll be back," I added. "And when we come back, she'd better be singing a new tune."

I wasn't sure if Ina would be singing a new tune or not, but from the look on Stephen's face, I only wished I could be a fly on the wall.

President of the United States, Stephen C. Jefferson

I wasn't up for any bullshit, especially since I still had to go deal with Levi before the night was over. I was already tired. This had been a long day. The last thing I wanted to hear from Ina was how she intended to move away and keep my son from me again. Yes, the choice would ultimately be his, but I felt like Ina was trying to sway him to follow her lead. That didn't sit right with me, and instead of displaying more anger in front of Joshua, I waited until he and my mother were gone. Now, I could deal with Ina how I intended to. I removed my suit jacket and tossed it on the sofa. And as I started to unbutton my shirt, Ina sat looking at me. Underneath my shirt was a white wife beater that revealed much definition in my arms. I cocked my tense neck from side-to-side, before tossing the shirt on the sofa too.

"Stephen," Ina said, keeping her eyes locked with mine. "I can tell by the look in your eyes that you came here seeking trouble. It's bad enough you had your henchmen meet me at the airport and bring me here against my will. I don't want to be here, and as soon as Joshua returns, we're leaving. "

I stepped forward and took menacing steps in her direction. She stood up. I could see her chest rise and fall. She appeared frightened by the devious gaze in my eyes.

"Stop looking at me like that," she said, backing away from the sofa. Before she got too far, I reached for her arm and pulled her in my direction. My grip on her arm was so tight that she squinted.

"Ooouch," she moaned. "You're hurting me, Stephen. Let go of my arm."

"I haven't hurt you yet, but I most certainly will if you do or say one more stupid thing that . . ."

Before I could finish my sentence, Ina reached up and slapped her hand across my face. My head jerked to the side; reflexes acted accordingly. I twisted her arm behind her back and quickly shoved her on the sofa. As she lay on her stomach, I pressed her face on the pillow and thought about suffocating her. I continued to twist her arm and couldn't understand a word she'd said because her words were muffled.

"What's that?" I asked with my knee pressed into the spine of her back. "Yeah, I know. This hurts, doesn't it, Ina? It really hurts and you want me to release you, right?"

I yanked her head back, lifting it so she could speak and catch her breath. She sucked in several deep breaths as more tears streamed down her face. "I . . . I can't breathe," she struggled to say. "Helllp meeee."

I pressed her face on the pillow again and held it there to muffle her screams. "You don't need help. What you need is a good ass kicking to make up for everything you did to me. I wish you weren't Joshua's mother. If you weren't, I would blow your brains out right now for hooking up with my enemy and allowing him to use you. Mr. McNeil saw a fool like you a mile away. He knew he could talk you into doing what you did, and trust me when I say I have no respect or love, none whatsoever, for a woman who could be as foolish as you are. You fucked up, Ina. Real bad and something has to be done for your fuck ups."

This time, I yanked her head back and pulled her off the sofa. Her arm was still twisted behind her back, and as I inched her toward the sliding doors to the balcony, her heavy breathing and cries continued. She tried to wiggle herself away from my grip, but with her head being pulled back, breaking my grip was hard for her to do.

"You . . . you're going to regret this!" She warned, as I dragged her to the balcony doors. She lifted her foot and kicked the glass, trying to break it. To get her to stop, I twisted her arm tighter. She yelped out in pain. "Nooo, Stephen! You need to stop this, nowww!"

Her words went in one ear, out the other. I released her head and slid the sliding door to the side. It was pouring down raining outside, and the gusty wind was pretty strong. I shoved her outside, and since the balcony was so slippery, she immediately fell on her ass. Her hair was flat on her head from the rain and smudged mascara ran down her face.

"What do you want from me?" she shouted. Her whole body shook as she yelled. I didn't bother to answer, but as I moved forward she rushed up and backed against the railing. She was right where I wanted her, and as I'd thought about flipping her ass over the rail, I thought about Joshua. I could make it look like she was so upset that she committed suicide, but I wasn't sure if he would believe me.

With rain pouring on me as well, I stood directly in front of Ina. There was no breathing room between us and I felt how fast her heart was beating. She moved her head from side-to-side. Her eyes were wide and showed much fear.

"I know you're not going to do this. Our son needs me! This balcony is twenty-six floors up, Stephen, and . . . and Joshua will never forgive you. You'd better think long and hard before you do something stupid."

I sucked my teeth while gazing at her. And when my hand clamped around her neck, her eyes got wider. She clawed at my hands with her long nails and made deep scratches that tore at my skin.

"Is that all you got?" I asked while leaning her back and making her fight to stay on the tips of her toes. A gargling sound came from her mouth as she tried to speak. I could hear an apology somewhere in there.

"Sorry my ass, Ina." I leaned her back some more. This time, her feet were off the balcony and she was trying to wrap them around me so she wouldn't fall. Her arms weakened and her scratches didn't even hurt anymore. At this point, all she could do was plead her case through her watery eyes that kept fluttering. The rain was beating on her face too, and when I released her neck to grab her legs, she started kicking and screaming wildly.

"No, my God, please no, Stephen! Put me down!"

My heart raced too as I struggled to grab her legs while holding on to her shirt at the same time. When one of her legs dropped, she lifted it to kick my knee. With the balcony being so wet, I slipped and almost fell. That was when she lifted her foot again and punted me in the groin. The kick caused me to back away from her and soothe my sacks with my hand. I squinted from the pain, but as Ina darted by me to rush back inside, I stuck out my foot and made her fall flat on her face. She crawled inside and quickly rolled on her back. By that time, I was already on top of her, pinning her to the floor by holding her shoulders down. She squirmed to get from underneath me, but her efforts had failed.

"If you want to exit," I said, lifting her from the floor and tossing her over my shoulder. "You need to exit from the balcony, not the door."

She kicked and screamed as I carried her back outside on the balcony. Her fists pounded against my back, and this time, I sat her on top of the rail. To prevent herself from falling, she threw her arms around my neck, squeezing it tight.

"If I go over, bastard, I'm taking you with me! So go ahead and push me, Stephen! Do it!"

Her grip around my neck was so tight that I couldn't pry my head away. Maybe a gut punch would send her backwards, but I didn't want to go there just yet. I leaned her back, and with every inch in her direction, she took me with her. She pulled on my wife beater, and it wasn't long before she ripped it from my back. I was now in my slacks and leather shoes that were slippery as fuck. Rage was in my eyes, and as I finally pried my head from her tight grip, I had her exactly where I wanted her. All I had to do was release her arms and it was fucking goodbye to Ina. Dying this way surely wasn't in her plan, and while staring at each other, we breathed heavily as rain ran down our faces.

"Please," she cried out. "I'm sorry, okay? Sorry for all of this, Stephen, and I regret what I did to you. I just wanted a fresh new start for our son. He's all I have, and if you kill me, you will destroy him!"

I winced as I looked at her. Couldn't think of anyone else that I despised more than her right now, other than Mr. McNeil. Then again, there was also Levi. The list in my head kept growing, and that made me release her other arm. As she fell back, I quickly grabbed her collar and pulled her face-to-face with me.

"I hate you," I spewed through gritted teeth. "And I'm willing to lose my son again, just so I never have to see your fucking face again."

Ina closed her eyes and sobbed like a baby. I pulled her away from the rail and shoved her back inside again. She dropped to her knees and covered her face with her hands.

"I hate you too, Mr. President!" she screamed and pounded the floor. "Damn you, Stephen, damn you!"

I walked away from her, and when I picked up my shirt to wipe down my wet face, she charged at me with something in her hand. I didn't realize what it was, until she hit me on the side of my face with it. It was a small crystal bowl that left me feeling dazed. I staggered back, but as I reached out to grab her, my vision was slightly blurred. She pushed me back, and when she hit me with the bowl again, we went at it. I was able to snatch the bowl from her hand and put her in a headlock. As I squeezed her head, she raised her fist to strike me wherever she could.

"You're not the only one from the hood," she barked. "I can fight back too!"

"I don't give a damn where you're from, nor do I care that you're a woman. If you act like a wild animal, you'll be treated like one!"

I lifted her high and slammed her on the coffee table next to the sofa. The legs on the table weren't strong enough to hold her, so the table crashed to the floor. As she held her back, I rushed in to finish what I started. By that time, Ina had snatched one of the broken legs from the table. She held it like a bat while daring me to come closer.

"This is going to hurt, Stephen. Back away from me now!"

I was willing to muster the pain, just to get at her again. And as I moved in, she struck me in the leg and made my knee buckle. It wasn't enough to damage me, so I grabbed her leg and dragged her across the floor.

"You will never be in Joshua's life, not if I can help it," she said. "Not you or your crazy ass mother! You both are crazy, and if you think I'm anything like Raynetta, you are sadly mistaken!"

To respond to her foolishness, I released her leg and fell over her. As I was face-to-face with her again, she caught me off guard and slammed her fist into my mouth, drawing the first blood. I licked the inside of my bloody mouth and growled as I banged her head on the floor, over and over again. I witnessed her eyes rolling in circles. She was dizzy and hurt, but not hurt enough. I wanted her to bleed too, so I leaned in and bit the shit out of her earlobe. She was in so much pain that she grabbed her ear and released an eardrum busting scream at the top of her lungs.

"Fuuuuuuuuck, aaaaaaaahhhhhh!"

Feeling satisfied, I rolled to my left and laid flat on my back. My chest heaved in and out as I stared at the high ceiling. Ina's cries echoed in the background. I crawled away from her, and as I sat against the wall with blood dripping down my chin, I watched her sway back and forth on the floor.

"Come over here and finish me off," she said. "You can't hurt me, Stephen. Nothing you can do to me will hurt me!"

"Well, you look pretty damn hurt to me. And shut the hell up talking to me, before I take you out there on that balcony again."

With blood pooling down the side of her neck, she made her way over to the back of the sofa and sat against it. That was when I noticed the big knot on the side of her head. I hated that a part of me felt bad about what I'd done to her. I didn't intend for things to go this far, but I couldn't let her get away with what she had done to me.

"Look at you, Mr. President," she teased. "You ain't shit! Nothing, Stephen, and you're not even man enough to come over here and finish me off."

For whatever reason, she was trying to provoke me. I spit a gob of blood from my mouth, before responding to her. "If I wanted to finish you off, I would have. Be sure to thank your son for saving your life."

"Whatever, coward. You're all talk and no action."

I looked at her with a smirk on my face. My arms were crossed against my chest and one leg was over the other. "I'll be whatever you want me to be, Ina. I'll also be a father to Joshua, whether you like it or not."

She laughed as she removed her shirt to wipe blood from her ear, neck and fingers. All she had on now was a white bra and a pair of jeans. "How can you be a father and you don't even know how to be a husband? You're also failing as president, and it's just a matter of time before you'll be impeached. All your crooked mess is going to catch up with you, and when you get what you deserve, I'm going to be somewhere jumping for joy."

I clapped my hands and continued to keep a smile on my face as we hurled insults back and forth at each other.

"I could be a good father and a good husband, if I hadn't messed around with a money hungry, low-life trick like you. A mother who did what you did to our son shouldn't even consider herself a mother. All you are is a tramp with a kid."

She fired back, calling me every name in the book. I did the same.

"And you have the audacity to be our president. The American people got suckered last time, but this time takes the cake."

"Before I am president, I am a man who will not put up with your shit and who will come over there and fuck you up, if you don't stop talking to me. One more word, Ina, and you're going to get your wish."

She didn't dare say another word. All we did was continue to stare at each other, until my mother and Joshua returned. Almost immediately, Joshua rushed to Ina's side. My mother and Secret Service rushed to mine.

"Are you okay, sir?" Lenny asked with concern in his eyes as he squatted next to me.

My mother pushed him aside while displaying a frown on her face. "What in the hell went on here? What did she do to you?"

"I'm fine," I said, pushing her away. "We just, uh, had a long and overdue *talk*."

Joshua's face was twisted as he helped Ina off the floor. All of a sudden, she was in so much pain that she could barely stand. Her tears were back and she held her stomach while crouched over.

"Do you need a doctor, mother?" he asked. "What happened and what did he do to you?"

My mother cocked her head back and was blunt with her reply. "I hope he beat her ass. That's what he should have done, and please tell me she did not put her hands on you."

She saw my lip bleeding and plenty of flesh revealing scratches on my hands. Scratches were probably on my face too. And with my shirt off, it looked as if I'd been street fighting. There was no question who had *won* the fight, and we both looked worse than what it really was.

"Grandmother," Joshua said. "Stop it. Can't you see my mother is hurt? She needs a doctor. Somebody needs to take her to the emergency room."

My mother snapped back. "Grandson, your mother can go to hell. Can't you see my son is hurt, and if he's severely hurt, she will need a doctor after I get finished with her."

Seeing that things were about to get more out of hand, I was already on my feet. "Let's go," I said to Lenny and my mother. I wiped my hand down my sweaty and wet face and sighed. "Ina and Joshua need to leave too," I said to Lenny. "Please take them to wherever they want to go."

"Joshua isn't going anywhere with her," my mother said. "Tell your father what we discussed on the way here."

Joshua looked at Ina who was still holding her stomach like she was in pain. "I . . . I know what we discussed," he said. "But I changed my mind. I don't want to stay here. I want to go with my mother. We all will never get along, and this is too much. I can't believe you did this to her. No woman deserves to be treated this way."

I looked at Joshua and had to bite my tongue. There was no way for me to defend my actions. I could say that Ina came after me first and that her tears were fake, but that would do me no good. He was on his mother's team and that was obvious.

"Whatever you decide to do is fine with me," I said then swallowed. "I already told you I will make no decisions for you, but please know everything that happened here tonight is not what it seems."

"Joshua, you need to listen to us," my mother said. "Going anywhere with your mother is a big mistake. All she's going to do is use you and . . ."

"Let it go, Grandmother," Joshua said, raising his voice. "I've already heard enough about what she's done. But staying here with you won't make things any better. We need to go and go soon."

Ina smiled and threw her arms around Joshua. "Thank you, sweetheart. I love you so much and you're right. We need to get out of here. Go far away, just you and me, and be done with all of this."

I could already see this was a battle I wasn't going to win. And instead of putting Joshua on the spot, I walked around my mother who was still trying to convince him to change his mind. After I grabbed my shirt and jacket, I tossed them over my shoulder and made my way to the door.

"Stephen, where in the hell are you going?" my mother yelled. "Don't you dare walk out and leave him here with this witch. Aren't you going to do something?"

I stopped near the door to look at her, then Ina. "You two have already done enough. Whenever Joshua wants to talk, he has my private number to reach me."

I opened the door and walked out. After I got on the elevator, I told Lenny again to take Joshua and Ina wherever they wanted to go, and the other agent to take my mother back to the White House. As for General Stiles, she and I had other plans.

Thirty minutes later, General Stiles had driven me to the underground bunker where she had taken Levi to. I couldn't help but to thank her for honoring my request to bring him here. She'd already told me Levi had put up a good fight at the airport and he refused to follow her command. Because he'd refused to cooperate, she had to Taser him just to get him inside of the car. After she handcuffed him, she mentioned that another scuffle had taken place. I didn't realize how bad it was, until I stood in front of Levi in the cold room surrounded by nothing but concrete walls. One of his eyes was swollen shut. Dried blood was on a cut above his bushy brow and his shirt was off. His big belly sat on his lap as he was positioned in a metal chair with his hands cuffed behind him.

"So," he said, licking across his dry lips. "This is how it's going down, huh? After all I've done for you, including saving your life, and you don't even want to hear my side of the story. You'd rather sick your Pitbull on me and let that slick mouth bitch do this to me. Come on, man. Really?"

As General Stiles stood silent behind me, I removed a chair from the corner and put it right in front of Levi. I straddled it backwards and held out my hands.

"Of course I'm going to give you a chance to explain yourself. I mean, what are friends for, Levi? I will never forget all that you've done for me, and I'm never going to forget what you didn't do either. So, let's hear it. Of all people, why did you have to betray me?"

Levi looked down and shook his head. "Man, look. It wasn't my intentions to betray you. I was ready to ride this shit out with you. But then Ina got at me. Said Mr. McNeil was willing to up the kind of paper I ain't never had in my hands. I listened to what the old man had to say, and as long as his plan didn't revolve around killing you, I didn't see no harm in it. I was just supposed to help Ina set this thing up with Joshua, and, eventually, disappear. The goal was to make you feel under pressure. You know, kind of stress you the hell out so you would resign and put the Republicans back in full control. All of this shit ain't worth it, man, and you couldn't be serious about trying to run this damn racist country. I know you want out. It was my way of helping you get out sooner. If you consider that as betraying you, I guess I did."

I sat silent for a few seconds, thinking about what Levi had said. He had me fucked up. It was apparent that he didn't know me as well as he thought he did.

"Anything else," I said with narrow eyes as I zoned in on the center of his wrinkled forehead.

Levi cleared his clogged throat. "Nah, not really. I just want you to know how sorry I am, and I hope like hell that our friendship don't have to end like this. From the looks of those scratches on your face and your fat lip, I guess you must've . . ."

"Yeah, I was in a fight earlier." I touched my swollen lip and thought about Ina. "But if you think I look bad, you should see her. And since I already had one fight today, consider yourself lucky because I'm not in the mood to fight again."

I turned in the chair to look at General Stiles. "How many people know about this little incident, or should I say how many people know we're down here?"

She moved closer to me and patted my shoulder. "Just you, me and Levi, Mr. President. That's it."

"Are you sure?" I wanted confirmation. "Don't lie. You know I don't like liars."

She laughed and looked me dead in my eyes. "I can confirm it, sir. Just you, him and me know. No one else."

I raised my hand and she slapped a 9mm in it. Tears streamed down Levi's face, sweat beads covered his body, and spit flew from his mouth as he yelled at me. "Stephen, it's me, man! Levi! This country don't give a fuck about you! Why you keep trying to save people who don't give a shit about you! Let the Republicans have this shit and get your black ass outta the Oval Office! All they want you to do is clean up their mess. You know the last election was rigged so you could come in and do Massa's work for him. That orange muthafuckah made a mess, and you need to turn the keys back over to those messy fuckers! Tell me, man. How many times we gotta step in and clean up their mess for them? The last black president did it and at look how they treated him. Like shit and they gon' do you the same way too. They don't want you there, and no matter what you do, you're still a nigger in all of their eyes! All of them!"

Offering no reply, I fired a bullet into the center of Levi's forehead. The chair flew back and hit the floor. A pool of blood ran from his head, and without an ounce of regret, I swung around to look at General Stiles.

"Please get someone who won't ask you any questions to help you clean this up," I said. "I'm leaving and I won't forget that I owe you one."

I slapped the gun back into her hand. She looked at it and smiled. "No, Mr. President, you owe me several. And I'm coming to get what I want real soon."

I didn't reply to her comment either. Just walked out of the room and made my way down the long, narrow hallway. My mind was all over the place. This was the first murder I'd committed on American soil, since I became president. I hoped there wouldn't be more—I was trying hard not to be the reckless young man I used to be while living in St. Louis. Memories of those days flashed before me, and for a split second I thought about Levi. I felt everything he'd said, and, yes, there was proof that the election process was rigged. But since I was the *chosen one*, they were now stuck with me. I intended to do things my way, and I wasn't going to let racist motherfuckers stop me from accomplishing the things I needed to do. I didn't care if they liked me or not, and unlike the last black president, I wasn't going to sugarcoat shit. Yeah, some people would say that a president needed to have the right temperament and be above pettiness, but disrespecting me and my family wasn't considered petty. It was personal, and I had to prepare myself to take some of the people who didn't want me in the White House head on.

I neared the exit door; my thoughts switched to Joshua. Never in my wildest dream could I have imagined the day I'd met him would turn out like this one. I still had so many things I wanted to talk to him about, but that conversation wouldn't take place tonight. I was exhausted. I didn't know if I was going back to the White House tonight or not. The one thing I was sure of was I needed a long hot shower and a comfortable bed to lie in. My body was aching, feelings were quite bruised. I needed to be by myself, so instead of getting back into the vehicle General Stiles and I came in, I decided to walk around for a while. Normally, at a time like this Michelle would've been a good person to converse with. But since I'd found out she'd been doing some foul crap behind my back with my mother, I had no desire to speak to her. She hadn't called, ever since the day I'd confronted her about knowing my mother. I guess she knew that reaching out to me again would be a big mistake.

I made my way through the barbed wire fence without anyone seeing me. And as I proceeded to walk down a curvy, two-lane road, only a few cars passed me. I spotted a small gas station on the corner, and with no cars parked outside, I went inside to get something to drink. At first, the Asian man kept squinting and watching me to see if was going to steal something. I guess my messy, blood stained slouchy clothes alerted him, as well as my fat lip and scratches. But when I made my way to the counter and asked for a bottle of gin, he slapped his hand over his mouth.

"Oh my, you, uh, aren't you the president?"

"No," I said without hesitating. "Everyone thinks I look like him."

The man scratched his head and kept looking at me. He reached for a bottle of gin from behind the counter, then scanned it on the register. Unfortunately, I didn't have any cash on me to pay, so I had to give him a credit card. He looked at my name, smiled and then he gave the card back to me.

"The gin is on me," he said. "A big thank you for stopping by, and while you're here, would you mind taking a picture with me? I go get my cell phone."

I was in no mood for pictures, nor did I want anyone else to see me like this. "Not tonight. When I'm feeling much better I'll come back to take some pictures and have a drink with you. Meanwhile, I need a ride somewhere. How fast can I get a taxi?"

"For you, Mr. President, I will close my store and take you where you need to go. Just tell me where, okay?"

I didn't want him to close up, but I needed a ride back to the White House. It was almost midnight, and after I downed a few swigs of gin, I knew I'd need a comfortable bed.

"Thank you," I said. "I would appreciate that very much."

The man rushed to close his business, and just as he was locking the door, a man in a truck pulled up to get gas. The Asian man told the man unless he was paying outside with a credit card, he wouldn't be able to get gas.

"Fuuuuck," the Caucasian young man shouted. "I'm on empty and I can't make it to another gas station. Come on, man, what's the deal?"

"The deal is I'm leaving," the Asian man said. "I have to take my good friend somewhere."

"Well, can't your fucking friend wait a few minutes so I can pay for my gas? I have twenty bucks in my pocket and I need to get some gas now."

I moved closer to the light so the man could see who I was. He looked at me and staggered backwards. I could tell he was drunk from the way his voice slurred. He slowly lifted his finger and pointed at me.

"Are—are you who I think you are?" His whole demeanor changed and a smile appeared on his freckled face. "I mean, this is so freaking cool. Your friend is the president? Like, how cool is that?"

"Real cool," I said, making my way over to his truck. He followed. I slid my credit card into the slot to pay for his gas.

"This is so freaking unreal," he said, laughing. "Nobody is going to believe this shit. Is it okay for me to snap a photo of you, or is like Secret Service going to pop out of nowhere and like kick my ass if I do?"

"Instead of taking a picture, why don't you come over here and pump your gas? I don't mind paying, but I'm not going to pump too."

He laughed. "Yeah, right, okay man. Thanks again, and just so you know, this is like . . . like one of the highlights of my life."

I shook his hand, and when the Asian man parked next to the man's truck, I got in the backseat.

"Don't you want your receipt," the Caucasian man said, before I shut the door.

"I chose not to get one. Be safe and no more drinking and driving tonight."

The man saluted me as I closed the door. The Asian man drove off, and as I popped the cap on the bottle of gin, he looked at me through the rearview mirror.

"Where to, Mr. President?" he asked. "And just so you know, this is a highlight of my life too. I feel like I'm dreaming. I can't believe you're actually sitting in the back of my vehicle."

All day, I'd felt so worthless. It felt good to hear such kind words. I thanked the man for saying them. I then took a swig of the alcohol and frowned from the taste. It wasn't long before I screwed the cap back on and laid the bottle on the seat. Drinking definitely wasn't for me—it never had been, especially after I witnessed what alcohol had done to my mother.

"Take me to the White House," I said. "Drive slow and turn on some music if you don't mind."

I laid my head back and closed my eyes. The Asian man cranked up the volume on a bullshit song I'd never heard. He kept talking to me, but I'd tuned him out. My thoughts were still on all that had happened today. I hoped that Joshua called me soon. I needed to hear from him.

"Mr. President, where would you like for me to let you out at? I can only get so close to the White House, you know."

"You can let me out near the security checkpoint. Not too close, because I don't want anyone to see you. And just in case I forget, thanks again."

"No problem. I've totally enjoyed this, even though we haven't talked much. I guess you have a lot on your mind. The explosion that happened at the hotel was horrible. It's a shame those people had to lose their lives over a stupid idiot with issues."

I just nodded and kept my eyes closed. It was a shame—all of it was.

Minutes later, the Asian man pulled over to a curb that was a few feet away from the White House security checkpoint. From a distance, I could see several reporters outside and a bunch of media vans. I assumed chaos was about to erupt, especially since I had slipped away from the press who often covered my every move. I took a deep breath and thanked the Asian man again. Before I exited the car, I allowed him to snap a photo with me. In his opinion, being in my presence was the best.

"Thank you, Mr. President. I can't wait to show my wife and kids. May I have your autograph too? You can put it on the bottle of gin, if you're not going to finish it."

"I'm not going to finish it, but I don't think it would be wise for me to put my signature on a bottle of gin."

He laughed, and instead of putting my signature on the bottle, I scribbled my signature on his leather headrest. He didn't appear upset, just smiled as I did it. After that, I exited the car and made my way toward the checkpoint gates. As he passed by me, he honked the horn and sped off. I buttoned my suit jacket, and with my hands in my pockets, I casually walked toward the gates. One reporter spotted me and it was all over with. As he rushed my way, so did the others.

"Mr. President, we thought you had been kidnapped. Where were you?" A reporter asked, before putting his mic close to my mouth. I smacked it away and the frown on my face deepened as I ignored his question and kept walking.

"Were you with your mistress?" A female reporter asked. "Does the first lady know who you were with?"

I cocked my neck from side-to-side and ignored her question too. I didn't speak up until one reporter spoke to me like she'd had some sense.

"Mr. President, are you okay? The American people are concerned about you, and many of us thought something tragic had happened."

I halted my steps to answer her question. "I'm fine. I went for a lengthy walk, and—" I couldn't finish my statement because Secret Service rushed to my side.

"We need this area cleared right away." David reached for my arm while several other agents attempted to clear the area. "Come this way, sir. Are you okay? You don't look okay."

I stressed again that I was fine.

"That's good to know, but it's dangerous for you to disappear the way you did. Everyone has been looking for you," another agent said while walking beside me. "We didn't know what had happened to you, and the director of Homeland Security is pissed. He's been on our asses all night. We were told you were with General Stiles, but when we reached out to her, she implied that she didn't know where you were."

"I was with her, but I decided to go for a walk by myself to clear my head. Maybe I should have informed someone."

"Yes, you should have. We all were panicking, especially after what happened earlier. In addition to that, the media is having a field day with this. Some outlets are reporting that you were kidnapped, others are saying you were killed. None of this makes our agency look good, and we've been catching hell for not protecting you like we should be."

I had a mess to clean up, and after we went inside, I turned to address the agents who appeared irritated by my actions.

"This will all be resolved by morning," I said. "I apologize for wandering off, but as I said, I just needed some time alone to clear my head."

As soon as those words left my mouth, Andrew came storming down the West Colonnade with a tight, red face. His suit looked slouchy, hair was wet and he really needed to shave his scraggly beard. He appeared upset with me too, and his tone was too up there for my approval.

"This is bullshit, sir! I can't do this with you anymore! I'm losing my freaking mind around here, and every time I need you for something, you can't be found! I've had it! You're going to have my resignation by morning!"

Andrew pivoted and marched back down the West Colonnade. I shrugged and shouted after him. "The earlier you can get that to me the better! And thanks for your service!"

He swung around and shot me dead with the look in his eyes. I could tell he wanted to say something else, but all he did was shake his head and stomp away. Secret Service quietly followed me to the Oval Office. You could hear a pin drop—no one said a word. That was until I went into the Oval Office and was reminded by Secret Service how my actions had everyone on pins and needles.

"Please be sure to release a statement from the White House," David said. "The sooner, the better."

I sat behind the Resolute desk and picked up the phone to call Sam. He was asleep.

"I know it's late, and I apologize for waking you."

"No problem, Mr. President. I'm well aware of what my job responsibilities require."

"Good. I need you to prepare another statement and release it to the Associated Press as soon as possible. Tell everyone I'm okay, and I'll be going to Camp David tomorrow for a quick vacation. Make it sound convincing for me, Sam, and let everyone know that I'll hold a press conference when I return."

"Will do, Mr. President. It's good to hear your voice and I'm glad you're okay. Have you spoken to Andrew? He was really worried."

"I've spoken to him. He's going to resign."

"No. Allowing him to do so would be a big mistake. Please don't let him resign, besides, we all make a really good team. I know there are times when you don't believe that, but Andrew and I are here because we want to be. We believe in you and we are with you every step of the way."

My level of trust was shot to hell. I didn't know how to respond to Sam about what he'd said, so I didn't.

"Just do as I asked. Thanks."

I ended the call, hoping that things settled down by morning. And as tired as I was, I still had to stop by Andrew's office to apologize. The truth is, I didn't want him to resign. He was valuable to my administration, even though I was reluctant to admit it. Secret Service stood near the corridor and watched me from a short distance as I entered Andrew's office. He was shoving some of his items into a suitcase with a scrunched up face. I also heard him mumbling something underneath his breath. He paused when he looked up and saw me enter his office.

"I heard what you said," I teased. "But say it louder."

"Asshole," he said. "You're a fucking asshole, Mr. President, and a jerk."

I nodded and walked further into the room. "Sometimes, yes, I am. But is that all you got? Seems to me that you need to get more than an asshole and jerk off your chest."

He lifted his finger and darted it at me. "I have a whole lot of shit to get off my chest, sir, and trust me when I say you don't want to hear all of it."

"No, really I do. At least let me hear some of it."

Andrew lowered his finger and walked behind his desk. He started slamming more items into the suitcase. "You're full of it," he said. "I'm sick of kissing your ass and trying to do the right things around here to protect you. You have no damn respect for me, and even when I call you, you don't even answer your goddamn phone! I can't work like this anymore. I refuse to work like this, and after I walk out of here tonight, you can kiss my freaking ass goodbye."

In a fit of anger, he lifted his chair and slammed it back down. I don't know why his actions made me want to burst into laughter. I tried to hold back, but as I looked at him, I couldn't help myself. I lowered my head and started to chuckle.

"What in the hell is so funny?" he said, slamming his hand on his desk. "Do you think this is some kind of joke?"

I looked up and cleared my throat. "No, I really don't think it's a joke. It's just that I've never seen you like this. I'm surprised by your choice of words, and it proves that you never really liked me much anyway."

"Ohhhh, go fuck yourself, Mr. President. And since I'll be out of the White House by morning, you'll have plenty of time to do it."

Andrew slammed his suitcase and tried to lock it. With so much stuff inside, he couldn't.

"Allow me to help you with that," I said. I made my way behind the desk with him. As I tried to assist with locking his suitcase, he shoved me out of the way.

"Move it. I don't need your help. Just leave and go back to wherever the hell you were."

"Where I was is really no one's business, but here's the truth. I should respect you more and I should have given you more details about some of the things I've been dealing with. I would like to discuss some of those things with you, only if you agree to stay and not resign. I have a funny way of showing people how much I appreciate them, and straight from the horse's mouth, I do appreciate you more than you will ever know. I want you to stay, and at this point in my presidency, you are the only other person I've come close to trusting. I've been betrayed by many people, Andrew. Every time I turn around somebody is trying to stab me in the back. It's kind of scary being me, and I just don't know who or what is coming my way next. All I know how to do is keep my guards up and try to protect myself from everyone around me."

Andrew sighed, then reached out to touch my shoulder. "I totally understand what you mean, Mr. President, but you have to trust me. There is no other way for me to continue working here, unless the two of us come to an understanding about certain things. I need to know where you are at all times, and I must be able to reach you. I don't like being left in the dark, and there is no way for the White House to function like this. I would love to stay, only if you can promise me that changes will be made. That you and I will have a better relationship, and that you'll be honest with me about what you're dealing with so I can help you."

I slowly nodded, before reaching out my hand to his. He grabbed it and we shook hands.

"I promise," I said. "I promise to kick your ass if you ever speak to me like that again, and I promise to adhere to everything else you said."

Andrew smiled. "Good. Very good, Mr. President, but no thanks to the ass kicking. I apologize for speaking to you in that manner, but I needed to get that off my chest."

I patted his shoulder. "Well, I hope you feel better. I must say that your approach was funny as hell. I needed a good laugh tonight, so thanks for that."

Andrew had to laugh too. And as he started to remove his items from the suitcase, I left his office. I made my way upstairs to the Executive Residence. It was after midnight, and when I entered the bedroom I saw Raynetta in bed asleep. I guess she wasn't as concerned as everyone else was about my whereabouts, especially after our conversation earlier. She knew I was going somewhere, but she wasn't sure where that was. I didn't even know yet, but the first thing I needed was a shower and some rest. I was so glad to finally be here, but the second I removed my clothes and stepped into the shower, my private cell phone vibrated. I walked over to the sink to retrieve my phone. The caller showed unknown, but I still answered.

"Hello," I said.

"It's me," Joshua replied. For some reason, after hearing his voice I felt relieved. "I just called to say that it was my pleasure meeting you for the first time today. It's something I will never, ever forget and I'm grateful to you and my grandmother for finally telling me the truth. But the more I think about this, I think it's best that my mother and me just go away and never come back to the states again. I know that's not what you want to hear, but we don't have many other choices."

My throat ached as he spoke. "You have plenty of choices, Joshua. I will protect you and make sure you and your mother are safe. You don't have to leave this country and you can stay here so the two of us can get to know each other better. I feel like I've been robbed. I always wanted a son, and something about this whole thing seems so unfair to me. It's unfair to you too, but we can . . ."

"No. I don't want to stay. I'm sorry, but I know for a fact that if my mother and I stay, there's going to be too much chaos, people trying to hurt us, and things happening that shouldn't be. Maybe if you weren't the president . . ."

"I'll step down then. I'll walk away from all of this, if it makes your life easier. I just want to be closer to you, son. If you move to another country, I won't be able to see you that much or maybe not at all. Is that really what you want?"

He hesitated before answering. "What I want is to get back in school, graduate and live a peaceful life. Living in England may be best, and at least you know where we're headed."

I swallowed the huge lump in my throat. My eyes filled with tears, but I blinked fast to wash them away. "Alright, son." I cleared my throat before I spoke again. "If that's what you want, who am I to try and make you change your mind?"

Joshua didn't respond. After a minute or two of silence, Ina spoke up. "Goodbye, Stephen. And don't come looking for us, because we don't want to be bothered."

She hung up. I looked at the phone, and as a rush of anger swept through my body, I threw the phone against the wall. It broke into pieces. I swallowed another lump in my throat, and right after I entered the shower, I let hot water and soap rain down my body. I was overcome by a flood of emotions. Tears fell fast. My stomach ached, but not as much as my heart. I was devastated. I covered my closed eyes with my hand, and tried to quiet my staggering cries. Unfortunately, I couldn't. I dropped to one knee and released the insurmountable amount of hurt I felt inside. It felt good to finally let it all out—this was long overdue. I didn't calm down until my shower was over, and after I wrapped a towel around my waist, I returned to the bedroom where Raynetta was still laying sound asleep. With narrow, fiery-red eyes, I looked at her while in deep thought. My eyes then shifted to her cell phone and pain pills on the nightstand. I couldn't help but to wonder if she had been in contact with Alex while she was at the hotel. Her fling with him was what led to her being at the hotel in the first place. I surely wanted to know if the two of them had been in touch. Seeking answers, I quietly made my way next to the bed and snatched up her phone. Her privacy code was our anniversary date, so I entered the numbers. I checked the call log, immediately noticing several numbers from the same caller. She had called the number twice, and when I looked at text messages, I saw that Alex had been reaching out to her. There were times when she hadn't responded, but she definitely responded today, telling him she was okay and there was no need for him to worry about her.

His reply: I CAN'T HELP MYSELF. ALL I THINK ABOUT IS U. I HATE THE WAY I'M FEELING INSIDE. I JUST WANT TO SEE YOU AGAIN. WE HAVE SO MUCH FUN WHEN WE'RE TOGETHER AND YOUR SMILE IS FOREVER WITH ME. I WON'T PUSH, BUT PLEASE

LET ME KNOW WHAT U DECIDE WHEN IT COMES TO THE PRESIDENT. HE DOESN'T DESERVE U.

Her reply: I'LL LET YOU KNOW WHAT I DECIDE. GOOD NIGHT, ALEX. THANKS FOR CHECKING ON ME.

I laid her phone back on the nightstand and got in bed. As the mattress waved around, Raynetta woke up and turned on her side to look at me. Her eyes fluttered. She forced herself to keep her eyes open. I assumed the pills she had taken for pain made her drowsy.

"Hi," she said softly. "I didn't think you were coming back tonight."

I lay on my back with one hand behind my head. "I had several meetings tonight. Needed some rest, but I'm leaving tomorrow."

"Do you know where you're going yet?"

"No, not yet, but I told you earlier I would call and let you know for sure."

"Okay, Stephen. Try to get some rest. You look tired. I know I am."

She moved closer and laid her head on my chest. I could tell she was already fading again, but I wanted to ask her a question before she went back to sleep.

"Raynetta," I called to her in a soft tone.

"Yeaaah," she moaned.

"Did you spend any time with Alex while you were at the hotel?"

I felt her body get tense. She didn't even lift her head from my chest, before replying, "No."

"Did you hear from him?"

Without hesitating, she replied, "No."

I left it right there. My wife was a liar. And because she was, she made me feel like I was sleeping with the enemy. I had recently learned something unfortunate about her too, and that piece of news caused me to plot against her like never before and sleep with one eye open.

President's Mother,
Teresa Jefferson

I was bitter about everything that had happened. There was no telling when I'd see my grandson again, and if I'd had a chance, I would've choked Ina to death. She'd won this round. I hated that because I didn't like to lose. I felt horrible. Not only for myself, but also for my son. He seemed so out of it yesterday, and there was something in his eyes that scared me. I knew for a fact he had already dealt with Levi. I didn't know any specifics about what Stephen had done, but I was sure, sooner or later, a missing person's report would circulate or Levi's fat ass would wash up on a beach somewhere. Whatever had happened to him, he deserved it. I was just disappointed that Ina walked away from this unscathed. Nonetheless, I assumed she and Joshua were gone, especially since he'd called last night to say goodbye. I didn't have much to say, but I wished him well. Then, when I reached out to Stephen this morning, he had left too. He mentioned something about a Hell House getaway in St. Louis. I didn't know any details about that, but he was on his way there. He asked me to stay at the White House and keep an eye on Raynetta, until he got back. He also wanted me to stay here because he was afraid there were other people conspiring against us. Yet again, I found myself being watched and guarded by Secret Service. I hated it too, because I had so many people I needed to deal with in private. One person was Michelle who had been calling me like crazy, trying to find out why I was now ignoring her. The other person was Mr. McNeil. I didn't know if he was still laid up in the hospital from his injuries or if he was home now. I would find out and pay him a visit soon. He needed to back off my son or else he would face dire consequences. I had finally had it with that racist, evil man. He'd already done enough damage, and after all he'd done to my son, I should've dealt with him a long time ago. If I had, there was a good chance we wouldn't be in this predicament.

I sat in the dining room eating breakfast and watching TV. A drunken fool who claimed Stephen purchased his gas last night was being interviewed by a reporter.

"The president was so down to earth. Not only did he pump my gas, but he sat in the car with me and we talked for about an hour or so."

"What did the two of you talk about? Did he tell you where he was when he disappeared?"

The man scratched his head and nodded. "We talked about the economy and all this racial bullcrap that's going on. He was real talkative, and he told me he had just left a bar or something. We shared a few beers, and after that he got in the car with another man and left."

"Was that man Mr. Chen? We spoke to him this morning too. He was ecstatic about meeting the president last night. His vehicle sold for two hundred thousand dollars this morning. Apparently, the president signed the headrest and there was a bottle of gin in Mr. Chen's car that belonged to the president too. We were able to verify the purchase."

"Yeah, that's so cool. I heard Mr. Chen sold his car. That's why I contacted you guys. I still have the beer can the president drank from. If anyone wants to purchase it, let me know. The starting bid is ten thousand bucks."

I rolled my eyes at the foolishness. Stephen didn't even drink, and who in the hell would be dumb enough to believe either of those fools? As one of the three servers around me poured my coffee, I looked up and saw Raynetta. She had a small bruise near her cheek and bags were underneath her eyes. There was also a scratch on her chin. Her eyes slightly rolled when she saw me, but she still came into the dining room and greeted me.

"Good morning to you too," I said. "Have a seat and let's chat."

One of the servers pulled back Raynetta's chair for her. He inquired about what she wanted for breakfast.

"I'm not that hungry, but some toast and fruit will be fine."

"Yes, Ma'am," the server said. "Will orange juice be okay?"

"Perfect."

Raynetta yawned as the server walked away. I never understood how the first lady could come to the table like this. Her hair was in a ponytail, clothes were wrinkled, and I doubted that she had even brushed her teeth. I was at the White House representing for my son. There was no way in hell I would be in front of anyone, not even the servers, looking like she was. Nonetheless, I left her appearance alone and tried to be nice.

"I haven't had a chance to speak to you since the explosion, but it's good to see that you're okay. Stephen was so worried about you. Maybe it wasn't such a good idea for you to temporarily move out of the White House to begin with."

"Just so you know, Stephen requested that I left. He was upset with me about a few things, but now we both know *his* decision was a big mistake."

I put a piece of buttered bread in my mouth and chewed. I wasn't quite clear about why Stephen had asked Raynetta to leave, but I knew it had something to do with Alex, based on media reports.

"It was a big mistake, and the last thing you need to be doing is chasing after another man. Stephen is going through a lot. He needs a strong woman in his corner right now. I don't know where the marriage stands at this point, but if you're not willing to play the part as first lady, I suggest you divorce Stephen and get on with your life."

Raynetta massaged her forehead while evil-eyeing me from across the table. "Teresa, I have a major headache this morning. I'm really not in the mood for this. Your guess is as good as mine when it comes to our marriage, and just so you know, I'm not chasing after any man, period. Meanwhile, I've done my part *playing* the first lady. And I'm going to keep on doing my part. That's because no matter what you think, I do love Stephen. I want things to work out, but everything about us is so complicated."

She was right about that. I couldn't agree more. "Maybe so, but please do your part around here to make things better. I don't know how long Stephen is going to be gone, but while he's away, do what you can to shine on his behalf. Don't sit around here moping. Show up and let the American people know things are good, even if they aren't. Many of the first ladies who came before you were some of the greatest pretenders. They had some of the same issues as you, but they made the best of their time here. I'm not going to be a thorn in your side, and whether you know it or not, I am rooting for you. But you have to start rooting for yourself too."

Raynetta sat silent as the server placed her food in front of her. "Is there anything else I can get you, Mrs. Jefferson?"

"No, this looks great. Thanks again. Your kindness is always appreciated."

The server smiled, nodded and walked away. Another server poured Raynetta some orange juice, before she, too, walked away.

"I can't believe you're rooting for me. That's the first time I've ever heard you say that. Make no mistake about it, I get what you're saying about being the first lady. We do have our challenges, but I never imagined mine would be like this. I had a different vision of what it would be like in the White House. I don't know if you realize it or not, but Stephen has been a changed man since he's been here. He's so angry all the time, and these ongoing relationships with other women drive me nuts. For the first time, I feel like I'm losing him. His feelings for Michelle are much deeper than I originally thought. I would put any amount of money on it that he's with her now."

"Your assumption would be incorrect. Michelle was only a fling. She was there for Stephen when you kept lying and he didn't feel like you had his back. As was that other hoochie reporter, Chanel Hamilton, who got her face cracked. I know that being with a man like Stephen isn't easy, but you have to take some responsibility for what has been going on too. After you take a step back and look at the big picture, you'll feel so much better. Get yourself back on track, and make Stephen regret some of the things he's done. Not necessarily by running off and having sex with another man, but by showing that you, as the first lady, have it all together, even when Stephen doesn't."

Raynetta seemed surprised by our pleasant conversation. The truth was, I had bigger fish to fry than her. While I wanted her to get it together, she still wasn't considered one of my favorite people. But I knew that in order for Stephen's life to get better, so did Raynetta's.

"I'm planning to get myself back on track, but it would surely help if Stephen wasn't so distant and angry all the time. I guess I'll be hearing from him soon, and, unfortunately, I haven't even had a chance to speak to him about Joshua."

I gave Raynetta the scoop on everything pertaining to Joshua. Even told her about how dirty Ina was and how Levi had betrayed Stephen. Raynetta mentioned that Stephen had told her about Levi too, and she stressed how worried she was about Stephen seeking revenge. Mr. McNeil's name came up again, and Raynetta admitted how bad she'd felt for lying to Stephen about Mr. McNeil trying to persuade her to do his dirty work. She was shocked and couldn't believe what had been going on with Joshua. She also appeared highly upset about Mr. McNeil's interference.

"That man has been a pain in the ass since the first day Stephen started on the campaign trail," Raynetta said. "Now I understand why Stephen needed to get away. This is too much."

"I'm glad you're finally opening your eyes. While you have insecure, pretty-girl problems, my son is seriously going through it. You and I are the closest ones to him. I think it's time for us to do whatever needs to be done to help make not only his world a better place, but our worlds too."

"I agree. But first, I think we should take charge and finally deal with Stephen's number one enemy."

I couldn't believe me and this bitch were finally on the same page and singing the same tune.

"You are definitely speaking my language. And I have a feeling that we're going to make a darn good team."

Raynetta smiled. We shook hands and continued to have a pleasant conversation during breakfast. After we were done, she informed me she was heading out later to make everyone aware that things were good with her and Stephen. As long as she cleaned herself up, her news was like music to my ears.

I had lunch later and was sitting at a cozy café, waiting on Michelle to arrive. I called her right after breakfast and told her to meet me here. Secret Service was sitting at a few tables to my left, and I was so glad they weren't paying too much attention to me. I reached in my purse for a compact mirror to make sure nothing was out of place and I was up to par. I wore a Saint Laurent polka dot blouse, black pants and ankle strapped heels. My salt-and-pepper colored hair was layered to perfection and not one strand was out of place. I teased the feathery bangs on my forehead and moistened my lips with more nude gloss. After I was done, I tucked the compact back into my leather handbag, then shielded my eyes from the sun with my dark sunglasses. The media considered me and the first lady fashion icons. I didn't necessarily understand why they viewed her as one, but I definitely understood why I fit that classification. I had already spotted several photographers who were standing across the street snapping photos of me. I paid them no mind and continued to sip on my iced tea while being shaded by an umbrella.

Michelle was late, and the second I glanced at my watch, I finally saw her. Her cocoa chocolate skin was flawless and her pretty brown eyes had to be what lured Stephen in. Her shapely figure was covered with a black-and-yellow, off-the-shoulder fitted dress. And with her natural hair held back with a band, in my opinion, she was much prettier than Raynetta was. She walked up to the table without a smile.

"Thank you for finally making time for me," she said. "Why did you hang up on me when I called to tell you about Stephen?"

I nudged my head toward the chair across from me. "Hello to you too, Michelle. Please have a seat and then we'll talk."

Displaying a slight attitude, she pulled back a chair and took a seat. After placing her purse on the table, she crossed her arms and legs. "I'm sitting. Now, tell me what's going on."

I finished sipping my tea through a straw, then cleared my throat. "What's going on is you got busted with my number in your phone, and Stephen doesn't want to have anything else to do with you. I will no longer give you any money and our little plan has concluded."

Her arched brows shot up. "No, Teresa. You mean *your* little plan has concluded. It wasn't a plan to me, because I care deeply for Stephen. I shouldn't have taken the money you offered me, simply because he and I were doing just fine without it."

All I could do was smile as I looked across the table at her. "Awwww, I'm sorry that you feel that way. But the truth is, Stephen doesn't give two-cents about you, Michelle. He never has, and I don't know why you side-ho's start get all delusional and think married men have feelings. If you had just stuck with my plan, you wouldn't have gotten so attached."

"I was attached before you discussed *your* plan with me. A side-ho I am not, and for your information, Stephen does care about me. He's always cared, and after I give him more details about my connection with you, I'm sure he'll understand my purpose for accepting your money."

I had to laugh. She was so young and naïve. "No, Michelle, he won't understand. He's had enough people lying to him and backstabbing him over money. You don't want to tell him anything about your thirst for cash, and if you approach him with a bunch of nonsense and excuses, you're going to get your feelings hurt. Now would be a great time for you to just move on like all the others have. Besides, Raynetta is never going to hand him over to anyone on a silver platter. He loves only her, and you're going to waste your time pursuing him."

"I don't intend to pursue him. All I want him to know is the truth. I owe him that, whether you like it or not."

"You can say what you wish, but it will go in one ear and out the other. I just hate to see a beautiful and intelligent woman like you get all worked up over a man who used you. Trust me when I say he did use you. It may have felt good at the time, but I'm sure it doesn't now. The after effects seem like they're starting to sting, but keep in mind that there are other dicks in the sea. From what I know, the size of Stephen's penis isn't all that anyway, so you should be able to find a satisfying replacement soon."

Michelle stood and reached into her purse. She pulled out a check and placed it on the table. "Here is every last dime that you gave me. I shouldn't have ever taken your money and I regret playing along with this little charade of yours. By the way, and before I go, I'm not interested in other dicks in the sea. I guess you haven't seen Stephen's penis since he was in grade school or something, because I assure you that the size of it is enough to satisfy any woman who finds herself lucky enough to get it.

Goodbye, Teresa. If you happen to see Stephen, please let him know I'll be in touch soon."

She walked off as I was looking at the check she'd written out to me. "I do take checks, but I hope this one doesn't bounce. If it does, I'll be in touch with *you*, soon."

Michelle didn't bother to turn around. I could tell she wasn't the confrontational type, but more than anything, I knew Stephen was finally done with her. Raynetta could thank me later.

First Lady,
Raynetta Jefferson

My conversation with Teresa left me feeling some kind of way about it. While I didn't trust that woman as far as I could see her, she was right about a great number of things. I needed to show up and show out as first lady, so right after breakfast, I made a commitment to myself to do just that. I had finally hired another assistant, Emme. She and I spent the entire day away from the White House. My first stop was on a late night talk show with a well-known host who had me cracking up. The show wouldn't air until later and everything was going great. He kept inquiring about Stephen, so I cleared up any misunderstandings about us.

"As with any marriage," I said, looking fabulous as ever. My hair was on point; it was parted through the middle with long curls flowing past my shoulders. The classy gray pantsuit I wore was an original. It melted on my curves and God had blessed me with plenty. "We have our challenges, but the president and I love each other. We want all Americans to live out their dreams and help us make this country suitable for all Americans, not just a few. That's what we're working towards, and we're both excited about what's to come."

Everyone in the audience applauded. The host inquired about the explosion and I commented on that too.

"It was a tragedy. I have never experienced anything like that in my life, and I regret there are people in this country who feel like they have to resort to things like that. The American people should know that the president and his team are working diligently to stop many of those kinds of acts, before they happen. Considering what happened during the last administration, we're already seeing much progress in the fight against terrorism. Just continue to pray for our country, and please keep the president and me in your prayers."

When all was said and done, the interview went well. I wasn't sure if Stephen would see it or not, but I hoped he would. Right after the interview, I went to a new school in the DC area to speak to fifth grade students. I then attended a ribbon-cutting ceremony for a new healthcare facility built to take care of more vets. I spent many hours there, thanking them for their service to our country. Being around so many brave men and women made me feel good. I was hyped when I left and was determined to spend more time away from the White House to attend events relating to the ones I had been to today.

"Your schedule is all clear for the evening," Emme said as we were in the car with a Secret Service agent. "Before we return to the White House, is there anywhere else you would like to go?"

"No, but I would like for you to set up a meeting with someone for me, while I grab a bite to eat in the dining room. Call Alex and tell him to meet me at my office around eight. I should be done eating by then, and let him know it's imperative that we speak this evening."

Emme did as she was asked. When we arrived at the White House, I had a wonderful dinner with two of Stephen's staff members. Then I headed to my office to see if Alex was there. He was. He reminded me so much of Daniel Craig, 007. My eyes scanned him as he stood in a tailored, tight-fitted navy suit, waiting to greet me. His beard was somewhat rugged, but his fine hair was trimmed nicely. Not once did he take his olive green eyes off me. He followed me into my office where I closed the door behind him.

"I need you to stop calling me so much," I said to him as he sat on the sofa. "You don't have to call me every day, Alex, and to be honest with you, your calls are getting out of hand."

"I only call because I'm always worried about you. Whether you realize it or not, the president has a lot of enemies.

I'm so afraid something is going to happen to you. I knew you weren't safe at that hotel and you should have never been there."

"I agree, but you know I have Secret Service to protect me. I don't need you too, but if you really want to help me, there is something you can do for me."

Alex crossed one of his legs over the other and tapped his fingers on his leather shoe. "What can I do for you?"

"I want you to find out where Mr. McNeil is. I want to know everything about him going forward, and I need some very damaging information against him. He's become Mr. Untouchable and he's utilizing his money to hurt too many people. I just want it to stop. I want to get him where it hurts, and I need your help with this."

Alex stood and strutted toward me. His shoulder touched mine as he leaned in to whisper in my ear. "Tell me. What's in this for me?"

"That all depends on how much information you can gather and how damaging the information is. I'll just say that the most damaging information may bring about great rewards."

"Oh, I'll get you some damaging information. But you can give me a little something before I start the investigation, can't you?"

The direction of my eyes traveled to his sexy lips. "A little something like what?"

Alex leaned in and stole a quick kiss. I backed away from him and held up my hand. "Listen to me, okay?" I said. "I don't want to go down that road with you again, and the last time we attempted to go there didn't end so well. But if you get me what I need, I may have a change of heart. Regardless, I'm sure I can figure out some way to reward you for your troubles."

Alex raked his fingers through his hair and smiled. "You're playing a dangerous game, sweetheart. You know the president isn't going to approve of this. He doesn't want me anywhere near the White House and the last time I was here I was kicked out."

"Well, this is a new day and you have my permission to be here."

Alex nodded and smiled. "Just so you are completely aware, I expect to be fully compensated for the work I do. So think long and hard about how you intend to pay me. Money won't do, because I'm already fully loaded."

"I'll worry about how to pay for your services when the time comes. As for the president, I'll handle him. Just keep this between us, and I don't want anyone . . . not anyone to know whatever you find out about Mr. McNeil. Can I trust you to do this for me?"

He was blunt and truthful. "No you can't, but what do you have to lose?"

I shrugged. "Nothing, I guess. So get to work and keep in touch. Not every day, but at least every other day."

Alex seemed hyped and up to the task. I didn't trust him, but I truly believed he was the only one who could help me bring down Mr. McNeil for good. My mother-in-law didn't stand a chance. She was all talk and no action. Then again, she had always been about her *son's* business.

President's Mother,
Teresa Jefferson

I couldn't believe how well Raynetta and me had been getting along. I was also proud of her for getting out of the White House more and committing to her duties as the first lady. She'd gotten some information about Mr. McNeil. She wouldn't share who gave her the information, but that didn't matter to me. People around the White House were always snitching and leaking information. Anything you wanted to know, someone around here was willing to tell you. In this case, Raynetta trusted the individual and said we would soon know more about Mr. McNeil's dealings.

With that tad bit of information, I was hyped. We were expected to attend a party that included many of the rich and famous in Washington. Everyone wondered if Stephen would attend, but I hadn't heard one peep from him. Every time I called, his cell phone went to voicemail. I had gone to Andrew's office to see if he'd heard from Stephen. He had, but he didn't provide any details about what Stephen had been up to.

"All I want to know is if he's okay and resting," I said. "When he left, he was down in the dumps."

"Yes, he was, but I think he's feeling better. At least that's what he told me. I can only hope so, because the sooner he can get back here, the better."

"Well, the next time you speak to him, tell him to call me. He needs to call Raynetta too. She said she hasn't heard much from him. The only thing she received was a brief text message."

Andrew displayed a fake smile. "I'll be sure to tell him. Meanwhile, will you be attending the gala tonight?"

"I wouldn't miss it for the world. I wish Stephen was here, but I guess he's not going to make it."

"Unfortunately not. But I'm sure he'll be in attendance at the next one."

I didn't say anything else to Andrew. He seemed reluctant to tell me anything, and the smirk on his face irritated me. I returned to the Queen's Bedroom to get ready for the gala tonight. For this country to be more than 23 trillion dollars in debt, I wondered how lawmakers had time to party. They all needed their asses kicked, and I was so sure that every single member of congress would be at the party tonight. There would be a few specks of black people here and there, along with numerous coons who did whatever to fit in. Raynetta and I knew many eyes would be upon us, so I made sure my attire was flawless. I prayed that she would get it together tonight, and if she didn't, I would keep my distance. The Elie Saab dress I wore was a champagne colored sheer gown with red silk flowers flowing through the upper half. It had a plunging neckline, and with silver accessories meshing with the color of my layered hair, I would slay every woman who crossed my path. Years ago, Stephen had purchased teardrop diamond earrings for me for Mother's Day, so I wore those. Glamourous defined me, and I didn't dare need a stylist to help me get ready. Raynetta, however, had one on hand tonight.

I was ready to meet up with her, so I sent her a text to see if she was ready. She said she'd be ready in ten minutes and asked me to meet her in the Yellow Room so we could exit the White House together.

The second I left the Queen's Bedroom, Secret Service was right there. All eyes were locked on me, and if I was blessed enough to capture the attention of these young men, I had to pat myself on the back.

"I'm not ready to leave yet," I said, prancing down the hallway. "And I won't be leaving until my daughter-in-law is ready."

They backed off, but kept their eyes on me. I went into the Yellow Room, admiring myself while looking in the mirrors. The ruby red lipstick I wore matched the flowers in my dress—this was probably the best I had ever looked. Just as I was teasing my feathery bangs, I could see Raynetta's reflection in the mirror. I swung around to examine her. For the first time ever, she had gotten it right. A smile washed across my face and my eyes were glued to her stunning dress and hair that was swept back into a loose twisted knot. The dress she wore was a cocoa colored, silk fitted dress with a sash around her perfect waistline. The ruffled collar traveled around her neckline, and with bare arms, smoky eyes, and just a sliver of her cleavage showing, she was one sexy diva. What really set her off was the high slit that started at her upper thigh and traveled all the way down the dress.   We complimented each other at the same time and laughed.

"You are slaying it," I said. "Girl, who made that dress?"

"The one and only Miss Vera Wang," Raynetta said, spinning around so I could check out the back. It was perfect. Wherever Stephen was or whatever he was doing, he was truly missing out.

"I wish you could look like that all the time," I joked, but was serious.

Raynetta threw her hand back at me. "Don't start, okay? We're on the right track so please don't veer off course."

"I'll try not to. In the meantime, let's get out of here and go get this party started."

With Secret Service surrounding us, we left the White House ready for some fun tonight. The moment we arrived at the gala together, people appeared shocked. There were many whispers as we exited the stretch limousine. Camera's flashed and Secret Service had to push away many reporters who wanted to know one thing—well, a couple of things.

"Where is the president? Will he be joining you ladies tonight?"

"Are you feeling better, Mrs. Jefferson? Do you have anything to say about the explosion?"

"Are you ladies getting along better these days?"

"Is the president on vacation with his other woman? Why aren't the two of you together, and to the other Miss Jefferson, are you still a heavy drinker?"

Raynetta's head snapped to the side, but before she lashed out at the white bitch who needed to be slapped in her mouth, I reached for Raynetta's arm.

"Don't let her distract you," I whispered. "Smile at that heifer and keep it moving."

Raynetta did just that, and as we paraded down the long red carpet inside, many people fawned all over us.

"You two look simply beautiful. Who are you wearing?" A fashion reporter from a magazine asked. Truthfully, who or what we wore was none of her business.

We just smiled, waved and kept it moving. The stares continued and everybody, particularly some of the filthy rich uppity women, couldn't help but to take double and triple looks at us. Raynetta was treated like royalty, and many reporters were trying to get one minute of her time. She didn't halt her steps until she spotted a reporter, Chanel Hamilton, who had hooked up with Stephen on Air Force One. On the other side of the red carpeted area was Michelle. I saw the smile on Raynetta's face vanish as she looked at her. That was when I leaned in and whispered to her.

"I guess ho's like to party too. Whatever you do, don't allow them to ruin your evening. You know why we're here, so focus. If they say anything to you, just flash your wedding ring and strut on."

Raynetta laughed and smiled. We finally made our way into the lavish ballroom where nothing but money was blowing through the air. Numerous chandeliers hung from the high ceilings, and the carpet was so plush that my heels sunk into it.

Several tables were set for dining, and with gold drapes covering the massive curvy windows, richness was on display. There was a band playing music in the center of the floor, and hundreds of waiters and waitresses scurried around to serve the guests champagne and caviar. It was time to meet and greet, so as Raynetta moved in one direction, I headed in another.

"My, my, Teresa," Senator Coleman said, moving too close to me. "Don't you look lovely tonight."

"Always, sweetheart," I teased and shook his hand. "You don't look so bad yourself."

That was all the conversation he'd gotten from me. I hurried away, and pranced around the room conducting small talk with a bunch of fake people.

"Teresa, you need to stop by next week so we can have tea," Senator Bell's wife
said while looking me up and down.

"I don't do tea, sweetie. Only alcoholic beverages, preferably white wine or Cognac."

Her mouth dropped open as I skirted away and indulged in another conversation with Senator Salvatore and his daughter.

"I saw that dress on the runway in Paris last week," she said, looking at me in awe. "My dad wouldn't purchase it because he said it cost a fortune. How did you, I mean, did you find it on sale somewhere?"

She was another ignorant bitch who needed to be slapped. And only because I wasn't in the mood to do so, I just walked away from her. She had the nerve to ask her father if she had said something to offend me. I started to go back and answer her question, but instead, I grabbed a flute glass of champagne from one of the waiters and tuned in to listen to Raynetta who had made her way on stage where the band was. She stood on stage looking like a million bucks. Many lustful eyes were locked on her. Jealousy was in Michelle's eyes, and far across the room stood Chanel with pursed lips.

"I apologize that the president couldn't be here tonight," Raynetta said in a professional tone. One never would've guessed she was born and raised in the projects. I had to laugh to myself because so was I. "He had a prior engagement that he was unable to cancel. He wanted me to encourage all of you to have a good time, and he promised that when he returns to Washington, some serious work will finally get done."

Nearly everyone chuckled, with the exception of a chunky fool next to me who said, "It's about damn time, lazy fuck."

I snapped my head to the side. It was one thing to say something about me, but saying something negative about my son triggered something horrible inside of me.
"At least we know your mouth isn't lazy, don't we, Mr. Piggy? If you ever speak ill about the president again, in my presence, I will make sure you never eat another snack."

He stood frozen with a cracker in his hand. I cut my eyes and moved in another direction. I didn't get far, before Andrew halted my steps to introduce me to a black senator who had been cooning on Capitol Hill for too many years.

"Teresaaaaa," Andrew said. I could tell he'd had too much to drink; a glassy film covered his eyes. "I'm not sure if you know Senator Belmar or not. He's single and he asked if I would introduce you to him."

"I know Senator Belmar very well. He's a Republican who has voted against nearly everything that could be beneficial to my people. In knowing so, Senator Belmar is going to stay single for a very long time."

Moving right along, I saw Raynetta step away from the bar and swish her way through the crowd. She stopped and conversed with several people, before she disappeared down a hallway. I followed, and the closer I got, I saw her speaking to Alex by an elevator. Just so they wouldn't see me, I moved to the other side of the hallway to listen in and watch them. Alex gave Raynetta an envelope.

"This is a start," he whispered. "Mr. McNeil is here tonight, but he's upstairs tying up a business meeting with two Japanese men. The information in the envelope will get the prosecutor's attention, but I don't know if it will prompt him to start an investigation or convince him to build a case against Mr. McNeil. The prosecutor is here tonight, so it would be wise for you to somehow get this information into his hands. You may want to have someone else deliver the envelope to him. He's going to get suspicious if you hand it to him, and I don't recommend mailing it."

Raynetta tapped the envelope against her hand and smiled. "This is exactly what I need. If you can get more information, please do."

"I will. My job is in no way finished yet, and as I said before, that's a start. Meanwhile," he said and moved closer to her. There was no breathing room between them. "Can I tell you how beautiful you look tonight? I can't keep my eyes off you and my heart is racing a mile a minute. I want you so bad I can taste it. I know what you said, but I don't know how much longer I can go on like this."

Raynetta placed her hand against his heaving chest. Her eyes flirted with him, but I couldn't tell if she was serious or not. "Be patient, Alex. Keep in mind what I said and let's not get ahead of ourselves, okay?"

He stepped back. I could see how deep Alex's feelings were for Raynetta. She'd better hope and pray this mess wouldn't bring about more headaches for my son. I appreciated Alex for getting the information for us, but when Raynetta mentioned she'd had someone working behind the scenes, I didn't know it was him. He rubbed his finger along the side of her face, and then he kissed her cheek. After he walked off, so did Raynetta. She headed back to the ballroom, and as I moved in that direction too, I finally caught up with her.

"I've been looking for you," she said. "I have some information about Mr. McNeil that needs to get into the prosecutor's hands right away. I need someone to give it to him, other than me."

I snatched the envelope from her hand. "I'll happily give it to him, but first, I need to see what's inside of the envelope."

Raynetta agreed, so we moseyed to the ladies room where several prissy women were standing around gossiping and boasting about how rich they were.

"Don purchased one of those big ole yachts last week and we've been sailing the high seas ever since. You ladies should join us. I promise we'll have loads of fun."

I cut my eyes and didn't bother to speak. Raynetta and I hurried to a sitting area in the restroom to view what was inside of the envelope. As I pulled out the papers and started to read, Alex had definitely done his homework. He had pertinent information relating to a multi-million dollar sex slave trafficking organization that had Mr. McNeil's name written all over it. Raynetta and I couldn't believe our eyes as we combed through the papers. It was disheartening to read. There were photos included as well. We both looked at the material with scrunched up faces, probably thinking the same thing. Mr. McNeil needed to be arrested.

"What more do we need?" Raynetta whispered. "This is enough to send him and anyone else involved away for a long time."

I wasn't as convinced as Raynetta was. Bringing down the rich and powerful wasn't an easy task, no matter what kind of mess they were involved in. "I wouldn't be so sure about that, but whatever additional information your friend has, be sure to get it. I'm going to make sure the prosecutor gets this envelope tonight. I'll give him a few days to review everything, but after that he needs to let me know something."

"I agree," Raynetta said. "In the meantime, I'll keep in contact with my friend."

I tucked the envelope underneath my arm, and as soon as we left the restroom, Michelle was leaning against a wall waiting for us. Wearing a blue sequins short dress, she looked decent too. I guess she'd thought Stephen would be here tonight.

"I'm sorry to bother you, Raynetta, but may I speak to you for a few minutes?"

I assumed Raynetta had no idea I'd offered Michelle money to shake up things with Stephen. I definitely didn't want them talking without me around, so when I didn't step away, Michelle looked at me.

"If you don't mind, I'd like to speak to the first lady in private," she said.

"I do mind," I said. "Whatever you have to say to her, you can say it in front of me."

Thankfully, Raynetta was on my side this time. "I don't have much time, so say whatever it is that you need to say."

Michelle released a deep breath and spoke sincerely. "I would like to apologize to you for getting involved with your husband. It shouldn't have happened and I will never interfere again. Enjoy your evening, and in case you don't already know it, you look amazing tonight."

Not even waiting for a response, she walked away. She was sweet. Too bad Stephen hadn't met her before he'd met Raynetta.

"She could've kept that to herself," Raynetta said. "How do you apologize for screwing someone's husband? Multiple times at that. I can only wonder why they're not messing around anymore."

"Because Stephen loves you and no other woman will ever replace you. That, my dear, is the truth."

Raynetta blushed. Unfortunately for me, sometimes, the truth stung a little.

While Raynetta was off mingling again, I saw Mr. McNeil gazing at her from a far. His old bushy browed, wrinkled face ass wanted a piece of her for sure. I could tell by the way he licked across his lips and touched himself down below. Probably couldn't even get his little wiener up anymore, but I was sure he was thinking dirty things to himself. Wherever she moved, his eyes traveled with her. His wife was too busy running her mouth to notice, but after I saw him step outside on the balcony, that was when I followed him. A fireworks display was in the works, and as he looked up at the red, white and blue performance, while holding a cane, I interrupted him.

"Beautiful, isn't it?" I said, looking at the fireworks display too.

He jerked his head to the side and looked at me. He didn't respond until he turned his head to glance at the fireworks again.

"Yes, it is beautiful." He coughed and sucked his teeth. Nasty bastard didn't even bother to cover his mouth. "But I assume you didn't come out here to discuss fireworks."

I snapped my finger. "As a matter of fact, I didn't. I wanted to see how you were doing. I heard about your little accident, and it's a shame that Levi didn't finish you off when he had a chance to. Or, was that a set up too? He really didn't try to injure you, especially since he was already on your payroll, right?"

His eyes widened. He was shocked to learn that I'd known about his connection to Levi.

"That bastard did stab me," he said with trembling thin lips. "I have the wounds to prove it. Do you need proof?"

"I don't care to see your wounds. Besides, there is no way for me to recognize a stab wound through all those wrinkles. If he did injure you purposely, you deserved it. You deserved more than that, and it's just a matter of time before you're going to pay for what you've done to my family, particularly my son."

Mr. McNeil smiled and wiped across his slick mouth. "Speaking of your son, where is he? I don't smell any niggers around here tonight, so I assume he's far away. I do, however, smell niggerettes." He chuckled, sniffed the air, then looked me up and down. "That's the name my associates and me made up for black women like you and the name we gave some of the servers around here. Since I can't find one right now, why don't you go fetch me a glass of champagne and bring back a chair so I can sit while watching the fireworks."

I laughed, before I reached out and squeezed his little penis so tight that his mouth dropped open. Saliva dripped from it; pain was visible in his evil eyes. His screech was loud, but it couldn't be heard over the booming sound of the fireworks.

"A bitch ass nigga, Mr. McNeil. That's who you are, and that's what we black women call any man with a pint-sized dick who screams and acts like a bitch like you do. The only thing I'm going to fetch you is a bullet in your head. It's coming and you've been warned."

I let go of his little bone, slapped the shit out of him, and then walked away. I knew it was time for me to go, so as soon as I saw the prosecutor, Mr. Blackstone, chatting it up with a group of senators, I moved in their direction. Mr. Blackstone was a tall and slim, older black man with nerdy glasses and a thick beard. He was an Uncle Tom too, but I needed him to come through for me in a major way. If he didn't, there were always other options. I didn't want to go that route, because I always knew killing Mr. McNeil would swing major heat Stephen's way. There was no question that Mr. McNeil was a formidable figure through the eyes of many in Washington. He had multiple people on his payroll, and nobody knew who those people were. That was one of the main reasons why no one in Washington could be trusted.

The second Mr. Blackstone looked my way, I waved at him. He turned his head and must've thought I was waving at someone behind him. Just to let him know I was waving at him, I walked up to him with the envelope still in my hand.

"I didn't mean to interrupt, but how are you? I didn't expect to see you here," I said, showing every bit of my pearly white teeth.

"I didn't expect to see you either, but I'm doing mighty fine this evening. Hope you are having a superb time too."

"I am and thanks for asking. I would be doing so much better if I could speak to you about something very important in private. Do you have a minute or two to spare?"

He looked around; I assumed he was looking for his ugly ass wife. She was a white woman with red hair and a face that looked damaged by too many Botox injections.

"Sure," he said. "I have a minute, but if you don't mind, I need to go to the men's room first."

"Please do and take your time," I said, cheerfully. "I'll wait for you nearby."

Mr. Blackstone excused himself from the other senators and me. He went to the restroom, and I waited near the door until he was finished. Almost five minutes later, he was still inside. I was ready to leave, so I opened the door to the restroom and went inside. I was lucky that no one was in there, with the exception of Mr. Blackstone. He was in one of the stalls, whistling. I knocked on the door then boldly shoved it open. He quickly pivoted with his zipper halfway down. A frown was on his face; he examined me with a frown on his face.

"What in the hell are you doing in here?" Irritation was in his voice.

I placed my finger over my lips. "Shhhh," I said. "There's no need to get all hyped and excited, but I have to admit that I've been keeping my eyes on you all night. First, I want to give you some important information I think you should know about Mr. McNeil. Look everything over and give me a call in a few days to let me know what you intend to do. At that time, maybe you and I can kind of get to know each other better. Or, we could possibly get to know each other better right now, especially since your slacks are already unzipped and part of *it* is already sticking out."

Catching him off guard, I squatted and unzipped his slacks even more. He almost had a heart attack, and he panicked when I touched his penis.

"Uh, Mrs. Jefferson, please, what . . . what should I call you? Please don't do that, unless we—"

I could only laugh to myself at his nervousness. He didn't have to worry about me stooping low and doing anything with him. Trust and believe, I never would. I stood, pressed my body against his and zipped his slacks.

"Something down there doesn't smell quite right, but when you clean that up, be sure to contact me. I'll be waiting for your call. My card is inside of the envelope, and I look forward to hearing from you soon."

I kissed his cheek, and with a wide smile on my face, I left the restroom and looked for the closest place I could find to wash my hands.

First Lady,
Raynetta Jefferson

The gala was fun. I thoroughly enjoyed being in the presence of the elite in Washington, but more than anything I was pleased that Teresa had gotten the envelope to Mr. Blackstone. She told me how she'd delivered the package to him. I couldn't stop laughing at how she described their little encounter. Now, however, we waited to hear something from him. Two days had already passed and he hadn't reached out to Teresa yet. We were sure we would hear something by now. I mean, how could anyone in their right mind have that kind of information and just sit on it? Teresa wondered the same thing, and I informed her more information was coming soon. There was no question that we could give the information to Stephen and let him handle it, but Stephen wanted Mr. McNeil dead. I didn't think he would trust anyone with the information we'd had, and he would ask too many questions about where we'd gotten it from. It was best that we did things our way. Besides, if things fell apart and I somehow went down for this, Teresa would go down with me. At this point, though, we were in this together. There was no turning back, and we were willing to do whatever to make sure Mr. McNeil would spend the remainder of his years on earth behind bars.

As I was having breakfast with Teresa, a Secret Service agent informed us that Stephen was on his way back to the White House. I wiped my mouth with a napkin and dropped it on the table. Teresa guzzled down her orange juice and we both made our way outside to greet Stephen. I couldn't wait to see him. I truly missed my husband, and we had only been sending a few text messages to each other. All he kept saying was he was resting, he was fine and he had been thinking about us. That was pretty much it.

As Marine One landed on the South Lawn, Teresa and I waited for Stephen to exit with wide smiles on our faces. She was just as happy as I was to see him, and when the door opened to Marine One, my eyes were glued to where he would soon stand. He appeared at the door, and as he made his way down the steps, I could only think dirty things to myself. His haircut was fresh, tailored blazer clung to his frame, slacks hugged his package in the right place, leather shoes had a shine, and his trench coat blew behind him as he walked. He saluted a marine who stood to his right, and as the media took photos of him, he waved with glee in his eyes. There was something about the way he looked that made me feel warm and fuzzy inside. Maybe it was how well rested he looked; his joyful expression implied he was glad to be home. I was surprised when I turned to glance at Teresa and her expression was now flat.

"What's wrong?" I asked her. "Why are you looking puzzled like that?"

At first she hesitated, but then she spoke up. "It's a shame that I know your foolish husband better than you do. Then again, I am his mother. What I do know is this. A man only looks that refreshed and energized if he's been smoking weed, just purchased a new car or if he's had some very good pussy. Since Stephen doesn't smoke weed, and he doesn't need a new car, I'd say you'd better wipe that smile off your face and handle this shit to the best of your ability. I'm going inside to call Mr. Blackstone. That sucker hasn't called me back yet and I'm getting worried."

Teresa pivoted and stormed away. I watched Stephen from afar as he shook hands with everyone who reached out to him, waved at more people and had even stopped to answer a few questions from reporters. The propellers from Marine One made the wind stir around, and as Stephen finally headed my way, his trench coat continued to blow behind him. I couldn't get the thoughts of what Teresa had said out of my mind. I wouldn't know if her words had any validity to them, until Stephen approached me and I could search into his eyes. When he stepped forward, he wrapped one arm around my waist and kissed my cheek.

"Hello," he said. I cocked my head back and stared at him. He was unable to look me in the eyes and his hold around my waist didn't last long. "You look nice."

"So do you," I said. "You also look rejuvenated. Are you glad to be home?"

"Of course," was all he said. With Secret Service following closely behind us, we made our way down the West Colonnade together.

"I have three meetings scheduled today?" he said. "Maybe we can have a late dinner this evening."

It was a little after ten in the morning. I assumed Stephen would be busy when he returned, but it was kind of disappointing that after being away for three and a half weeks, he didn't feel obligated to spend, at least, one hour with me. I now believed every word Teresa had said. But in no way would I sweat it. One day, and in due time, he was going to regret everything. Maybe one day I would have some regrets too.

"I have a few things on my schedule as well," I said. "So a late dinner sounds good."

He reached for my hand and held it with his. Right before we made it to the Oval Office, he lifted my hand and kissed the back of it. "See you later," he said.

He walked off, and when I called after him he turned around. "Welcome back," I said. "I missed you."

He winked at me. "Missed you too."

That was it. I guess I was supposed to wait until later to spend time with my husband. Like hell I was. I went to the bedroom to change clothes, and after I snatched up my cell phone and purse, I went to my office. I called Alex who had reached out to me earlier to tell me he'd had some more information to give me about Mr. McNeil.

"Where are you?" he asked.

"I'm at the White House. Where are you?"

"At home, but I can meet you somewhere."

"No. Stay right there. I'm coming over."

"It's not a good idea for you to come here."

"Maybe not, but I'm coming anyway."

I hung up the phone, and when I looked in the doorway I saw Teresa standing there gazing at me.

"I'm not going to ask who that was," she said. "But, sometimes, us women have to do what we have to do. I'm on my way to go chat with Mr. Blackstone. The stupid fool said he didn't know how to reach me, but I could've sworn I put my card in the envelope."

"Well, keep me posted on how it goes. I may have some more information for you to share, and let's keep our fingers crossed that this all works out in our favor."

"I'm sure it will. Meanwhile, may I say one more thing to you before you go?"

"I'd rather you didn't, but I know you will probably say it anyway."

Teresa chuckled then stared at me with a straight face. "Figure out how to get him where it hurts and do to others what they do unto you. I'll leave it there, but I do think you know what I mean."

Without replying, I knew exactly what she meant. And after I slipped away from Secret Service during a meeting I was supposed to attend, I went to Alex's place. He opened the door without a shirt on. The top of his jeans were unbuttoned and smooth hair was right above the good stuff. From the look in my eyes, he already knew why I was there. He slipped his arms around my waist and pulled me into his apartment. After he slammed the door, he pressed me against it and yanked my blouse away from my breasts. One popped out, and as Alex leaned in to tackle my nipple, I rubbed the back of his head. His hands squeezed my thighs, and with my assistance, we both lowered my lace panties to the floor. His jeans hit the floor next, and after he hiked me up to his waist, he backed away from my breast to look at me.

"Are you sure you want this?" he asked.

"Positive," I replied then directed his head to my breasts again.

While holding my legs open in his arms, Alex sucked and massaged my breasts at the same time. He parted my moist slit with the tip of his head, before driving his thick muscle right in. It felt so good, I quickly shut my eyes. I raked my fingers through his sweaty hair, and as he aggressively took charge of my insides, my backside pounded against the door. He groaned, so did I. My breasts were getting a workout, until he backed away from them and pressed his lips against mine. I was the one who slipped my tongue into his mouth; the sweet taste made me go all in. I finally opened my eyes to look into his. They were the prettiest things I had ever seen. So was his smile, and I smiled back as his steel finally hit the mark. I gasped, pulled at his hair and yanked his head back. I was now the aggressor, and I soaked his lips with the saliva building in my mouth. Alex loved the taste. He softly bit my bottom lip and made a confession.

"I . . . I want more of you," he whispered. "And whatever you do, please don't stop this like you did last time."

The look in my eyes, and the fact that my fluids had started to rain down my thighs, that confirmed he could have all of me. He carried me away from the door with my legs secured around his waist; my arms were tightened around his neck. I surely didn't want to let go, but I had to when he carefully laid me back on the sofa. Instead of steering his muscle back in, he laid over me, taking rough bites at my neck. His tongue traveled from there to my belly button. After that, he journeyed south and slipped his tongue between my folds. I rubbed his soft hair, moaned out loudly and regretted how long I had waited to feel like this. Alex was a beast, and for the next few hours I had stepped down from my position as the first lady.

President of the United States,
Stephen C. Jefferson

Upon my return, I didn't have time to do anything but get back to work. Andrew and I had been in touch every day. He'd already told me VP Bass and the Republicans were trying to push through legislation regarding an infrastructure bill that was loaded with more tax cuts for the wealthy. That damn sure wasn't going to happen on my watch, so as soon as I ended my conversation with Raynetta, I made my way to the Oval Office. I went inside and saw VP Bass, along with six other Republicans sitting around talking. Everyone had a stack of clipped papers in front of them. I assumed they were discussing something pretty serious.

"I don't want to be rude, but this meeting is over. Get out." I held the door open for them to leave. "I have plenty of things to do and I need some privacy."

"Mr. President, we were in a meeting," VP Bass said. "Do you mind waiting until we're finished?"

"I do mind, and since you failed to comprehend what I just said, let me repeat myself again. Get the *fuck* out. Thanks."

VP Bass didn't expect to see me back so soon. She had been plotting since I was away, and after she and the other senators walked out, claiming how disrespectful I was, I slammed the door behind them. I buzzed Andrew so he could come into my office, and within the hour, he was there with numerous other people from my cabinet.

As I casually strolled around the room, they listened in. "While I was away, I had time to examine more executive orders that were put in place by my predecessor. I've already reversed a number of those orders, but I needed time to review all of them. After careful evaluation, many more orders will be reversed.

Some of that shit doesn't even make sense, and the American people have suffered long enough." I looked around the room and addressed each of my cabinet members who were tasked with creating a detailed outline for improving their areas within the next six months. Some people were able to relay their plan to me, many others like head of the Department of Education, head of the Department of Housing and Urban Development, and head of the Department of Justice weren't able to provide specifics.

"By tomorrow," I warned. "You all have until then to show me an outline or a detailed plan for improvement. If I don't see those plans, please be prepared to turn in your resignation letters. We can't afford to sit around and do nothing any longer. Not when our educational systems around this country are failing our children, and not when our justice department is still broken as hell. Too many things are in disarray, and instead of pointing fingers at the previous administration, let's get to work and make some real differences."

Everyone nodded. I had already spent nearly three hours discussing the changes I wanted to see, so I dismissed everyone and advised them to get to work. I had some work to do myself, and to be honest, it felt good to be back. Being away for a while helped. No, being in Hell House helped. After things settled down, I was able to have real discussions with a few Americans who supported me and who were all rooting for me. They let me know what they expected from me as their president, and the whole experience opened my eyes. The unfortunate thing was I had to bring down one person; someone who plotted to cause major damage in the house. Other than that, it was all good. I sat at my desk in deep thought about another thing that had happened— that maybe shouldn't have happened. But from the moment I'd entered Hell House, I suspected she and I would find ourselves in *situations* like we did. She had no idea what those moments did for me, and sometimes, all I needed was good conversation and sex that came with no attachments.

My phone buzzed and interrupted my thoughts. It was my secretary.

"Your mother is here to see you. Should I allow her to clear Secret Service and send her in?"

I didn't have much time on my hands, but I figured a few minutes with my mother wouldn't hurt. "Sure. Tell her to come in. The door is unlocked."

I looked at the door, and when my mother came in there was no smile on her face. She didn't appear happy to see me; I could tell there was something on her mind. I stood as she walked over to my desk.

"Welcome back," she said. "I know you don't wish to hear this, but your marriage is so messy. More so you, Stephen. The moment I saw you I could tell that you—"

I quickly cut her off. "My marriage is none of your business. And to be truthful, nothing that I do is your business, so you should learn to stay out of it." I sat on the edge of my desk with my arms crossed. "Have you heard anything from Joshua or Ina?"

"Unfortunately, I haven't. But getting back to your messy marriage, it is my business. A man of your caliber should know better than to indulge in sexual escapades with a former stripper who use wealthy men to climb the ladder. You are president of the United States, and you need to stop acting like a male whore. This is getting out of hand!" She raised her voice and shook her head. "We already had one president running around bragging about grabbing women by their pussies, and now . . ."

I placed my finger over her lips. "Shhhh. There is no comparison, so do not insult me. I guess people are starting to run their mouths again, but you can't believe everything you hear. My marriage *looks* good compared to many others who have occupied the Oval Office, so let it go and stop interfering. You've done enough of that already, and I assume, by now, you've already spoken to Michelle."

Her brows shot up. "Michelle who?"

I stood and gave my mother a look like she should've known better. "Don't you dare try to pretend that you don't know who I'm talking about. I already know what you did, and yet again, you're poking your nose where it doesn't belong."

I walked away from the desk and sat on the sofa. My mother followed and sat in a chair next to me. She continued with her lies.

"I don't know who or what you're talking about, so try again. What I do know about is Joshua. What are you going to do about him?"

"Nothing. Nothing at all. I guess I'll hear from him if or whenever he calls."

She rolled her eyes and crossed her legs. "That's a shame. I can't believe you're not going to do anything about getting him to come back here. He needs you, Stephen. And if you think I'm going to have a life without seeing my grandson, you're sadly mistaken."

"I told you what I was going to do. Let me repeat it again. Nothing. If you want to see him, go find him in England, apologize to Ina and ask her to forgive you. I want no part of it, unless I hear from Joshua again."

"You are so stubborn. I hate when you act this way. I love you, but there are times when I feel like Raynetta needs to leave you high and dry."

"She's already done that, and for the last time, Raynetta and I are none of your business."

"As long as you are my child, you are my business. So get over it, dear child, and hurry and clean up your mess. I'm starting to approve of Raynetta. The two of us had some interesting conversations while you were away. She's growing on me, and she's not as bad as I thought she was."

I got up to touch my mother's forehead. "Are you feeling okay? You couldn't be. And please, please tell me you haven't started drinking again. Have you?"

She smacked my hand away from her forehead. "Don't touch me. I don't know where your hands have been. I can only imagine what you did while you were gone."

I laughed and she stood to address me on a serious note. "Go ahead and get back to work," she said. "I'm staying one more night at the White House, and then I'm going home. Think long and hard about how you and Raynetta plan to move forward. If you don't love her anymore, Stephen, release her. There could be a chance that both of you deserve better. I don't know, but I do know you better not ever leave here again without her."

I kissed her cheek and held her hand as we walked to the door. "The only time I'm leaving is when I go on vacation again. Until then, I'm back and I'm about to show out for the American people. So sit back, watch and enjoy. You're going to be real proud of me in the upcoming days and months. Even more proud to call me your son."

She smiled and released my hand. "I'm always proud to call you my son, Mr. President. I can't wait to hear more about your plans. Meanwhile, I have something instore for you too. It's a surprise and I'm not ready to spill the beans just yet."

I didn't bother to elaborate because my mother was always up to something. She gave me a tight hug and told me she loved me before she left the Oval Office. I closed the door, and when Andrew returned with numerous executive orders for me to sign and reverse, I didn't need an audience. The media wasn't required, and this wasn't about getting a photo op. An hour later I was almost done, until I was interrupted by a phone call that in no way surprised me.

"I made it happen," he confirmed. "Now what, Mr. President?"

I didn't respond. Just ended the call and reached out to Sam so he could set up a press conference for me later. I needed to address the American people and share some of my objectives going forward. Thirty minutes later, it was show time. I stood behind the podium in the Press Briefing Room and didn't hold back on anything, starting with my marriage because people always wanted to know about that first for some reason.

"I can't say where things stand with myself and the first lady, but be patient with me as I attempt to work through a very difficult time. We are going through some unfortunate things, but please respect our privacy. That's all I ask, and I will not elaborate on much more. My priorities revolve around all of you. Whether you're Caucasian, African American, Hispanic, whatever, I need you to join together and mobilize like you've never done before. I need to work with a new congress, and many of the long serving muthafuckas on Capitol Hill need to be voted out next year. You all know who those cowards are. They are the ones who refused to stand when Russia tampered with our democracy. They rallied behind another war that we didn't need, and gave each and every one of you the massive bill. They minimized your healthcare, cut programs that were beneficial to you, told women what you should do with your bodies, and left our seniors fending for themselves. More children are living in poverty, the unemployment rate is on the rise again, not even a dog can survive on minimum wage, and when blacks are still being treated unfairly, they remained silent. The only ones satisfied right now are the wealthy. This isn't what I had hoped for America, but it's never too late to reverse the damage. Do your part, and I will continue to do mine. While many of our allies have turned their backs on the United States, I will find a way to make peace again. Along with our strong military, I will deal with our enemies one by one. But the truth is, we have major problems within this country. Problems that I can't resolve alone. I need each and every one of you to stand with me, please. For the love of every man, woman and child in this country, stand with me and say goodbye to the hypocrites who no longer belong in Washington. Democrat or Republican, send me people I can work with, not racists idiots who will find my foot swallowed in their asses. As your president, I refuse to tolerate the ongoing disrespect, and if anyone expects me to be politically correct, after all I've been through, wait on it. It's not going to happen. This is as presidential as it's going to get, until I have a congress who can work with me, instead of against me."

As the room fell silent, I continued to stress the need for action. I touched on some of the future plans I'd received from my cabinet members, and spoke about some of the new executive orders I'd signed. I wasn't sure how energized the American people would feel after this, but from the smiles in the room, I got a sense that something big was about to happen. If anything, congress would be forced to get on board and ride this wave with me. I was well aware that real change took time. It took a certain kind of president to shake things up and make the impossible happen. It had been promised too many times before, but many hadn't delivered. Even with all my flaws, maybe I would be able to.

"Unfortunately, I'm not going to take questions tonight. I'll be back tomorrow to answer any questions that you have. Enjoy your evening and don't get used to me being on good behavior."

Many of the reporters laughed and fired off questions at me anyway. I couldn't help it that my eyes shifted to Michelle, before I stepped away from the podium. Therefore, I wasn't surprised when I was walking down the hallway and Sam rushed up to tell me Michelle wanted to speak to me. Like before, I went into a private meeting room where she stood nibbling at her nail. I closed the door behind me and stood with a stern expression on my face.

"I guess you're ready to come clean," I said to her.

She dropped her arms by her side. "Come clean or whatever you want to call it, I do owe you an apology. I never should have accepted any money from your mother, and to be truthful, there really wasn't a reason for me to do it. I make decent money as a reporter. But after my divorce, things got a little tight. I kept thinking about my kids, and when your mother approached me about doing what I could to dismantle your marriage, I wasn't thinking clearly. It was never my intentions to go that far and I hope you know that. When I told you how I felt about you, I meant every word. I have fallen in love with you. This hurts so bad because I put myself in a situation that makes me look like a horrible woman. I'm not the kind of person you may think I am. You must know that, Stephen, please tell me you know I would never do anything to hurt you."

"Well, lies do hurt, and accepting money from my mother is unacceptable. You have no idea how this makes me feel, and it would've been wise for you to simply tell her to go to hell when she approached you. At this point, it doesn't matter. It's not like I ever had any intentions of divorcing my wife so you and me could ride off into the sunset and go live happily ever after. That wasn't going to happen, so now we can both just move on sooner than expected."

Michelle stood and stared at me. She blinked several times to clear her watery eyes.

"So, I guess it's over," she said as her lips quivered.

I didn't want to stand there and watch her fall apart, and even though I wanted to walk out on her, I couldn't. All I could do was speak the truth. "Months ago, I told you I didn't want to hurt you. I asked you not to get so attached to me. You knew I could never . . ."

"Yes, you said all of that, but you never stopped coming to see me. You made me feel like there was something there. Like you cared for me, just as much as I cared for you. Was it all fake, Stephen? Did you just use me? Is this thing with your mother an excuse for you to walk away from this? I need to know and you darn well better tell me the truth. Even if it hurts, just tell me!"

Her voice cracked as her tone went up several notches. I didn't want to answer her questions, and I didn't care if she would think I was a coward for not answering them. Instead, I made my way up to her and wrapped my arms around her. I tried to console her, but she pushed me away and demanded to know the truth.

"Answer me, Stephen. Was I just a piece of ass like your mother said? Did you really use me to help take away the pain you experienced due to your broken marriage? I've been through so much this year and you know exactly what I'm talking about. First my husband, and now you. I thought you really cared. But you didn't, did you? You never cared and now you just want me to forget that this—"

She paused to wipe her tears. Not saying anything else, she darted toward the door to exit. I rushed toward the door too and grabbed her wrist. I swung her around to face me, finally spilling my guts to her.

"I did care, but maybe not as much as you may have needed me to. It was more than just sex for me, but this thing with my mother has left a horrible taste in my mouth. I feel like I can't trust anyone. No one, Michelle, not even you. I'm sorry that it can go no further than this. I need to focus on what's really important. Shit has gotten out of hand and the American people are counting on me to make some major changes in their lives. I can't concentrate if I keep thinking about us. If I keep thinking about my marriage and how my personal life is so fucked up. So if you really love or care about me, I want you to walk away from this with an understanding of what my priorities must be. Are you willing to do that for me?"

She answered when she grabbed my face and hit me with a wet, juicy kiss that sent me staggering backward. I grabbed her waist and pulled her close to me. The taste of her tongue was so sweet, and it took everything that was in me not to spread her legs and indulge.

"Please," I said, looking into her eyes. "Can you please do that for me and just . . . just walk away from this?"

She slowly nodded and backed away from me. As our eyes stayed connected, she opened the door and then walked out. I wiped down my face and shook my head. "Fuck," I whispered. Now that I'd gotten *some* closure with that situation, I had to work on getting closure with another one.

First Lady,
Raynetta Jefferson

I was beat when I walked into the master bedroom around eleven o'clock that night. I'd missed dinner with Stephen, and I honestly didn't expect to see him there. He was sitting in bed while reading a book. He removed his glasses away from his face and looked me up and down. My wrinkled clothes implied I had been about my business, and without a drop of makeup on, he knew what time it was. The direction of his eyes traveled with me as I made my way across the room.

"I didn't know the duties of the first lady required you to be out this late at night," he said in a calm tone. "Where have you been?"

I yawned as I removed my heels and tossed them in a corner. "I think you already know that I wasn't representing as the first lady tonight. And please don't pretend you don't know where I was or who I was with."

"I don't know. If you care to share, I'm willing to listen."

I stood at the edge of the bed, contracting my eyes as I looked in Stephen's direction. "You haven't perfected lying as good as I have, Stephen, so try again. But if you think you have that's cool too. I'll just update you on a few things, starting with the night you came into this room and looked at my cell phone. You knew I had spoken to Alex; therefore, it made no sense for you to inquire. You're always trying to catch me in a lie, just so you can have a reason to run off and do what you do best. I know that you contacted Alex while you were away, and even though he told you he and I spent no time together at the hotel, you threatened him and dared him to keep pursuing me. You knew he would come after me, because that's the kind of man Alex is. Your threats energize him, and you were hoping that we hooked up so you could do your dirt while you were away and have something to throw in my face. More so, something to justify your actions." Having his full attention, I started to unbutton my ripped blouse. "But you know what, Stephen? It would take me a looooong time to get even with you. I would have to really put myself out there, so don't act surprised when you happen to see a new me. My actions won't be for revenge or anything like that, but maybe because your behavior proved to me that you have no problem with another man screwing your wife. It doesn't bother you if he made me come three times within an hour, compared to your one lousy time that proves I'm not excited about you anymore. I thoroughly enjoyed myself tonight, and whenever I feel as if we're equals, I'll give you a call and tell you all about it. On another note, if I find out you had anything, whatsoever, to do with that explosion at the hotel, I'm going to participate in your downfall. I don't trust you anymore, and I never thought the day would come when you willingly handed me over to another man on a silver platter."

Stephen didn't say one word. Just stared at me as I went into the bathroom to take a hot shower and wash Alex's scent off me. My shower lasted for thirty long minutes, and after I was done I changed clothes and slipped into a new pair of heels. I brushed my hair into a ponytail, refreshed my makeup, and then returned to the bedroom. Stephon was now sitting up with his hands behind his head. He looked straight ahead without shifting his eyes in my direction.

"I'll see you tomorrow," I said. "Sleep well, if you can."

He finally looked at me. "For the record, I've made you have more than three orgasms within an hour. Sometimes more than that, so get your facts together."

I clapped my hands and smiled at him. "I figured you would comment on that and nothing else. Interesting, Stephen, very interesting to say the least."

I rolled my eyes and left the room. With a Secret Service agent in tow, he drove me to a nearby hotel where I spent the night. I had no intentions of staying there for more than one day; tonight I just needed some space. I rested well that night, and getting back to my business as the first lady, my schedule for the following days thereafter went something like this:

Day 1: Spoke at a women's conference in Washington, and then I helped several families of soldiers put together care packages to send overseas. At the end of the day, I met Alex for drinks and we went back to his apartment to have sex.

"I was afraid that you wouldn't be back," he whispered in my ear while tampering with my hotspot. "I don't think I'll ever get enough of you."

"I wouldn't be so sure about that, but we'll see."

I rolled on top and gave Alex the ride of his life.

Day 2: I left the White House early with Stephen so we could attend a senator's funeral. It lasted for about an hour, and afterward I attended a picnic with several kids at two elementary schools in Washington. At the end of the day, I met Alex in a park. He gave me some additional information about Mr. McNeil, and it wasn't long before we started having sex on a bench. I straddled his lap and held his head as he dropped it back and moaned.

"Why are you doing this to me?" He gripped my hips that moved at a tranquilizing pace. "You're going to have me hooked, Raynetta. I'm going to be sooooo disappointed when you go back to the president."

"I never left the president, but there's no need for you to worry about him. Just focus on us and all that we're doing right now. Doesn't it feel good?"

He nodded, and after two orgasms, I was the one who couldn't get enough.

Day 3: Emme and I didn't leave the White House until noon. I attended a baseball game and threw out the first pitch. Had a blast that day, but wound up with a sore ankle when I left the ballpark and tripped in my heels. I was seen by a doctor at the White House, but at the end of the day, Alex took good care of me. He massaged my ankle while we were in the shower, and shortly thereafter we had sex. As he stood behind me, massaging my breasts and biting my neck, I sucked in a deep breath and closed my eyes.

"I could get real used to this," I confessed. "Are you tired of me yet?"

"No," he rushed to say. "Never. I want this to go on forever."

I wished it could too, but all good things, eventually, came to an end.

Day 4: Emme and I traveled to Florida to rally Senator Jenkins' constituents. She deserved to win the upcoming race more than the Republican who ran against her. I made the case for why everyone needed to get out in a few more months and vote. Emme and I didn't return to the White House until late that evening, but at the end of the day, I met Alex in the lobby at a hotel. He gave me some more information about Mr. McNeil, and as we made our way to a suite, we settled for sex on the elevator. Alex was down on his knees with one of my legs thrown over his shoulder. I could barely keep my balance as he feasted on my insides.

"What am I going to do with you?" I cried out and pulled at his hair. "This is tooooo much!"

He backed away from my goodness and pecked my thighs with his soft lips. While looking up at me, he smiled.

"I'll show you what I'm going to do to you when we get to the suite. I hope you're ready because it's going to be a long and eventful night."

It took a minute to get to the room, because when Alex dropped his pants and turned me around to face the wall in the elevator, I bent over and allowed him to indulge. My healthy butt cheeks slapped his thighs as he scooped his hard muscle into me. I came more times that night than ever before.

Day 5: This was the busiest day of all. I entertained groups of visitors at the White House, Stephen and I had a luncheon with several leaders from the Black Lives Matter movement, I participated in a parade and I joined several tourists at the National Museum of African American History & Culture. At the end of the day, I met Alex for dinner. We laughed and ate our hearts out. We resumed our conversation in a private room that had a California King bed and a Jacuzzi. Soft music thumped in the background as I faced him in a lounging chair with no clothes on. We had just gotten out of the Jacuzzi and our wet bodies were close together.

"How did you know I like Jazz?" Alex asked.

"There are numerous things that I know, Alex, and the kind of music you enjoy is just one of those things."

"Well, I know plenty of things you enjoy too. I also know that I've fallen in love with you. And shame on me, because I knew this would happen."

As he laid over me, I touched his face again. "I figured it would happen too, but, unfortunately, I won't be able to do anything about your feelings. I have feelings too, but I could never fall head over heels for a man who works for my husband. You do still work for him, don't you?"

Alex moved to the side of me and released a deep breath. "Saying that I work for him is a bit of a stretch. I . . . . I just handle some important matters for him when I'm asked."

"You mean important matters like screwing me and keeping me busy so I don't get in his way? Or are you paid to do other things for him like fake an explosion at a hotel so the president can keep the American people on his side and force them to unite."

Alex lay silent. He pondered what to say, and when he opened his mouth his words appeared sincere.

"I've been very helpful to the president in telling him things he needs to know. But I haven't been asked to keep you busy, nor was I behind the explosion. Other agents were, but please know I can't discuss details about that incident with anyone."

"I don't expect you to go into details, but I was there. The explosion seemed so real. There were dead bodies and everything. How can . . ."

"Everything is not always what it seems in this country. You were in shock that day, and you were eager to get out of there. The images shown on TV, well, even a director can make a movie appear real. There is a reason for everything, and maybe the president will tell you more. In reference to us, yes, the president told me I could never have you. He said you would never give yourself to a man like me, and I didn't like that he threatened me."

"So, you had something to prove. And now that you've conquered the president's wife, you can throw it in his face and wear your badge of honor, right?"

"It's not like that. It was never about me throwing this is in face. I'm being completely honest with you about how I feel."

"I believe that you are, Alex. After all, you win, right?"

"I win because you make me feel like a winner. I am in love with you, Raynetta, and that is the truth. I just didn't want to share any details with you about the conversations I've had with the president. They haven't been good, and I do believe his threats are serious."

"If you believe they are, why are you here? Do you not fear what he will do to you?"

"Honestly, I don't. I used to, but not anymore."

I knew there was so much more to this, but for now, our conversation ended on that note. I rolled on top of Alex and made sure the camera caught my pretty, smooth cheeks when he slipped his hardness into me again. I laughed at the way it tickled my insides, and I also chuckled when I thought about Stephen's face when he'd have an opportunity to see the explicit photos of Alex and me from the past five days. Those photos didn't arrive at the Oval Office until the following day. They were inside of a nicely wrapped gift box with five pair of my moist and sticky panties, compliments of Alex who had definitely taken me there. While speaking to Stephen over the phone, I asked him to carefully open the gift box.

"There's not a bomb in here, is it," he said, jokingly. "The way you're rushing me to open this, I can only assume what's inside."

"No. No bomb, but it may cause an explosion."

"Not in this nicely wrapped box. Whoever wrapped this did a good job."

"I'll be sure to thank the lady at the store later."

There was silence, followed by more silence. Nothing was said for, at least, two or three whole minutes. I assumed he was admiring the photos or possibly sniffing my panties.

"Nice, isn't it?" I asked. "And now, Mr. President, I think we're finally even."

After those words left my mouth, he hung up the phone. All I heard was the dial tone.

Day 6: My explicit photos with Alex were on the front page of the *National Enquirer*. Stephen was the only one who could've leaked the photos to the press; I was livid. When he called, I snatched up the phone and listened to him speak in a soft and calm tone.

"Don't fuck with me, Raynetta, you will lose every time. If you don't believe me, ask Alex. By now, he should be at the gates of hell where you're headed, if you ever try some shit like that again. And for the record, you are now considered an enemy to me."

Right after he ended the call, I rushed to call Alex. I was surprised—shocked when Stephen answered his phone.

"I guess you must be in hell with Alex," I said. "If not, by this time next week you will be, especially when I tell the media about the fake explosion and about all the dirt you've been doing behind closed doors. So, don't *you* fuck with me, Stephen. Think wisely, and you can start by telling the American people those photos of me and Alex were doctored. Better yet, tell Alex to do it. He's your puppet, and if you expect me to believe you killed him, please. I'm not as stupid as you think. There's a reason why I'm married to the most powerful man in the world, and from the first day I met you, I knew you would be someone special. Going along with the ride hasn't been easy, but by the time I get finished with you, all of this, Mr. President, will be worth it."

There was a long silence, followed by laughter. I hung up on Stephen, and just as I walked to the other side of the hotel room, there was a knock at the door. I had recently called room service, but when I opened the door, I saw a gun aimed directly at my face.

"Two options," General Stiles said. "Come with me or find out what a bullet tastes like. The choice is yours."

I opened my mouth, but just as I started to speak, I was smacked across my face with the gun. After that, darkness followed.

President of the United States, Stephen C. Jefferson

I hated it had come to this, but Raynetta's actions, words and threats didn't sit right with me. She'd been on my shit list for a very long time, and I didn't feel good about anyone who had ties with my number one enemy, and then turned around and smiled in my face. Wife or not, I had to find out what her motive was, if she actually had one. I wanted to know what her reason was for staying married to me, the most powerful man in the world, and was this all along a plan of hers that included someone else? So for now, it was back to the underground bunker for me. I wasn't sure how the night was going to end, and if my precious wife failed to say the right things, the world would hear about the unfortunate demise of the first lady.

Once again, I entered the cold, concrete room with General Stiles right by my side. Just like Levi, Raynetta had been placed in a chair with her hands cuffed behind her. Her head was slumped, hair covered her bruised face and part of her shirt had been ripped away from her chest. She glared at me with much anger in her eyes and spoke through gritted teeth.

"Un-cuff me now, Stephen. What are you doing and where in the hell are we?"

I turned to General Stiles and lifted my hand. She smiled and slapped in my hand the same 9mm I'd killed Levi with.

"Un-cuff her and then give us some privacy," I said to her.

General Stiles did as she was told. "No problem." She removed the cuffs from Raynetta's wrists. "I'll be outside if you need me."

After she left the room, I gave Raynetta my undivided attention. I grabbed a chair and sat directly in front of her, calm as ever. "It's time for some real talk, baby, or some real action." I placed the 9mm on her lap, then retrieved another one that was tucked in the front of my slacks. I aimed the gun at her while looking at the one on her lap.

"Go ahead and pick it up." I said. "There's one bullet inside, and on the count of three, we're going to exchange gunfire. My advice, don't miss."

Raynetta didn't hesitate to pick up the gun and aim it at me. Our eyes focused on each other as I started to count.

"One, two—"

She fired off a bullet that whistled as it blew past my ear and landed into the concrete wall. I quickly turned around to look at the broken concrete pieces on the ground.

"Shit!" I said. "You didn't wait until I got to three and you almost took off my damn ear." I turned around and touched my ear to make sure it wasn't bleeding.

"Unfortunately," Raynetta said. "I missed. Give me another bullet and I won't."

I stood and walked over to the concrete wall where several other holes were visible. "You have no idea how historic this concrete wall is," I said, touching the holes in the wall. "These four holes right here are symbolic. So are the two down there, and the one furthest to the left is the most recent."

"Good, Stephen. I don't need a lesson on bullet holes, but thank you very much. Let me out of here, now!"

I smiled as I returned to the chair and faced her again. "I can't let you out of here, because you're in a safe place where you can't tell anyone my secrets. And as long as you're down here, no one will know the truth about the explosion. What you don't understand, Raynetta, is being president of the United States of America is the most difficult position ever. You have so many critical decisions to make, and whatever you do, sometimes, it never seems like enough. People flip on you at the drop of a dime, and after a few years in office, many people start to hate you, maybe even your own wife. So, many years ago, one of my brilliant predecessors created the presidential playbook. Every president has read it, and it gives us tips on what drastic measures to take to get the American people on our side. It tells us how to be creative and concoct certain incidents to cause distractions. It informs us when and when not to go to war. How to really deal with our enemies, and when to make certain announcements to shake up things. It even informs us how to deal with our marriages, and when our wives threaten to reveal our secrets, well, the playbook warns us that things can get a little sticky." I turned to face the wall again. "So the holes you see back there are from first ladies, like you, who purposely missed their target. Only once did a president get shot, and no one ever knew about it because we only tell the public what we want them to know. So, according to the playbook, congratulations, you passed the trust test. I still, however, have too many doubts about you. I would never do anything to hurt you, but if you attempt to cripple me, my views will change. The playbook says a president should never divorce his wife, under any circumstances, and if he does, the American people will never forgive him. So, the bottom line is, I need you. I need you to put your big girl panties on and ride this shit out with me until I'm done. If your motive all along was to use me to get here, then you're going to stay here. I don't give a damn if you love me or not, nor do I care what your intentions were for marrying me. I guess you don't want to tell me, but like everything else, the truth always comes to the light."

Raynetta narrowed her eyes as she looked at me, exemplifying much hatred. "It does come to the light, but just so you know, I have plenty of more secrets you will never know about."

"Of course you do, but there is one little other secret I need to go ahead and share with you."

I removed an envelope from the inside of my shirt and reached out to give it to her. "If Alex was here," I said. "He would've delivered this to you. But since he's long gone, allow me to break the news to you."

Raynetta hurried to open the envelope. She probably thought the inside contained photos of Alex, but it didn't. Inside were photos of her family. Of her grandfather in particular, and seeing his photos and background information caused her eyes to grow wide.

"The only reason I decided to spare that bastard's life was because of you. It is his poisonous blood that runs through your veins, and when I recently found out who you were to him, I was devastated. Maybe that's why you can't love me like I need you to. Maybe you hate me at times because there is something in you, just like him, that triggers you to despise me due to the color of my skin. He's going down soon enough, but it will be on my terms. I—"

"Stop it!" Raynetta screamed. "Stop your lies, Stephen, you are such a liar! Mr. McNeil is not my grandfather! There is no way in hell he is, so stop telling lies!"

"If you don't believe me, go ask him. He knows who you are, and he hates the hell out of me because I'm married to his granddaughter. If he lies to you, all the proof you need is right there in your hand."

"Like hell it is," she shouted. She ripped the papers and photos to shreds and threw them at me. "This is just something else you fabricated. And if there is any truth to it, why would you stay married to me?"

"I already told you. The presidential playbook says I can trust you, and I must prepare myself for the duration of—"

"Fuck the presidential playbook and screw you too! I . . . I need to get out of here. You will not hold me here against my wishes!"

Raynetta rushed to the door and banged on it. "Open this door, bitch, and let me out of here!"

"Unfortunately, General Stiles doesn't follow your orders, only mine. So, come back over here, have a seat and chill. Allow everything I've said to you to sink in. And if the chair gets too uncomfortable for you tonight, just pretend you're in Alex's bed where you appeared real relaxed and more flexible than you've ever been."

Raynetta rushed up to me, but after a little arm twisting and necessary force, she was back in the chair with the cuffs tightened on her wrists again. I rubbed the tips of my fingers along the side of her face where the bruise was.

"Remind me to get at General Stiles for putting this mark on you. She's supposed to respect the first lady, but since you haven't been representing, maybe she thought it was okay. I'll tell her we're good, and now that we both know where things really stand, maybe shit will get better between us."

Raynetta didn't say anything until I reached the door.

"You will pay for this," she threatened. "If you think I'm going to fall in line and continue my role as first lady, you are out of your damn mind."

I chuckled and stroked the hair on my chin while looking at her. "I know you're going to fall in line, because you invested a lot into this. And if you wanted me dead or you wanted me to pay for this, you would've killed me when you had the chance."

I unlocked the door and walked out. In a few days, I was positive that Raynetta would have a change of heart. As for tonight, I had other plans. General Stiles headed in one direction, and Lenny took me to Michelle's place. It was the weekend, so I knew her kids wouldn't be there. She, however, was standing in the kitchen in front of the sink while filling a pitcher with water. All she had on was a pair of white cotton panties that sat high on her curvy hips. Her white bra was partially unhooked in the back, and her beautiful chocolate skin looked moisturized with oils. I leaned against the doorway to the kitchen, admiring her beautiful mountains that had my steel standing at attention. She carried the pitcher of water to the refrigerator, and as soon as she put it inside, I cleared my throat. Her head snapped to the side; a frown instantly appeared on her face.

"No," she said, moving her head from side-to-side. "No, Stephen, you can't do this. I won't allow it. You need to leave right now."

"I just stopped by to say hello. Am I not allowed to . . ."

"No. You're not allowed to do anything and I mean it, Stephen. Leave and don't ever come here again."

She wanted to exit the kitchen, but the only way out was through me. I held up my arm to block her from exiting.

"I came to apologize. I know that I put you in a bad position, and what I asked of you was very unfair."

"You're darn right it was, but it doesn't matter anymore. You told me to move on, and I want you to do the same."

Michelle ducked underneath my arm and rushed to the front door. She opened it and pointed out the door. "Go," she said. "Please and stop showing up like this. I heard what you said loud and clear. I also accept your apology, and I do understand that your plate is full and you have a country to run."

I stood by the door and examined her actions with my hands in my pockets. "You're right. I shouldn't have come here, but I couldn't stop thinking about you. I . . ."

"You mean, you couldn't stop thinking about those photos of Alex and Raynetta in the *National Enquirer*. I'm so hip to your game, and you should be ashamed of yourself for doing this crap." She opened the door wider. "Out. Go now or else."

I took several steps forward, but turned around as I was on the other side of the door. "Just so you know, I didn't come here because of Raynetta and Alex. This is no game, and if it was all about sex, I do have other options."

"Good. Go seek those options and don't you dare come back here."

Michelle slammed the door in my face. My feelings were slightly bruised, but I was never one to give up without putting up a fight. I lightly knocked on the door, and the second she opened it, she yelled at me.

"What, Stephen? What do you want?"

"You, damn it. I want you."

Before she responded, I rushed inside and flipped her over my shoulder. I kicked the door shut with my foot, and as I carried Michelle down the hallway, she wildly kicked her legs and tried to make me lose my balance.

"This is not going to work!" she shouted. "Put me down, Stephen, and just . . . just leave me the hell alone!"

I laid her on the bed and hurried to remove my suit jacket. As I eased between her legs, I held her hands above her head so she wouldn't strike me. I could feel her heartbeat racing against mine. Frustration was visible in her eyes and she fought hard not to give in. Her voice was up there.

"So, you're just going to ignore what I said to you, right?" She tried to pull her hands away from my grip. "Is that what you're going to do, Stephen? Just come in here and take what you want."

"No, I'm not going to take anything. It is my hope that you forgive me for being so stupid and give us what we both want."

With the tip of my nose touching hers, she gazed into my eyes and tried to speak her truth. "I don't want us anymore."

"Yes you do." I pecked her lips then lowered my head to suck her neck. "Tell me you want us or should I say how badly you want us to continue on like this."

She moved her head to stop me from sucking her neck. "I don't want us to continue. You don't know how much this hurts and . . ."

I placed my lips over hers to silence her. "I know it hurts. But give me a chance to stop the pain."

"You can't stop it. Nothing you can do at this point can stop it."

"Yes I can. Open those pretty legs wider, give me a few hours and I will make everything feel so good."

"A few hours with you isn't what I need."

"Then tell me what you need so I can give it to you."

She turned her head to avoid looking into my eyes. "I need for you to go."

"I can't do that. Not now, especially since I can't help myself. I'm selfish and I just want it all. I have to have all of it."

I released her hands, lifted her bra and went for it. From her breasts to her belly button, I tasted her sweetness. She squirmed around underneath me, and when I pulled her panties aside to swipe her moist folds with my tongue, she widened her legs and provided much access to all of it. I removed my clothes and didn't hesitate to go all in. I had discovered Michelle's weakness that night, and, unfortunately, she'd tapped into my weakness as well. The only thing I hoped was my desires for wanting to have it all—to have everything—wouldn't lead to me being left with nothing at all. I could never envision that happening, and as long as I continued to adhere to the presidential playbook, I was on track to becoming one of the most successful and productive presidents ever. Then again, I guessed that depended on who you asked.

"I surrender, Mr. President," Michelle whispered as I slow stroked her so well. "You . . . you got me."

I halted my moves, pecked her lips and locked my eyes with hers. "I know, but you got me too."

The lights went out, and as I made love to Michelle, I could hear several reporters in the background, conversing over the television.

The president is riding high. His poll numbers continue to increase, and the American people agreed with his assessment the other day. They are prepared to take action, and this upcoming midterm election is going to be brutal for numerous members of congress, both Democrats and Republicans. It finally feels like this country is moving in another direction. We have to give the president credit, and whether we agree with his approach or not, he seems to be getting the job done.

The other reporters agreed. All I could do in the moment was smile as I listened to Michelle on the verge of an orgasm and the reporters kind words. As president, it simply didn't get any better than this.

Season 2: Episode 2
Change is Coming to the White House

President of the United States,
Stephen C. Jefferson

For now, I was riding high and things were going according to my plans. Raynetta had come to her senses, and after four lonely days and nights in the bunker cell, she was ready to come out and continue on in her role as the first lady. She wasn't happy about it, but she understood that leaving the White had consequences. Divorcing me had consequences too and the truth was, we still needed each other. I needed her so the American people would stay on my side. She needed me because, no matter how bad things were, being the first lady positioned her to make a lot of money and be set for life whenever we left here. I wasn't sure how she intended to handle the situation with Mr. McNeil being her grandfather, and a part of me felt like she was still in denial. We were barely speaking to each other and many of my nights were spent in the Oval Office. I didn't want to sleep in the same bed as Raynetta, especially since she had given herself to another man. Of course I was upset about it, and I had to find out if Raynetta was as loyal as she often claimed to be. There were times when I purposely pushed her buttons, just to see how she would react. I guess she must've had enough of me being with other women. But for some reason, I thought she knew, deep in her heart, that none of the women I'd been with meant that much to me. Yes, I liked Michelle Peoples, a lot. If anyone had tampered with my heart, it was her. She was *sweet*, but being sweet was not enough to make me fall in love. I wasn't even trying to go there, and the only people I'd have love for, right now, was my son, Joshua, and my mother. I missed the hell out of him, but he and his mother, Ina, were long gone. I had ways of finding out where they were, but since Joshua asked me to let him leave in peace, that was what I intended to do.

After my morning workout, I took a shower and changed into a navy suit that hugged my frame. My face was clean shaven and my waves were flowing. I had a meeting scheduled with a few members from my administration this morning, and after that, I was expected to join Senator Hines for a women's rally in North Carolina. They were counting on me to make some changes with women's health and equal pay. The prior administration had dropped the ball on women, and I had to do what I could to get congress to vote on legislation that was as fair to women, as it was to men. I certainly knew that making such changes was important, but as always, I was disappointed in Vice President Bass who was pushing back against these changes as well. With her being a woman, it didn't make any sense to me. But nothing in politics made sense. Special interest groups controlled many members of congress, as well as the wealthy. They had a grip on VP Bass and ever since we'd worked together on gun control legislation, things had stalled.

It was my intentions to skip breakfast, but when I saw Raynetta in the dining room eating, I decided to join her. She appeared ready to go handle some business too. Her gray pantsuit had a belt that tightened at her waist and part of her hair was pinned up. Her makeup was caked on pretty thick; I assumed she wanted to cover the bruise on her face, compliments of General Stiles. As soon as I took a seat, I questioned her plans for the day. Without lifting her head, she stirred her grits that were topped with butter.

"Where I go is none of your damn business," she barked.

I chuckled and looked at the server next to me. "Can I get you anything to eat, Mr. President?"

"Some coffee will be fine, along with a bowl of fruit."

Raynetta added her two cents and finally looked up. "If you happen to have some poison, put some in his coffee. No one will ever know and your secret is safe with me."

With a frown on his face, the server walked away. I wiped my lips with a napkin and smiled as I looked across the table at Raynetta. "Just so you know, threatening the president can get you jail time. And so can trying to get someone to harm me. Be real careful about what you say and how you treat me. I'm still your husband, and I am, indeed, the president."

"That doesn't mean anything, whatsoever, to me. Through my eyes, you're a murderer, a liar, a cheater and a lousy ass husband. The American people have no idea who you really are, and once they figure it all out, I feel sorry for you. They're going to chew you up and spit you out. So enjoy your time here as much as you can. I'm going to enjoy it too, but in the meantime, all I ask is that you keep your distance from me."

"I promise you I will, and I'm slightly disappointed in you. By now, I thought you would've calmed down and come to your senses. But I guess you're still upset about Alex, huh?"

"I couldn't care less about Alex. He was your puppet and I'm sure he's still somewhere alive and well. As for me coming to my senses, trust me, I have."

Raynetta dropped her napkin on the table and got up. As she walked by me, I reached for her hand. In an instant, she snatched up a knife from the table and held it close to my face.

"Your days of touching me are over. I hate you Stephen and I should've killed you when I had a chance. Don't make another opportunity present itself, and you can make sure that doesn't happen by keeping your distance, as I kindly asked."

She dropped the knife and it bounced on the floor. After she walked out, the server came in with my fruit and coffee. I sat in silence, enjoying breakfast without any more drama from my so-called wife.

Several hours later, I was done with my staff meeting and was on my way to North Carolina on Air Force One. The meeting was what I considered productive, and we had an outline of some of the items we wanted to see implemented in the bill for women's equality. VP Bass griped the whole time, but with so many Democrats on my side, I ignored her suggestions that set women back, instead of moving them forward.

"Did you see the look on her face when you mentioned the meeting was adjourned?" my chief of staff, Andrew, said as we sat in my office. "She is going to be a problem for us. I wish there was some way to replace her."

"Replace her with who? Another pain in the ass republican. No thanks. I'll take my chances with her, and we may get her to come on our side this time. Especially, since this legislation pertains to women."

"I wouldn't be so sure of that. As the VP, she her vote may be needed to get us over the threshold. Too many members of the freedom caucus are planning to sit this one out. We need all the votes we can get, and unfortunately, we don't have the support of every democrat."

"Well, we just have to keep pushing. This rally is going to stir things up and many democrats won't be able to buck their party and say no."

"I hope you're right, but you know how Washington works."

I nodded because if anyone knew, I certainly did. It didn't work, and we had so many issues looming.

The rally had me feeling high. After witnessing a sea of cheering women with signs waving in the air, I was ready to address them. Secret service surrounded me, and after I was introduced by Senator Hines, I strutted to the podium to speak to the roaring crowd. The thunderous applauses were so loud my eardrum felt like it was about to burst. A smile covered my face as

I looked at the thousands of women gathered before me. I waited for the cheers to cease. That didn't happen until nearly ten minutes later, and after everything quieted down, I lowered the microphone to my lips and prepared myself to let the women of this nation know whose side I was on.

"What's up, ladies? It feels good to be here," I said while nodding. "I can't think of any other place I would rather be right now, and when I come, I always come with good news."

The crowd roared again. And when things quieted down this time, I started to speak about many of the changes I had discussed with my administration earlier. The women cheered when I spoke about equal pay, they groaned when I mentioned what the previous administration had done and they chanted "leave our bodies to us" when I touched on the subject of women's health. My speech lasted for nearly an hour. Everyone was hyped, and as I made my way through the crowd, shaking hands and signing autographs, several secret agents followed me.

"We love you, Mr. President," one woman shouted from afar as I stopped to sign another woman's T-shirt.

"I love all of you too," I said and continued to sign my autograph on numerous pieces of papers that were shoved in my direction.

"Mr. President, can we come visit you at the White House," another woman said. "We heard you be having some live parties. Why don't we ever get invited?"

I laughed. "I wish that was true, but it's not. I don't have much time for partying."

As those words left my mouth, one woman reached for my arms and snatched me closer to her. "I . . . I just want to fuck the—"

She paused when secret service pushed her back and threatened to arrest her. I kept it moving and when I felt someone touch my package, I looked up and saw a white chick smiling at me.

"Mr. President, do you have an internship available?"

She was also pushed back by Secret Service. One of my agents offered a suggestion. "I think we should go, Mr. President."

I shrugged and kept moving through the crowd, shaking hands. One woman held on tight and squeezed my hand as I attempted to pull it back. When I looked at her, evil was in her eyes. Her stained yellow teeth were rotten and her dirty blonde hair needed conditioner and shampoo.

"Get out of my house, Nigger. You don't belong there."

As secret service grabbed her, she gathered spit in her mouth and released it directly in my face. I could feel it sliding down the right side of my cheek. Seconds later, secret service had wrestled her to the ground. A few other women in the crowd started to throw punches at her, and as the situation turned chaotic, I was rushed away by three other agents. One of them gave me a napkin to wipe my face.

"Thanks. Arrest her ass and do not release her until I give the order."

That fast, I was pissed. Talking ill to me was one thing, but spitting in my face would bring about death.

President of the United States, Stephen C. Jefferson

While on my way back to Washington, I had calmed down. I was disappointed, though, that today's news wasn't about the thousands of women who had shown up at the rally. It wasn't about the proposals I had drafted with my administration to improve the lives of women. The coverage was all about me being spit on. About the numerous fights that had happened and about how many people had been arrested. There was a video being played over and over again, showing the man spitting in my face. It was downright disgusting, and it angered me on so many different levels.

"Who is he?" I asked Andrew while on Air Force One.

"According to his social media pages, he belongs to one of those white nationalist groups. His name is Paul Macon and he's a loser. He's unemployed, depends on the government for a disability check and he lives in a trailer park. His criminal record is long. Several assault charges, robbery charges and a possession of illegal substance charge. He did six months in jail and it appears that he coordinated with a few other people to attend the event and disrupt it. I'm upset about his actions, but I have to say this, Mr. President. If Secret Service can't stop spit, how can they protect you from a bullet? I think they're getting too relaxed again. Maybe some more heads need to roll."

Before I could respond, there was a knock at the door. One of my Secret Service agents poked his head in the doorway to tell me someone from the press had asked to see me.

"Screw the press," Andrew said and threw his hand back. His cheeks were red. I could tell he was frustrated about being interrupted. "Tell them the president is busy. We're in the middle of an important conversation."

"It's a reporter," the agent said. "She said it was urgent."

"What's her name?" I asked.

"Michelle. Michelle Peoples."

Andrew released a frustrating sigh. I sat up in my chair and rubbed my waves back. "Andrew, let's finish this conversation later."

"How much later?" he snarled. "I need to discuss a few other things with you. And no disrespect, but I just want to know how long you're going to be."

"Not long. Wait for me in the communications suite. Get something strong to drink and find out more about Mr. Paul Macon for me."

Andrew nodded. As he left my office, Michelle sauntered in. Her arms were folded across her chest. She wore a peach blouse and a tight tan skirt that hugged her P-shaped backside. Her natural hair was pulled back into a ponytail, and there wasn't a drop of makeup on her blemish free, smooth chocolate face. I glanced at her model-shaped long legs that were poured over my broad shoulders about a week or so ago. I didn't have time to reminisce about that night, because the somber look on her face told me something serious was on her mind.

"Two things," she said after the agent shut the door. "I wanted to know if you were okay, and I need to open up to you about something, pertaining to this thing we have going on."

I massaged my hands together while checking her out as she stood in front of my desk.

"Spit isn't going to kill me, but he did catch me off guard. I assume everyone sitting in the press corps area can't stop talking about it, right?"

"That's all everyone is talking about, and I assure you that it will be on the front cover of every newspaper tomorrow morning."

"That wouldn't surprise me one bit. And since we both already know that will be the case, let's switch to the other subject which pertains to us."

Michelle pivoted and took a seat on a sectional sofa that faced my desk. She crossed her legs and bit into her bottom lip.

"We need to end this," she said bluntly. "I want you to stop coming to my place and persuading me to do things with you that make me feel so horrible afterwards. There was a time when I felt like I didn't care what happened between us. My feelings are now way too involved in this, and I know this thing between us isn't going anywhere. I think you know that too, so let's just stop while we're ahead and let it be."

"I have no problem with that, Michelle, and I want you to make the call going forward. If that's really what you want, your wish will be granted."

"Your words don't hold much truth, because every time I look up, you're coming to my place, making me feel like I really matter to you and . . . "

My reply was stern. "You do matter, and I asked for you to make the call going forward. You said you would like to end this, and I'm in agreeance with you. The truth is, I don't have time for this. I don't have time to deal with us and I agree that what's been going on between us needs to cease. You have my word that I won't come to your place again. Even if you invite me, I won't come. Is that what you needed to hear?"

There was silence as she stared at me. Seconds later, she responded. "Yes. It's exactly what I needed to hear, so don't let me waste anymore of your time."

She stood and as she made her way to the door, I spoke again.

"Thanks for putting up with me. I know this hasn't been easy for you, and if you change your mind, the door remains open."

She walked out. I released a deep sigh and fell back in my chair, thinking about her and about what I was going to do with Mr. Macon.

The moment I returned to the White House, my mother was waiting for me in the Oval Office. She was sitting behind the Resolute desk while resting comfortably in my chair. A glass of alcohol was in her hand, a frown was on her face.

"Before I tell you how I feel about that clown-ass fool spitting on you today, I have to tell you that sitting at this desk makes me feel like a very powerful woman. Maybe I should run for president one day. You know I would get so many important things accomplished."

"I have no comment, but if you don't mind, I would like to have my chair back. After you allow me to sit at my desk, can you please tell me why you have that drink in your hand?"

She jumped up from the chair, yet remained by the desk with the glass in her hand. After tossing back the brown liquid, she placed the glass on my desk and cleared her throat.

"What else am I supposed to do? You have me worried sick about you. I've been waiting for two hours for you to return. I need to know if you've heard anything from Joshua, what is going on with you and Raynetta, and why in the hell didn't you slap the mess out of that white, racist fool for spitting on you today? He was well within your reach. All you had to do was snatch him up and deal with him right there at that rally."

I plopped down in my chair and reached for the empty glass. After turning it upside down, not one drop came from it.

"I don't expect to hear from Joshua or Ina for a very long time. You should prepare yourself for their absence, and you have no one but yourself to blame. That's probably why you're drinking again, and Mama, I really wish you would not . . ."

She snapped her fingers to cut me off. "How many times do I have to tell you that I'm grown and I will do what I wish? I only had one drink today. I needed something to calm my nerves. I'm upset about a lot of things, Stephen, and this stuff with Mr. McNeil, along with everything else is driving me nuts."

Appearing emotional, she stepped away from my desk and took a seat on the sofa. I knew she had been experiencing some setbacks, but the last thing I needed was for her to start drinking again. I got up from my desk and sat across from her on the other sofa. As we faced each other, she looked at me with a glassy film covering her eyes.

"Answer my question," she said. "What are you going to do about that idiot spitting on you? I know darn well you're not going to let that slide."

I removed my suit jacket and laid it across the arm of the sofa. After removing my tie and unbuttoning several buttons on my white crisp shirt, I relaxed and crossed one leg over the other.

"I have bigger fish to fry, so change the subject."

"Fine then. Where is Raynetta?"

"As I said, I have bigger fish to fry so what else do you want to know?"

"Go ahead and fry your fish, bake it, stuff it or do whatever you have to do to it. I want to know where Raynetta is at. She and I have some business to tend to."

I nodded and snickered at the same time. "I don't know and don't care where she's at. Maybe she's out somewhere with Alex, trying to cook up some more damaging information about Mr. McNeil. You should know where she is, especially since the two of you have gotten rather cozy with each other lately."

"That's because I was wrong about Ne-ne. She's nice and she deserves more of your attention. So does Mr. McNeil, and since you know that Raynetta and I been working together to find dirt on him, I guess you must know what we found out."

I pretended as if I didn't know. "What exactly did you find out?"

"We discovered that he's involved in some kind of sex slave ring. I'm trying to get the prosecutor, Mr. Blackstone, to handle some things for me. After I pay him one more visit, he'll be eating out of the palm of my hand."

I sat up and had to laugh. "You and Raynetta haven't discovered anything. Don't you know when you're being played? I hate to be the one to break the bad news to you, but the information Alex gave to Raynetta about Mr. McNeil was false. He's not involved in anything dealing with sex slaves, and if you turned any tricks to get Mr. Blackstone to file charges against Mr. McNeil, you wasted your time. It's not going to happen. I told you before that I will deal with Mr. McNeil. You and Raynetta need to stay the hell away from him. He's dangerous."

She adjusted herself in the chair while contracting her eyes as she looked at me. Her facial expression implied that she wasn't happy about what I'd told her.

"So, you're telling me that you knew Alex gave us false information? That you knew I've been in contact with Mr. Blackstone, and I lowered my standards to sleep with his ass, just so he would do me a favor? Basically, my time and efforts to make sure Mr. McNeil caused you no harm were wasted? Is that what you're telling me?"

I clapped my hands. "Bingo, you finally got it. That's exactly what I'm telling you, Mama, so halt the investigative nonsense with Raynetta and go join some kind of social club, if you want to keep yourself busy. I didn't think you would be foolish enough to have sex with a married man like Mr. Blackstone, but nothing you do these days surprise me anymore. That man can't help you, and he's not going to help you do anything to Mr. McNeil. If he told you he was going to do something, he lied. Also, if you're thinking about sticking to your plan with Raynetta, you may want to have a serious conversation with her about her connection to Mr. McNeil. Since the two of you are so chummy now, maybe she'll tell you who he is to her."

She folded her arms across her chest and crossed her legs. By now, a full attitude was on display.

"First of all, don't you dare sit there and tell me what I need to join. You need to join the respect-yo-mama club before you find my foot swallowed in your ass. I don't know what's up with your foul mouth, and just because you speak to Raynetta any kind of way, you will not do the same to me. I call myself helping you, but if you don't appreciate . . ."

Irritated, I interrupted her. "I don't need your help, okay? You helped enough with Joshua and look where it left me. I haven't forgotten about what you did, Mama. The more I think about it, the more it upsets me."

This time, she clapped her hands and stood up. After walking around the table, she stood in front of me.

"Let me make myself real clear, nigga, okay? I don't care how upset you are, but you'd better thank your lucky stars I went out of my way to find out what Levi and Ina had done behind your back. You'd better thank your lucky stars that I always show up at the right time to save your black ass. In those moments, I never hear you complaining. I don't care what your status is or who you've become. You'd better learn to respect me, because the last person you want to go to war with is me."

I didn't flinch, and without a single blink, I stared into her eyes showing no fear whatsoever. "Just so you know, your threats mean nothing to me. I have work to do, and I think it's time for you to pack up all that unnecessary noise and leave."

As I leaned forward to get up, she moved her face close to mine, purposely spraying it with her spit.

"Since my threats don't work, maybe my specks of spit on you will get a reaction."

I jumped up from the sofa, and as I squeezed my fist, she raised her hand. "Come on muthafucka, I dare you. Put your hands on me, just like you did that white man today. You handled him good, didn't you? And if you even think about *handling* me, I got something for you, son."

I opened my hand and wiped down my face to clear her spit. "Get out, now. I have nothing else to say to you, Mama. What kind of mother spits in her own son's face? That alcohol must be doing quite a number on you."

"A mother who feels disrespected. You lucky I didn't pull out my piece and shoot your ass. Maybe I'd better get out of here, especially if the American people want to see you alive after tonight."

I didn't say one word as she marched toward the door, slamming it behind her. I hated that I still allowed her to get to me. My insides were boiling. I plopped down at my desk and quickly reached for my cell phone. I hit one button and was very pleased to hear her voice when she answered.

"You already know where he is," I said. "Be sure to take care of this situation for me, and as always, thanks."

"Will do, Mr. President. It's lights out for him tonight."

I hit the end button and laid the phone on my desk. For the next few hours, I read a few letters I'd received, reviewed the notes from my meeting earlier and returned several calls. When I was ready to call it a night, I stripped down to my briefs, grabbed a blanket from the closet, turned on some soft music and chilled on the sofa. The television was on; I watched breaking news flash on the screen. The news anchor reported that the man who had spit on me earlier, hung himself while in his cell. *What a shame?* I thought. *Humph.* I pulled the blanket over my head and closed my eyes so I could get some sleep.

President's Mother,
Teresa Jefferson

See, sometimes, men needed to be put in their place, including my son. Steam poured from my ears as I left the White House in a rage. With Secret Service trying to keep an eye on me, I hissed at them and drove off. I was mad at myself because I'd made a big mistake. I'd gone to see Mr. Blackstone about prosecuting Mr. McNeil, and unfortunately, one thing led to another that day. I had no intentions of giving him anything; after all, what I'd seen in the bathroom stall one day wasn't worth my time. My only excuse was I'd been drinking. Drinking too much to be honest, but as I'd told that stupid son of mine, I needed something to calm me down.

As I made my way to Jeremy Blackstone's house, I breezed my Lexus through traffic. I reached for a bottle of gin in my glove compartment, and after tossing back a few swigs, I laid the bottle on the seat. The road ahead looked blurry. I kept blinking my eyes because my eyelids felt heavy. Once I arrived at Jeremy's house, I swerved my car in his driveway, almost hitting his white BMW in the rear. There was another car parked next to him; I guess it belonged to his wife.

Before exiting my car, I teased the feathery, salt-and-pepper bangs on my forehead, slid on some bright red lipstick, and to free my breasts, I opened a few buttons on the silky blouse I wore. My slim-fit jeans tightened at my ankles and the red-bottom heels I wore added much height to my small frame. I always represented for older women, and even though my mouth was slick at times, it was required to deal with some of these idiots who lived in Washington.

With my purse tucked underneath my arm, I stumbled to porch. Jeremy lived in an upscale neighborhood; every house on the block was, at least, 6,000 square feet. The two-story brick house stretched around the corner, and with a well-manicured lawn, the house was fit for a magazine. I pressed my finger on the doorbell, and then glanced at my watch to see what time it was. It was almost midnight, but his car was evidence that he was home.

I peeked through the double glass doors and could see Jeremy coming down the arched staircase, yawning. A burgundy robe covered his tall and slender frame, and his bald head had a shine. Black-framed glasses covered his eyes and his full beard looked very rugged. Before he opened the door, he turned around to see if anyone was behind him. Seeing no one, he opened the door with a scrunched face.

"Are you serious? What are you doing here?" he asked in nasty tone. "Do you know what time it is?"

"It's time for you to get a breath mint, now, back up and lower your voice. I came here because I need to know what you intend to do with the damaging material I gave you about Mr. McNeil. Somebody informed me today that you aren't planning to do anything."

He glanced at my breasts, then turned his head to look behind him again. Seeing no one, he gave me his attention.

"I told you I would review the information and let you know what I decide."

"That's what you told me, but I get a feeling that you're playing games with me. Are you?"

He straightened his glasses, then tightened the belt on his robe. "No, I'm not. I don't play games with people."

"Are you sure about that? Maybe I should ring the doorbell again so I can wake up your wife and ask her. She would know if you play games with people, wouldn't she?"

"There's no need for you to do that, okay? It smells like you've been drinking, and I think it would be smart for you to get in your car, go home and wait for my call tomorrow. I'll let you know what I decide to do then."

"That sounds like a plan, but I don't think you'll follow through. Are you or are you not going to prosecute Mr. McNeil? You've had enough time to review the material I gave to you. I need to know, right now, what your next move will be."

He rubbed his hand across the top of his sweaty bald head and sighed. "My next move is, I'm going inside to get back in bed with my wife. I said I will contact you tomorrow, but if you wish to make a scene out here tonight, I'll have to call the police. That would be a shame, because I'm sure the media would be here in a flash."

I laughed and shook my head. My finger touched the doorbell again. This time, I punched it, at least, ten or twelve times.

"Don't do that!" he shouted. "Leave now, Teresa, or else."

His threats didn't scare me away. And when I looked inside, I was pleased to see his white, red-headed wife coming down the stairs with a twisted face. She also had a silk robe on, and by the time she'd reached the door, Jeremy had already gone back inside and was standing in the foyer. The door was open; I remained on the porch.

"What's going on down here?" she questioned while raking her hair back. She looked at me for answers, all I did was shrug.

"Ask your husband what's going on. He knows for sure."

She didn't say one word to him. All she did was open the door wider to get a closer look at me.

"Aren't you the president's mother, Teresa? Why are you at our home at . . ."

Jeremy reached for her arm and attempted to pull her away from the door. "She came to tell me something important about the president. Our conversation is done and now we can go back to bed."

He tried to shut the door in my face, but I pushed on the door and let myself inside. They both appeared shocked by my aggressiveness. Mrs. Blackstone was the first one to speak up.

"What in the hell is going on here? You can't push your way into our home like this. Who do you think you are?"

"I was your husband's sex partner, but I'm here tonight looking for answers."

She gasped and touched her chest. With tears trapped in her eyes, she turned to her husband for answers.

"Is she telling the truth? She couldn't be Jeremy, and is she, the president's own mother, another one of your side-chicks?"

As he stood there looking silly with his mouth open, I replied to her question.

"Don't insult me, okay? A side-chick wants to hang on to a man and get what she can from him. I don't want anything else from Jeremy. You can keep that pint-sized penis. I have no idea how you stay married to a man with that little thing. You are way better than me for sure."

"Enough," Jeremy shouted and darted his finger at me with spit flying from his mouth. "Don't you stand there lying to my wife about us! I have never, ever touched you, woman! Are you out of your freaking mind?"

I had to laugh at his performance. His wife looked at me like she believed him. Her anger was now geared towards me.

"You need to march your ass out of our house right now! Don't bring your filthy lies over here, and as my husband warned, we will call the police if you don't leave."

I cocked my head back, looking at both of them. "Am I supposed to be scared of the police? Trust me, I'm not. I'm the one who needs to call them on your husband. He's a criminal, liar and a cheat. You can believe what you want, but you can't deny how small *it* is. Sex with him only lasted five minutes and there is a tiny mole on his right butt cheek that blends in with some of those dents. I noticed it when he got out of your bed last week. The same canopy bed you're sleeping in tonight with the pretty, silk and ruffled pink sheets on it."

Her head jerked in her husband's direction. With fury in her eyes, she barked at him. "You piece of shit! How dare you screw this woman in our bedroom? Did you invite her over while I was at my parents' house last week? For God's sake, Jeremy, my mother is dying and you were in our home screwing another woman?"

"Correction," I said. "He didn't screw me. He just poked me with a pencil. I'm so sorry to hear about your mother. What a shame?"

She growled and stormed toward the stairs, threatening to leave. Jeremy turned to me with fury in his eyes.

"See what you've done? I told you to get out of here, didn't I? I warned you and now you must pay for bringing this bullshit into my house."

He reached for his phone to call the police.

"I don't know why you're so bent out of shape. Her ass isn't going anywhere, and as long as you keep paying the bills, she's good. Now, hit the end button on that call and tell me what you plan to do about Mr. McNeil."

He ignored me and spoke to the 911 operator. "Yes. An intruder and she won't leave. Send someone right away."

He ended the call, and as he reached for my arm, shoving me toward the door, I pushed him away. He pushed back, and as I stumbled and almost fell, that's when I let him have it. I took off my shoe and charged him with it in my hand. I was able to strike him one time in his head with my shoe, but he managed to grab it and fling it near the stairs.

"You are fucking crazy!" he shouted and grabbed my shirt. This time, he pushed me on the porch and elbowed me in the chin when he released me.

"You can wait out here for the police! Don't you ever come back here again, Teresa, and hell no I will not prosecute Mr. McNeil! Not now, not ever!"

As he turned to go back inside, I took my fist, pounding it against his back. He crouched down, his glasses flew off and he attempted to grab my waist to get control of me. I was swinging too wildly. He couldn't get control of me, but two police officers surely did. They pulled me and Jeremy apart from each other. With a heaving chest, he yelled for the officers to arrest me.

"I want to press charges," he said. "She assaulted me. Threatened to harm me and my wife."

The officers held my arms while waiting for me to respond to the accusations. "I did not threaten anyone. He invited me to come here tonight for sex. His wife came home and now he's upset that he got caught. We got into an argument and he put his hands on me. I wasn't about to let him put his hands on me, so I threw my shoe at him. After that, he pushed me outside and here we are." I wiggled my arms from the officers' tight grip. "Release me, please. Obviously, you two don't know who I am."

Jeremy made my status clear to them. "She's the president's mother. Regardless, I want her arrested, now!"

They were reluctant to arrest me, and with him and me going back-and-forth, they couldn't decipher who was telling the truth.

"Miss Jefferson," one officer said. "Have you been drinking tonight?"

"I had one drink. That's it and it has nothing to do with him putting his hands on me. He's the one who needs to be arrested. Arrest him now, before I call my son."

Just then, Mrs. Blackstone appeared in the doorway. Tears streamed down her face and she could barely catch her breath as she spoke.

"Officers, we want this woman arrested. She just . . . just rushed into our home, threatened us and we couldn't get her to leave. I'm afraid for my life. I don't know what she came here to do, and her accusations against my husband are false."

After that, it didn't take long for the officers to grab my hands behind my back and cuff me. With one shoe off, I limped my way to the police vehicle, cussing and shouting.

"How in the hell does she have more clout than the president? I know what this is all about and heads are going to roll for this. I can promise you that!"

One of the officers put me on the backseat of the police car, but before he shut the door, I asked him to get my shoe for me.

"Those are some expensive shoes. We're not leaving here until I get my shoe. I can't walk around like this. I need my shoe!"

One officer ignored me, but the other one went inside and got my shoe. He tossed it on the backseat, but I wasn't able to touch it. When we arrived at the police station, the media was already there. Reporters swarmed the police vehicle, banging on the windows, snapping pictures and questioning what had happened.

"Move back!" the officers yelled as they escorted me out of the vehicle and towards the police station. "Move back or you people will be arrested too!"

One reporter put her mic close to my mouth. "Miss Jefferson, did you have an affair with the prosecutor, Mr. Blackstone? Is that why you were at his house tonight?"

"Yes. We had an ongoing affair that his wife just found out about tonight. Things turned ugly and I'm the one being arrested. While I'm not proud of myself for this, there is no reason why I was the one arrested and Jeremy Blackstone is the one who put his hands on me. I mean, where in the hell is the justice? Is this how women in this country are supposed to be treated? After all, he's the one who assaulted me."

I was sure that would give everyone something to debate. They surely debated it, and with so many people agreeing with my assessment of unfair treatment of women, the officers released me almost an hour later. My car had been towed to my new apartment complex, but I took a taxi to my next destination, before going home.

I knocked on the door, and within minutes, Michelle opened it. It was in the wee hours of the morning; I guess she thought I was Stephen. She displayed an attitude and didn't allow me to come inside. All she did was step into the hallway and shut the door behind her.

"If it's not your son coming here in the middle of the night, it's you. What do you want, Teresa? My children are inside sleeping. I don't want them to wake up."

"I don't either, but you and I haven't talked in a while. I wanted to know how things are going between you and Stephen. He's been real irritable lately. I don't really know what's troubling him."

"It's called running a country, having a mother who is trying to run or ruin his life, and being married to a wife who doesn't always support him. That's what troubling him, so there's no need for you to come here and ask."

"Well, we can thank you for being so perfect and giving him all the pussy he needs. I'm not trying to cause him no harm, and shame on you for thinking you have the facts. The one thing I do know is troubling him is not being able to see his son. I know how close you and Stephen are, and whether you realize it or not, he cares deeply for you. I've said some things before which implied he doesn't care, but I was wrong. Dead wrong, and when I spoke to him about you, I saw something deep in his eyes. Something I've never seen before. It is you, only you, who can give him what he wants."

Michelle rolled her eyes, but it was obvious that she wanted to hear more. "What do you think he wants from me? I haven't figured it out yet, and as a matter of fact, we agreed not to see each other anymore. I think it's best, and I truly wish everyone would just leave me alone."

"I know how you feel, but you have so much to gain from all of this, Michelle. You have the president's heart and he has never felt this way about another woman, not even Raynetta. You need to have his child. Give him a child and make him the happiest man in the world. I will pay you whatever you want. I would hope that I wouldn't have to give you anything to do this, but just to see him happy, I would give you anything. You do want to see him happy, don't you?"

Michelle's brows were scrunched inward as she frowned. "Of course I do, but I'm not having any more children. Not for him and definitely not for you. Goodbye, Teresa. I don't know what kind of game you're playing, but you need to exclude me from your plans."

She went back inside and closed the door. Maybe I'd have to come up with another plan to shake Stephen up. When I returned home, I called Raynetta. She hadn't been answering her phone; I could only imagine what she had been up to.

First Lady,
Raynetta Jefferson

Whoever said there was a thin line between love and hate surely didn't lie. My wake-up call came the moment I sat in that sweltering bunker with Stephen and saw with my own eyes exactly who he was. He didn't care about nobody but himself. I couldn't believe it had come to this, and I could honestly say that the man I had been married to for many years was totally out of control. Power had caused his head to swell. He truly believed he was invincible. He was going to obliterate any and everything around him, but in no way was he going to destroy me. I'd had enough, but you'd better believe I was going to use the situation I was in to benefit myself to the fullest. It was time for me to start being the woman I always yearned to be and start building more wealth for my future. Whenever we left the White House, I expected for Stephen to leave me high and dry. He'd already told me why he needed me; it was to simply protect his reputation. What he didn't know was, at this point, I cared about my reputation as much as his. I fought back against those accusations about me and Alex being together. And every time anyone asked me about Alex, I denied everything. They pointed to the salacious photos that had been released, but since the photos were fuzzy, I insisted the woman in them wasn't me. Basically said someone was out to destroy me and had been doing so since day one. Day by day, the news cycle changed and the story about me and Alex faded. Stephen was on the front page of every newspaper, and people were talking about the white man who'd spit on him committing suicide while in jail. After that story was released, a story about Teresa being arrested followed. Once again, things were chaotic at the White House, and I had no idea how Stephen intended to deal with his or his mother's mess.

Quite frankly, I didn't care. I needed to find out the truth behind my supposedly connection to Mr. McNeil. That was my priority, because the truth was, my background had always been shaky. There were so many missing pieces and I didn't know much about my family. I never had anyone to turn to, but when Stephen and I got together, I felt as if I had found a man who loved me and would be there for me forever. At that time, no one else mattered. Where I came from didn't matter, and it didn't bother me that I didn't know much about my family. Now, it mattered. In no way did I want to be related to a man like Mr. McNeil, but if I was, I saw it as being beneficial to me too.

A Secret Service agent drove me to Mr. McNeil's mansion. On my way there, I reached for my phone to call Teresa. She had been calling me like crazy. I was eager to find out the details of what kind of trouble she had gotten herself into this time.

"It's about damn time," she said. "What took you so long to call me back? I had something important to tell you."

"I've been busy. Besides, ask your son why I couldn't talk to anyone for almost a week. He knows. I'm sure he's probably already told you about my little stay in a bunker."

"Listen. He doesn't tell me anything about the two of you. But he did mention that the information Alex gave you about Mr. McNeil wasn't true. I don't know where that bastard Alex is, but it appears he was told to give us that information so we'd look like fools."

I rolled my eyes as I thought about being tricked. "Why doesn't that surprise me? I've been given a lot of false information lately, and I don't know who or what to believe these days. I do know that I'm tired of being your son's puppet. I honestly do not care what happens to him anymore."

Teresa remained silent for a few seconds. "I don't know what to do about him either, but he mentioned something to me about a connection you have with Mr. McNeil. What's that about, if you don't mind me asking?"

"Stephen seems to think I'm somehow related to Mr. McNeil. He says that I'm his granddaughter, but I tore up the so-called proof he gave me. I don't know what to say. I'm anxious to find out what's going on, and Mr. McNeil is the only one who can tell me."

There was more silence on the other end. But this time, the silence remained. Teresa had either hung up or the battery on her phone went dead. I called her again, but my call went directly to voicemail. I didn't bother to leave a message. She was probably upset about my breaking news. She was a person who'd never had my back before, so I wasn't too worried about how she'd felt. The news, however, about Alex giving me false information stung a bit. It confirmed for me that he had been working behind the scenes with Stephen after all.

The hefty agent with black hair and chubby cheeks pulled in front of Mr. McNeil's mansion. He buttoned his jacket as he got out of the black Suburban and opened the door for me. With dark shades on and with my hair in a sleek ponytail, I stepped out of the car. The jean jacket and waist-high jeans I wore were simple. The pink shirt and shoes added vibrant color to my attire, yet I wasn't there to impress anyone.

"Mr. McNeil is expecting us," the agent said as he closed the door. "He said he would be around back by the pool area."

"Thank you. And if you don't mind, I'd like to go alone. I'll be okay. If I need you, I will holler loudly."

"Are you sure? I don't want to leave you by yourself. The president would be very upset about that."

"What the president doesn't know doesn't hurt. Just keep this between us."

I swayed my hips from side-to-side, leaving the agent behind. As I made my way down a long concrete path that took me to the back of Mr. McNeil's mansion, I saw him sitting in a lounging chair, smoking a cigar. There were two young kids splashing water on each other in an Olympic-sized swimming pool, and the resort-style backyard area was filled with lounging chairs, tables with umbrellas and an outdoor kitchen where a chef was preparing food. From a distance, Mr. McNeil saw me coming. He contracted his eyes as I strutted his way, then he sat up to put his cigar in an ashtray.

"I don't have much time," he said in a grouchy tone. "What do you want?"

I remained cordial, even though he seemed ready to attack me. "What I want to know is the truth about our connection. I'm not going to beat around the bush, and I want to know if you really are my grandfather."

The old man struggled to get up, and when he did, he stood face-to-face with me. His wrinkled, pale face shook as he spoke. "You were disowned by me before you were ever born. My son made one of the biggest mistakes of his life and no one in this family is allowed to sleep with dirt. I don't want my blood running through your veins. I want no part of you, and when you married that nigger you're married to now, I hated you even more. I hope that answers your question. And if money is what you came here seeking today, you will never get one dime from me."

My stomach rumbled. I'd be lying if I said his words didn't hurt. They cut deep, but I would never allow him to see how deep.

"Listen up, you foolish old man. I don't want your dirty money, nor do I want to be a part of your family in any way. I'm embarrassed by you. To know you're my grandfather makes me feel ill. The truth, however, is important. I plan to keep on doing my homework, and all I wanted to do was start here. I'm done, so have a good day and enjoy the rest of your day with family."

I walked away, feeling like I wanted to throw up. By the time I'd reached the Suburban, I hadn't shed one tear. What I intended to do was use my connection with Mr. McNeil to open a few doors. It was exactly what I intended to do as first lady, and my days of playing nice with the people around me was over.

The second I returned to the White House, reporters were everywhere. I was questioned about the situation with Teresa and asked to share my thoughts about my husband being spit on. I didn't answer one question. I was escorted inside, and as soon as I sat at my desk in my office, I called my assistant, Emme, to help me with a few things.

"The first thing I want you to do is help me research some of the items on this list." I reached across my desk and gave her a long list of things I'd been working on, pertaining to Mr. McNeil. "Find out what's true and what's not. After that, I want you to find me an agent who is willing to sell my tell-all book to a publisher. The least I will take is sixty-million-dollars. Anything less than that is non-negotiable."

Emme sat across from me with wide eyes. Her hands trembled as she read the items on my list.

"Are . . . if these things are validated, are you going to tell everyone about all of this? What about the president? I'm sure there are things about him he doesn't want the American people to know."

"Yes, I'm going to tell it all. My relationship with two of the most powerful men in the world will be beneficial to me. And after how they've treated me, why in the hell should I keep their secrets?"

Emme shrugged. She seemed reluctant to participate in this, but her loyalty meant nothing to me. I intended to push ahead with my tell-all book, no matter what.

President of the United States, Stephen C. Jefferson

To no surprise, after Mr. Macon's suicide in jail, the heat came my way. Some people assumed I had something to do with it, but my lips remained sealed. I didn't even bother to offer my condolences to his family, and since I hadn't said anything about the incident, many white supremacist groups decided to protest around the country, even in front of the White House. Andrew and my Press Secretary, Sam, were upset and afraid. They begged me to say something to calm things down. Thus far, a few brawls had happened, but many more white supremacist groups started to show up in areas where they knew serious confrontations would arise.

"Mr. President," Sam said while sitting on the sofa with his beer belly touching his lap. I stood next to a bookshelf, gazing at a photo of President Lincoln that was beside it. "You have to say something. I've been doing my best answering reporters' questions, but the American people want to hear from you."

"I agree," Andrew added. "Many more news outlets are reporting that you had something to do with Mr. Macon's death. His family doesn't believe he committed suicide, and they're starting to make a lot of noise. You need to quiet the noise and confirm that you had nothing to do with his death."

I touched the gold frame around Lincoln's picture and rubbed my thumb across his name that was engraved. "*Whenever I hear anyone arguing for slavery, I feel a strong impulse to see it tried on him personally*. That's what Lincoln said, and another one of my favorite quotes of his is when he said, *I do not wish to be misunderstood upon this subject of slavery in this country. I suppose it may long exist. Perhaps the best way for it to come to an end peaceably is for it to exist for a length of time. But I say that the spread, strengthening and perpetuation of it is an entirely different proposition. That we should in every way resist it as a wrong, treating it as a wrong, with a fixed idea that it must and will come to an end.* I believe he said that during a speech in, uh, 1858 or 59, one of those years. What I can't believe is hundreds and hundreds of years later, we have people in this country who honestly believe that we're going back. That by protesting, they're going to make a point or resolve something. Asking me to speak out in regards to their foolishness is a fucking insult to me. I don't have to say one word, especially when they travel to those inner cities and the shit really hits the fan."

"But you can put a stop to this now, Sir," Sam said. "You don't want shit to hit the fan, do you? A lot of people could get hurt. You are capable of calming things down, and I really think you should do it."

I slipped my hands into my pockets, then turned to face Sam and Andrew. "Understand that people are sick of the bullshit. Not only black people, but people from all races are sick of being treated like they don't belong in this country. That motherfucker spit in my face, and president or not, his actions should be condemned. I'm not offering my condolences to anyone. People can believe what they want; too damn bad. If the two of you want me to take action, go get me about a hundred Tiki torches. Contact every member of the Congressional Black Caucus and ask them to join me in front of the White House tonight. If anyone else wants to join us, feel free."

"Mr. President, you couldn't be serious," Andrew said. "There are hundreds of white supremacists out there right now, and if you go out there, you will put your life at risk, along with the lives of many others. That's a very dangerous move."

I shrugged. "Dangerous, maybe. Smart, hell yes. Now get me those torches and start making some phone calls for me. If not, I'll make them myself."

Sam and Andrew left the Oval Office with disappointment written across their faces. They didn't return until two hours later. By then I was casually dressed in denim jeans and a button-down black shirt. An assault rifle was strapped across my chest, and with comfortable tennis shoes on, I was ready to go speak up as Sam and Andrew had suggested. They both looked at me like I had lost my mind.

"Sir, please don't do this," Andrew said, pleading with me. "You don't have to go out there and do this. Your bully pulpit allows you to stay safe and address issues like this from right behind that desk over there. I fear this is going to send the wrong message to the American people."

"You mean, you fear I'm going to send a clear message to people who go out there and stand against this bullshit every day. I'm no different from them. At the end of the day, we are all striving for the same thing."

I walked around Andrew and headed toward the door. "Are those Tiki torches here yet?"

"They're on a truck near the security checkpoint."

"What about members of the Congressional Black Caucus?"

"Some of them said they would meet you outside."

I turned to face Andrew and Sam with a stern look on my face. "What about the two of you? If you say you have my back, now would be a damn good time to show it."

"We do, Sir," Sam said. "But we think you're making a big mistake."

I didn't bother to respond. I marched out of the Oval Office, and within minutes, my Secret Service detail followed me. I also heard many gripes from them.

"Bad move, Mr. President," said one agent. "We can't protect you like this."

"We don't mind if you do this, Sir," another one said. "But maybe you should consider planning this out more carefully."

I ignored them all and kept walking. By the time I made my way to the exit door, I turned to face them.

"Either you're with me or you're not," I said. "I don't care either way and no one is going to stop me."

I pushed the door open, and as I moved toward the checkpoint gate, I could see numerous members from the Congressional Black Caucus waiting for me. Secret Service followed. I shook hands with some of the members of the BC; they were surprised to see me.

"What's the plan, Mr. President?" Senator Fletcher said. "We got Andrew's call and we're waiting on you."

"The plan is to just stand before them, show no fear and don't say one word. Just look them in the eyes. They'll understand our purpose. No fighting, no arguing, no throwing things . . . nothing. Understand?"

Everyone nodded, and after we removed the Tiki torches from several trucks, we lit them and headed towards a large area around the White House were hundreds of protesters stood, waving Confederate flags, holding up insulting photos of me and carrying negative signs relating to, mostly, blacks and Jews. As we neared the crowd in small numbers, they couldn't believe it. We were definitely outnumbered, simply because every member of the Congressional Black Caucus didn't show up. Nonetheless, our appearance had many of them in shock. Their mouths were dropped open, eyes were wide and anger swept throughout the crowds of people who headed our way. We halted our steps and stood on a large grassy area in silence. The lit Tiki torches were lifted high in our hands and no one was smiling, barely even breathing. Not even my Secret Service detail, who for the first time appeared nervous as crowds of white supremacists rushed our way. Within a few minutes, many of them stood before us grunting with mean mugs on their faces and using racial slurs. Screeching cars could be heard in the distance; the media had shown up. Cameras flashed as we all stood there, staring each other down. No one from my side moved. I was barely breathing and my eyes were locked on one man in front of me who waved a Confederate flag.

"It was nice of you to show up, Mr. Loser. I know what you did to my brother and there is no way in hell he committed suicide while in jail! You gon' need to tell us what really happened to him or else things around this country gon' turn real ugly for you and your kinfolks."

It was considered a crime to threaten the president, and as two Secret Service agents stepped forward to confront the man, I stopped them.

"Let it go this time. Allow him to exercise his first amendment right and do not arrest him. Suicides happen a lot while people are in jail. Especially, to black people who all of a sudden decide to take their lives. It's a shame, and I regret that your brother felt like he had no other options."

My words and calmness angered him. He moved forward, Secret Service pushed him back.

"Spit on that nigger, Frankie! Spit on all of them!"

"Burn'em! They all need to burn!"

The crowd got rowdy, but the side I was on remained silent. Water bottles were thrown; some of the bottles hit a few BC members, but they didn't budge. Insults were being hurled at us, and the one word they continued to reach for was nigger. Nigger this, nigger that. Go back to Africa and never come back. It was a pathetic sight to see, but as the clock ticked away, all of it was being televised for our nation to witness. It wasn't long before other people started to show up—more members from the BC, people who lived and worked in the area and a bunch of young people who refused to stand for this. People from all races stood behind and beside us. And in less than an hour, our side outnumbered theirs. The crowd was massive and every single person stood silent.

"Nigger lovers," the white supremacists chanted. "White lives matter," they screamed at the top of their lungs and they laughed when more people showed up.

"How special is that?" said one man. "You must feel real good to have all these nigger lovers on your side. Come election time, I guarantee you they won't be there for you. This is all for the cameras, and you'd better believe your ass will be out of our house!"

I smirked as I looked at the fool in front of me. Kind of felt sorry for him—just a little bit. My unfazed expression angered them even more, and when they realized we weren't going to entertain their foolishness, the crowd started to disperse. One by one, they moved in another direction and eventually left the premises. They promised to be back, and if they came back, I planned to be out here again. I couldn't believe how massive the crowd with me had swelled. I thanked everyone for showing up and shook many hands. I had to cut my time with the crowd short because Secret Service was on pins and needles.

"Thank you, Mr. President," many people expressed their gratitude. I waved, and when I saw Sam and Andrew standing with Tiki torches, I cut my eyes at them. I made my way back into the White House, without incident.

"You made us real nervous out there, Sir," said one agent. "I'm glad things turned out as they did."

Another agent chimed in. "We are very pleased about the outcome. We've never had to stand there and participate in anything like that. I hope you never advise us to do it again, because our number one job is to protect you."

"It is," I said while moving towards the Oval Office. "But next time, somebody needs to catch that spit."

They chuckled, but I didn't see shit funny. Some members from my administration clapped their hands and pat my back as I opened the door to the Oval Office. I wasn't sure if they had stood with me or not, but it didn't matter. My approach was a success and the media was going crazy. People from other cities had started to do the same thing. No fighting, no shooting, no arguing . . . just looking them straight in their eyes and showing no fear. It worked in many places, but some people in the inner cities weren't having it. A few fights had broken out, two people had been shot and one officer had been injured from trying to break up a fight. I watched the news, until Andrew and Sam returned to my office with Tiki torches in their hands.

"Okay," Andrew said. "I was wrong, Mr. President, and I apologize for not following your lead. Hopefully, you can forgive me and Sam for not listening to you. We did, however, stand with you tonight."

"We sure did, Sir. And I apologize too," Sam said.

I reached for a piece of gum in my drawer, then closed it. I replied without looking at them.

"Exit. I want some peace tonight. I need to prepare for my visit to the United Nations in a few days, and I could really use some sleep."

They left my office on what we all considered a good note. I knew it was difficult for them to follow my lead this time, but next time no excuses would be accepted.

As a routine, I got some work done, talked to several Congressmen and women who were pleased about what had transpired tonight. Even VP Bass had reached out to me.

"I was on my way there, but traffic was so crazy that I didn't make it on time," she said. "And even though I don't like to get in the middle of all that racial stuff, Mr. President, I do applaud you for taking a stand against white supremacy. We don't have time for that in this country. We're not going back and the only way is forward."

"I agree. And after you make your way through traffic, we need to discuss some things tomorrow. There is too much legislation pending and we need to work on a budget and talk about the debt ceiling before Congress goes on break."

"We definitely will. I'll see you tomorrow. Have a good night, Sir."

We ended the call on a positive note, which was rare. I couldn't believe the pleasant mood so many people were in. The phone calls I'd gotten were positive, the media was speaking good things about me and people across America weighed in on TV.

"See, that's the kind of president we need," a black man from Baltimore said. *"One who ain't afraid to stand with us. I feel proud tonight. Real proud and I do believe a change is coming."*

Another lady weighed in. "I feel proud to be an American. We are at our best when we stand together. I didn't always understand that, but I sure as heck do now."

While lying on the sofa, I stayed up until almost one in the morning watching what was happening around the country. What I saw made me feel proud. I felt that a change was coming; it was coming one day at a time. That's what I'd told myself, until a knock on the door interrupted my thoughts. Andrew walked in; Michelle was behind him.

"I wasn't sure if you were asleep or not, but you always told me if she called to make sure—"

I sat up and lifted my hand to halt his explanation. "That's fine. Thanks."

He walked around Michelle and closed the door behind him. She stood for a moment, staring at me. I didn't say anything to her until she moved closer and remained in front of me with a silver mini-dress on, showing her pretty brown legs that looked dipped in oil. Her tiny hard nipples poked through the top section of the dress—I could tell she wasn't wearing a bra. I wasn't even sure if she had on panties, but I would soon find out. I looked up at her; she looked down at me.

"I thought you didn't want this to continue," I said. "I'm surprised you changed your mind already."

She touched the side of my face with her finger, while gazing into my eyes. "I told you to stop coming to me. I never said

I wouldn't come to you. Even though I'm fighting like hell to stay away from you, I can't. I'm in love with a brave man who consumes my mind too much. There are days when I'm so done with you and days when I just have to see you. It's a battle, and tonight, I lost the battle. I had to hold you, and I want you to make love to me all night, if you're feeling up to it."

Her admission garnered no response from me. But when she straddled her legs and squatted on my lap, I had to say something.

"You're wet. Real wet, and it's apparent that you started having sex with me before you got here."

"Only in my head." She reached down to remove my steel from my briefs. It plopped out long and rock hard. "And now, your head will have the pleasure of feeling everything I was thinking about on my way here."

I wanted to feel all of it, so I lifted my buttocks from the sofa and removed my briefs. Michelle pulled her dress over her head; her shapely body sent me to La-La Land. My hands traced her curves, but as I lifted her round cheeks so she could squat on me again, she stopped me. She also lifted my head, before I had a chance to tease her nipples that were right in front of my face.

"What?" I questioned. "Don't tease me and please don't change your mind about this."

"I'm not going to change my mind, but there's something important I think you should know, just in case we get interrupted and I have to leave quickly. It's about your mother. She came to my place to express how unhappy you are. She offered me money to have your child and she encouraged me to keep seeing you. I want you to know that I'm not here because of her. I don't want another child, but if there is anything else I can do to make you happy, please tell me because I'm willing to do it."

Hearing about my mother's ongoing shenanigans frustrated me, but I shook it off. I showed Michelle how she could make me happy, and as she secured her soft legs around me, I indulged. Our bodies rocked fiercely together in sync. She rode me so well that I gripped her cheeks tighter and dropped my head back. My eyes were shut tight as she grinded her hips to a rhythmic pace that locked me in a trance. I relieved myself when I lifted my head and covered my mouth over her breasts. My tongue turned in speedy circles around her nipples, making them even harder. This time, her head was dropped back and she whined her words loudly.

"Do you really want another child? Just tell me and I'll—"

"No," I quickly said. "All I want right now is you in every way possible."

I wrapped my arm around her waist and laid her back on the sofa. With one of her legs poured over my shoulder, I plunged deep into her insides, causing her juices to squirt all over me. She bellowed out after every long stroke that I gave her, and with her creamy fluids building more by the seconds, I had to return the favor. My downtime didn't last for long, and honoring her request, I made love to her throughout the Oval Office. We ended up near the east door that led to the Rose Garden. Michelle was on her hands and knees, rocking her beautiful body back-and-forth in a doggy style position, while I dipped into her tightened folds. I couldn't get enough of watching her mountains bounce against me. I felt high as a kite. Her folds tightened on me, and seconds later, she sprayed me again too cool us down. As she laid flat on her stomach, I laid over her. I kissed the nape of her neck, before my tongue traveled down her sweaty spine. I planted kisses on her soft butt cheeks, and after I parted them, I took my time cleaning up the sticky little mess she'd made. After each swipe of my tongue, she lifted her mountains higher and higher, giving me more access to the good stuff. I felt so energetic that we resumed on the sofa, where she saddled up and rode me again. This time, her back faced me. My body weakened, especially when she fell forward and touched the floor. We fought hard to make it to the finish line, and in the midst of expressing ourselves, there was a light knock at the door. Seconds later, in walked Andrew. General Stiles was behind him. I quickly reached for a sheet next to me, throwing it over Michelle to cover her naked body.

Andrew spun around to face the door, but General Stiles didn't budge. She looked at us with a blank expression on her face while biting her bottom lip. Even I was speechless.

"We had a seven o'clock meeting scheduled," General Stiles said. "I guess time must've gotten away from you. We can always come back."

"Right," Andrew said, slightly turning his head. His eyes were glued to Michelle, but she was already covered with the sheet. "We . . . We can come back later, Sir."

I wiped the sweat from my face with my hand. "Give me about an hour. I need to shower and change."

Without saying a word, General Stiles saluted me and walked out. Andrew, however, turned around again. He spoke to me, but his eyes were still on Michelle.

"One . . . One hour, Mr. President. We'll see you in one hour, and I apologize for the interject—I mean, the interruption."

I slowly nodded and watched as he left the room. While holding the sheet close to her chest, Michelle sat on me with bugged eyes.

"Oh, my, how embarrassing was that? I thought when the door closed it locked? I'm sorry for keeping you up all night, and with the curtains being closed, I had no idea what time it was."

"I didn't either, but now that we know and I still have another hour, why don't we finish what we started?"

Michelle laughed and jumped up from my lap. "Uh, no. I think I've had enough to last me for a long while. Besides, you have work to do this morning."

As she saw me coming towards her, she rushed over to my desk with the sheet wrapped around her. I stood on one side of the desk, she stood on the other. The direction of her eyes journeyed to my package.

"You couldn't have anything left to give me," she said. "I know for a fact there is nothing else left in there."

I laughed and rushed around the desk to catch her. She moved again, and as she raced to the other side of the room, I reached out and grabbed the sheet. She almost tripped on it, but managed to keep her balance.

"See, that's what you get for trying to run from me," I said. "All I was trying to do is make sure you left here with a smile on your face."

I wrapped my arms around Michelle's waist; she wrapped hers around mine. She planted a kiss on my lips then cocked her head back to look at me.

"You don't have to do anything else to make me leave here with a smile on my face. I'm good, real good, and thank you so much for a wonderful time, Mr. President."

"You're welcome." I kissed her again. Our lips stayed locked for a while, and the taste of her tongue was sweeter than any berry I'd ever had. "That was memorable. Now get on your clothes and get out of here before I change my mind about this meeting and cancel it."

"I don't want you to do that, but be sure to call me later."

We kissed again, before Michelle backed away from me and put on her dress. She straightened her hair with the tips of her fingers, and after sliding into her shoes, she left the Oval Office. I put on my wrinkled shirt and pants, before heading upstairs to the Executive Residence to shower and change clothes. On my way to the bedroom, I saw Raynetta sitting in the Yellow Room with a cup of tea on the table in front of her. A thick notebook was in her hand; she was busy writing something. I cleared my throat so she would look up.

"Yes," she said in a snobby tone.

"I wasn't sure if you were here or not, but good morning."

She cut her eyes at me, replied "morning" and started writing again. I was in a decent mood, so I hurried to take my shower and changed into my gray slacks and a purple shirt. This time when I passed by the Yellow Room, Raynetta was gone. I hurried to the Oval Office so I wouldn't be late for my meeting. Since I'd had ten or so minutes before Andrew and General Stiles returned, I straightened up a bit. I fluffed the pillows on the sofas, straightened the rug, organized the papers on my desk and took the sheet to a laundry room. When I returned, Andrew and General Stiles were in the Oval Office waiting on me. I closed the door behind me and walked over to the sofas where they sat.

"Let me apologize for pushing this meeting back an hour, but I had no idea what time it was. I guess we can get started without Sam, but when he comes I'll have to pause for a minute and tell him a few things I want him to communicate to the American people during his press briefing today."

"That's fine, Sir," Andrew said. "Before we get started, I hope you're not troubled by the way I looked at Miss Peoples. She's a gorgeous woman. I couldn't help myself. I just wish things weren't so complicated between you and the first lady."

"No problem, Andrew, and if you don't mind, I don't care to elaborate."

"Please don't," General Stiles said. "Our meeting is already running way late and I need to share some important things with you before your meeting at the U.N. I'm sure you'll be meeting with the Secretary of State later, but I thought it was important for us to have a discussion first. If your mind is clear and you're ready to hear what I have to tell you, please say so."

I didn't appreciate her jab about my mind being clear. "My mind is always clear. Please share, and as always, thanks for your time and service."

General Stiles provided me with vital information to share at the U.N., but during our conversation, she seemed irritated. I knew she'd had a crush on me, but I wasn't aware of how serious it was until I saw her reaction today. I now knew I had to watch my back when it came to her as well.

President's Mother,
Teresa Jefferson

I was too pissed about everything to call Stephen and congratulate him on confronting those racist fools in front of the White House. I didn't want to converse with him, and I surely didn't want to hear no mess from Raynetta about Mr. McNeil being related to her. I couldn't believe it. Then again, yes I could because she had always been a snake in my book.

What upset me the most was Jeremy and his wife calling the police on me. They thought they'd made my life miserable, but when I say the media tore that man to shreds, I mean it. Just this morning, he was forced to resign. I cracked up while watching his poor explanation on TV, while his silly-looking wife was by his side. I predicted she wouldn't be there for long, but that was now their problem, not mine.

The last gripe I'd had was pertaining to Michelle. How dare she reject my offer about having Stephen's child. She knew good and doggone well she wanted his baby, and if she could move her and her children into the White House she would. I couldn't quite figure her out. But if things turned out to be what I predicted they would be with Raynetta, Michelle was my only hope for having some more grandchildren. I missed the hell out of Joshua. Every time I called him or Ina, they didn't answer. It was as if they had disappeared, and after all I had done for them, I was disappointed.

Hell, I was disappointed in everybody, including my son. I had to do something to shake him up; he didn't even call to check on me after I had been arrested. Those police officers could've done anything to me. Stephen wouldn't know, because he hadn't even checked. I figured he was still upset with me about Joshua, and since Ina wasn't around for him to attack her, he attacked me. He overlooked everything I'd done for him as a mother; the shame was on him.

Right after I finished watching the news, I decided to put on some casual clothes and go join some of the protesters I'd seen on TV all week long. Things were ugly. Even though Stephen had settled things down in some cities, not all cities followed his lead. The people in Baltimore, Maryland weren't having it. A black woman had been killed by a cop who claimed she was waving a knife around when he arrived at her apartment. It was a messy situation, and unfortunately, the woman had some mental health issues. Still, in my opinion, the cop had other options. He didn't see it that way, but nonetheless, people took to the streets to protest. I knew that my being there would cause a scene, and the media would definitely want to speak to me. This was a grand opportunity for me to follow Stephen's lead, but to also get his attention. I tossed back a strong drink before I left, and then I hit the highway. Listened Stevie Wonder while in the car, and just as I arrived at my destination, Aretha was crooning about respect. I waited until the song was over, and after taking another swig from a bottle in a brown paper bag, I popped a breath mint in my mouth. I exited my car, and within fifteen minutes, I started walking with an energized group of protestors who were highly upset with the police. Many protestors were young, some older. I saw signs from "Stop Killing Us" to "Black Lives Matter." Some protestors carried guns, some wore masks over their faces, and I couldn't believe how many people had brought their children. It was a peaceful protest, and after I marched nearly six blocks with an older couple next to me, and plenty of younger people surrounding me, I was noticed by a reporter who pointed in my direction. She rushed through the crowd to question me. The cameras followed and cell phones were up.

"Miss Jefferson, how are you today?" the reporter asked. "I never thought in a million years I would see you protesting. Are you trying to set an example like the president?"

I stepped aside to answer her questions. "No I'm not, but why wouldn't I be here? The entire city needs to be here, and I'm glad to see this many people standing up for what is wrong."

"Does the president know you came today and will he be joining you?"

"I don't know what the president's plans are, but I'm here because it's a shame what that cop did. Losing his job isn't enough. We want to make sure there is a conviction."

"But nobody has all the facts yet. Why not wait until the facts are in, before you decide the officer is guilty?"

I didn't like her tone, so I told her what she needed to hear and decided to move on. "The fact is, too many black people have been killed by cops who already know there will be no consequences. Another fact is we have ignored these issues for too long. So many people are afraid to open their mouths and admit that we do have killer cops in this country who have hatred in their hearts for people of color. The last thing I want to share pertains to privileged people like you who continuously make excuses for these cops. You know doggone well that a man with a gun is not fearful of a woman with a knife. That's bullshit. He shot her because she was unprivileged and black."

The crowd surrounding me started clapping and cheering.

"You damn right he wasn't scared!" A man shouted. "Ain't none of them scared, because they know what the end result will be!"

More people made comments, and with a frown on her face, the reporter was frustrated.

"I won't dispute anything you've said, Miss Jefferson, but let's move on. You were arrested the other day for assault, and then you were released. Mr. Blackstone recently stepped down from his position. Can you share with us how you feel about him resigning?"

"I don't wish to talk about that situation right now. The crowd is moving, and I prefer to get back to protesting."

As I started to walk away, she hit me with another question. "What about your alcohol problem? Are you in rehab? Mr. Blackstone stated that you were intoxicated when you showed up at his house. Were you?"

My face twisted and I pursed my lips. "Bitch, you can smell my breath, can't you? I'm intoxicated now, but I handle myself very well. Now, this interview is complete. I've given you enough of my time."

I walked away with a crowd of people following me. Many people used their phones to snap pictures/videos and upload them on social media. I was given numerous signs to carry. I waved them in the air and proudly marched in my red bottom heels and jeans that hugged my curves.

"Dang, Mama," a young black activist said to me as I held my fist in the air, swaying my hips in the process. He was too cute. Had dreads in a ponytail, muscles stretching his T-shirt, loose jeans that displayed a nice print, and tinted glasses on that made him look smart. I appreciated his pearly white teeth as he smiled.

"You out here representing," he said. "I love a woman who's down for the cause, especially a sexy, classy woman who don't mind sweating a little."

Like I said, he was too cute to ignore. I needed a little excitement in my life, so instead of ignoring him, I asked what his name was.

"Malik Henderson. Nice to meet you."

We shook hands and when he asked me to call his cell phone so he could have my number for future protests, I surely did. Right after that, a fight broke out. I didn't know who was fighting who. All I know was people were running and falling. I had to remove my heels, and just as I crossed the street, someone threw a brick into a glass window, shattering it. Things quickly turned chaotic. Mace was sprayed and the fumes went right in my face. My eyes burned; I started coughing. The next thing I knew, I was being handcuffed by the police. For what, I didn't know.

"Wait a minute," I shouted while squeezing my eyes together. Smudged mascara ran down my face and my arms were hurting from the officer holding them too tight. "Please tell me why I'm being arrested? I didn't do a damn thing! How dare you treat me like this. Do you know who I am?"

The officer didn't say a word. I was shoved into a paddy wagon with numerous other people who were rowdy as hell. One man kicked the inside of the vehicle while his hands were cuffed behind his back. Another banged his head, and nearly everyone was shouting vulgarities at the officers. We were all taken to the police station, and after being "processed" I found myself inside of a muggy, musty-smelling cell with nearly fifty other people. My body was sweating; my shirt stuck to my skin. Hair laid flat on my head, and I still hadn't had a chance to wipe my smeared makeup. What I needed was a drink, a cold shower and my bed. In that order. Maybe this protesting stuff wasn't for me after all.

Everyone stood around chit-chatting, as if this was no big deal. I wanted out, and I let it be known to the officer that he needed to release me.

"May I use a phone?" I said to an officer who stood outside of the cell. "I need to call my son, the president."

The officer didn't respond. A man behind me laughed, and when I turned around, he shook his head.

"Call the president," he said. "That's a good one. Maybe I should call him too."

A few more people laughed, but another man vouched for me.

"Fool, that is the president's mother. Haven't you seen her on TV?"

The sarcastic man snapped his finger. "Yeah, I've seen her on TV. She was on that, uh, crazy TV show Snapped, right?"

He giggled and so did a few other people. I was about to snap on his ass, but when I heard my name being called, I turned to look at the officer.

"Let's go," he said.

"Go where?"

"Wherever you want to go, lady. Your bail has been satisfied."

I was glad to hear that. I rushed out of the cell and went to the waiting area, expecting to see Stephen. I figured he'd seen me getting arrested on TV, especially since the media was everywhere. Instead, the person I saw was Malik. A smile was on his face and he stood by the exit door waiting for me.

"When I saw them put you in the paddy wagon," he said. "I hurried to come get you. Our organization is able to pay numerous protestors' bail. I'm glad we were able to help you."

His swift actions put a smile on my face. I was impressed. He opened the door for me, and I stepped outside in the rain. Representing how polite he was, he removed his jacket, putting it over my head.

"Can I drive you to your car?" he asked.

"You sure can, because I'm not about to walk."

He laughed and walked with me to his car. I wasn't thrilled about riding in a Honda Civic, but his car was nice and clean. It smelled good too; the smell of pines infused the inside. Malik pulled away from the curb, and knowing that my makeup was a mess, I lowered the visor to look in the mirror.

"You wouldn't happen to have any napkins in here, would you?"

"Open the glove compartment. I may have some napkins or tissue in there."

I opened the glove compartment and found exactly what I needed. I wiped my face with a napkin, removing every drop of makeup from it.

"You don't need to wear makeup," Malik said. "Your skin is already pretty."

I blushed, but I had to let him know his charming words were unnecessary. "I appreciate your words, but please don't

160

start all that sweet talk that sounds like game to me. I've been around for a long time, and I've heard it all. Compliments are cute, but they can also be tacky sometimes."

Showing his sense of humor, he laughed again. "Okay. I won't tell you how beautiful and sexy you are. But if you don't mind, I'd like to know how old you are. I already know you're the president's mother. I've seen you plenty of times before. Every time I see you, well, I won't say because you'll think it's game."

"Much game, and my age is none of your business. I never tell my real age, it doesn't matter. Also, I am so much more than just the president's mother."

"I believe that you are. You don't have to convince me."

We made small talk as he drove me back to my car. Some of the protestors were still hanging around, but Malik said him and his organization always left before it got too late. It was already ten o'clock. I wasn't looking forward to the long drive back home.

"When can I see you again?" Malik asked.

I shrugged. "You'll probably see me on TV. The media tries to cover my every move. If I don't hurry up and get out of your car, I'm sure one of those reporters will see me and come running over here."

"I'm sure they will, but I don't want to see you on TV. I'd like to see you in private. Just you and me, alone, having some fun."

My eyes scanned his sexy self. Just for a few seconds, I visualized him naked. "Before I reply to your question, my question is how old are you? I don't want to waste my time with kids. You do look pretty young."

"I'm thirty-six. And you see how easy that was? I don't mind telling you anything about me. I'm sure you can find out anything else about me you want to know."

"Thirty-six is too young for me, but I thank you for paying my bail and driving me to my car. I honestly need to get home and get some rest. It's beyond my bedtime and this old lady can't hang."

"I know you can hang, but how far do you have to drive?"

"Too far. Back to Washington."

"I don't want you to drive all by yourself. Let me drive you home. I'll bring you back here tomorrow to get your car. Then we can have breakfast together."

I was reluctant to let him drive me home, but to be honest, I didn't want to be alone. Malik seemed like very good company. He proved to be just that as we found ourselves in a joyful and interesting conversation on the way to my place. He seemed intelligent, had a business degree and lived alone. He had a three-year-old daughter, and according to him, he and his child's mother didn't really get along. His parents were still married, father was his hero and his best friend was his dog. I had to ask why a young man like himself, with good attributes, wasn't in a relationship with anyone.

"I was in a seven year relationship with a wonderful person, but I made some mistakes that caused me to lose her. I got another chick pregnant, and the one I was with wasn't having it. She left me and the rest is history. I broke her heart, she broke mine."

"I know how that is, but that shouldn't stop you from dating. Things happen and you just have to keep on keeping on."

"It's not like I stopped completely dating. I just haven't found a person who excites me and makes me want to do the relationship thing again."

I didn't say much after that. A relationship with me was out of the question. I already knew that Malik would be good for one thing and one thing only. I wasn't sure if I wanted to find out if he was even good at that.

When we arrived at my apartment, I unlocked the door and we went inside. Malik looked around at the lavish white furniture in my living room area, and at the shiny, hardwood floors that ran throughout the apartment. The open space viewed my kitchen with stainless steel appliances and an island topped with black granite. Black and white photos of Stephen and me were here and there. I also had photos of Joshua on a unique circular bookshelf I'd had handmade for my books. There were colorful throw pillows on my sofa, and the crystal clear windows in my apartment viewed Washington D.C.

"This is real nice," Malik said. "Do you stay here all by yourself?"

"I've only been here for a short time. Had to give up my house because of an unfortunate incident. When I'm not here, I'm usually at the White House. I have a room there too," I boasted.

"I'm impressed," he said, still looking around. "I hope to live like this one day."

Honestly, I didn't think my place was all that, but if he liked it, so be it.

"Can I get you something to drink?" I asked, then removed my shoes. I was dying for a shower, but I wanted to make sure he was okay.

"Nah, I'm good on the drink thing. But if you got some chips or something to snack on, I'll take that."

I pointed to the pantry. "Help yourself to anything in there and make yourself at home. I'll show you the guestroom, after I take a shower. While I'm in there, you can watch TV, turn on some music, but please do not eat in my living room area."

"I wouldn't dare," he said. "Enjoy your shower. I'll be right here when you get done."

I don't know why I felt at ease with Malik being in my apartment, but you'd better believe that my security cameras watched his every move. If he tried anything tricky, he wouldn't get away with it. I would have him arrested and make sure he spent time behind bars.

I went to my bedroom, removed my clothes and put on a white, soft cotton robe. After sliding into my house shoes, I headed to the bathroom. I turned on the waterfall showerhead; the bathroom quickly filled with steam. I couldn't wait to indulge, and for thirty-or-so minutes, I did. I felt like a new woman. My hair had been washed and Dior moisturizing body milk had done the job. This time, I put on a silk robe after I was done, and when I opened the door that led to my bedroom, I saw Malik chilling on my king-sized bed with his shirt off. He sat against the tuft headboard while flipping through a book I had been reading. I cleared my throat, causing him to look up.

"It's about time," he said. "That was a long ass shower."

"Excuse me, but what are you doing on my bed? I don't recall telling you to come into my bedroom."

"You told me to make myself at home, so I did. If I was at home, I would be in my bed, probably chilling and watching TV. If you would like for me to exit your bedroom, I most certainly will without any hesitation."

"Yes, I would like for you to exit. I already told you I would show you the guestroom. That's where you can sleep tonight."

Malik got off the bed and tossed his shirt over his broad shoulder. My eyes were locked on his carved chest that displayed multiple tattoos. He moved in my direction, then he stopped right in front of me.

"Are you sure you want me to chill in another room? I prefer to be in here with you tonight."

Hell, at this point, I preferred him to be in here with me too. "If I let you stay in here with me, tell me what I can look forward to."

He answered by inching me back to the bed and placing his soft, buttery lips over mine. I was so caught up with the taste of his sweet tongue. The way he kissed me sent shockwaves throughout my body. He was gentle as gentle could get, and as he lay on top of me, one hand held up my leg, his other hand massaged my breast. He planted multiple delicate kisses on my neck, between my breasts, inside my bellybutton and right above my goodies. I was shocked when he dropped to his knees, and after securing my legs on his shoulders, his tongue traveled deep. So deep that a high arch formed in my back. I gasped out loudly to catch my breath. I had no idea that young men gave head like this, and this motherfucker had brought tears to the rims of my eyes. After this, I was going to beg for forgiveness and get back in church real soon.

President of the United States, Stephen C. Jefferson

My mother was a trip. I tried to ignore her as best as I could, but seeing her protesting last night and being arrested was too much for me. Everybody in my administration kept talking about it. Sam couldn't even focus in the press briefing room, without reporters asking him questions about my mother. She was a mess. Had started drinking again—I surely didn't want to go down that path with her again.

"You need to get your mother," Raynetta said as we sat at the table, eating breakfast while trying to ignore each other. "She's out of control. If you don't stop her, something tragic is going to happen."

"I agree, but don't sit there as if you care about me or my mother. Nonetheless, I'll deal with her soon."

"You're right. I don't care anymore, but can you blame me?"

"I don't blame anyone for anything, but myself."

It was obvious that Raynetta wanted to argue and get my day off to a bad start. I wasn't going there with her, especially since I needed her to attend two functions with me this week.

"I'll be meeting world leaders at the United Nations in New York tomorrow. While I'm there, I have a fundraising event to attend. I would like for you to join me, if you don't have anything else to do."

"I have plenty to do, but I know how important it is for you to keep on pretending that we love each other. I'll go, just make sure I have my own suite at the hotel. My rest these days is important."

Raynetta couldn't stand to be around me much longer. She grabbed a bagel from the table and picked up a binder in front of her. She winked at me and walked away. I couldn't help but to wonder what she was up to. It never took me long to find out what was up in the White House, and whatever Raynetta was doing behind closed doors would come to the light. For now, I needed to go see what was up with my mother. I'd called her twice, but she didn't answer her phone. And while I was in the Suburban, on my way to her place, I called her again. Still, no answer. I was somewhat worried, especially since she'd been drinking so much. Then, I figured this was her way of getting my attention. As usual, it worked.

My cell phone vibrated; I thought it was her calling me back. Instead, it was General Stiles calling. I answered right away.

"How did your meeting with John go?" she asked. "I'm asking because, at times, he seems clueless about what's going on. I just want to make sure he went over some of the details we discussed."

"He covered everything. I kind of know what you mean about him seeming clueless, but many of us are new at this. There's a lot to learn. We're all a work in progress."

"I won't disagree with you on that. So true, and when you get back from New York, I want to meet you somewhere so we can have a heart-to-heart talk about my position. I'm starting to worry about some of the things I've been doing too, and I want to get your take on how you think I should move forward. If you can pencil me in somewhere on your schedule, it would be much appreciated."

"Will do. I'll have Andrew give you a call and set something up."

"Thanks. I'll be watching you at the U.N., and good luck with those world leaders. Stay away from the fake ones and the ones who want to cause our country harm. I'm sure you already know who they are."

"I do, but thanks for the advice."

By the time our call ended, Secret Service had parked in a parking garage where my mother lived. The place was highly secured because several famous people resided in the same building. Only a few people saw us coming. That was the security guard at the front desk, and a lady who was on her way out with her daughter. She stopped to thank me for joining the protest the other day.

"I couldn't believe you were out there," she said. "My husband has mixed feelings about it, but what other choice did you have? The protests are still happening, but they seem more controlled now."

"They are and I hope they stay that way."

The lady's daughter asked for my autograph so she could show it off at school. I signed one of her notebooks, before I headed up the elevator with two Secret Service agents. As we exited the elevator, I asked them to wait for me right there. I walked to my mother's door that was the second one to the right of the elevator. Since I'd had a key, I let myself in. All I heard was a loud TV coming from her bedroom. The living room area was tidy, but I saw a Cognac bottle on the kitchen's counter, next to two glasses.

"Mama," I said as I proceeded down the hallway. I glanced into the guestroom; it was empty. When I made it to her bedroom, I had to take two or three steps back. I was shocked to see her lying naked in bed with a young man who was somewhere in his twenties or thirties. He was sitting against the headboard, watching TV. She was partially on top of him; their legs were intertwined.

"What's up?" the young man shouted with bugged eyes. "Teresa, wake up! Yo . . . Your son, the president is here!"

Without saying a word, I stood in the doorway with a stern expression covering my face. My eyes were contracted; palms had already started to sweat.

"Teresa," he said, shaking her shoulder. "Wake up!"

She lifted her head from his chest, yawned and wiped the corner of her mouth. As she slowly backed away from him, he eased out of bed and reached for his pants.

"What are you yelling for?" she said, still not seeing me in the doorway. "Come on, Malik, get back in the bed. I have a hangover and I'm not ready to get up yet."

With an embarrassed look on his face, Malik's eyes stayed focused on me.

"I . . . I apologize for presenting myself to you like this, but uh, I just, we didn't know you was coming."

My mother's head snapped to the side. The second she saw me standing there, she reached for the comforter on the bed to cover herself. She sat up, raking her messy hair back with her fingers.

"What do you want, Stephen? Why are you here and you shouldn't come here without calling first."

Malik zipped his jeans as I walked further into the room and stood at the edge of the bed.

"What I want is for you to stop making a fool of yourself. You're out of control, Mama, and sleeping with young men who are only trying to use you won't solve your problems."

"Man, look," Malik said. "I'm not trying to use anybody. Your mother . . ."

She quickly interrupted him. "Malik, you don't have to say one word. You are a guest in my home. My son has no business coming here and making assumptions that are insulting to me and to you as well. If you can't tell, I'm busy, Stephen. Go back to the White House and run the people in your administration. Your look doesn't intimidate me, and being ugly all the time doesn't suit you."

Without even knowing it, she was about to catch hell. I looked at Malik who stood there like a damn puppet.

"Get out. I need to speak to my mother in private. And when I say get out, I do mean exit the building."

He looked at my mother, as if he needed validation. She moved her head from side-to- side.

"He's not going anywhere. You're the one who needs to leave. Don't make me disrespect you in front of my guest."

"I'm warning you, Mama. I'm about to do more than show my disrespect. I told him to leave."

She pointed to the door with fury in her eyes. "I told you he's not going any damn where. You don't run anything over here, so march your ass out that door and save this conversation for another day."

"Look," Malik said, calmly. "I don't want to cause no trouble. I can just go and give you a call later."

"Good choice," I said. "And don't bother to call her later. She'll be in rehab where she belongs."

"And you'll be in a dick control center where you belong. Malik, don't you dare leave this room. If you do, it would be a cowardly act and I would be so disappointed."

"I know you would, but I . . . I can't diss the president. I got much respect for this man. If he wants me to leave so he can holler at you, I can't stand in the way of that."

His words didn't *charm* me. And since he was still there, I moved his way and demanded that he left immediately.

"I appreciate all the smooth talk, but it's not needed. Now go. Go before you get hurt and you witness a side of me that you won't appreciate."

Malik shot me an evil stare; his left eye twitched. I could tell he was a piece of shit, and when pushed, every man showed his true colors.

"Man, you need to step back," he said. "I've been real cordial, but I'm not gon' stand here and let you punk me."

I shrugged and moved face-to-face with him. "You shouldn't let me punk you, but what are you going to do about it?"

My mother pulled my arm, telling me to move back.

"This is stupid. You're not in the streets anymore, Stephen. Back the hell up and keep him out of this. This is between you and me."

I snatched away from her hold and kept my eyes focused on Malik. "This is between us, Mama, and I intend to deal with you in a minute. Or should I say, after Malik put all of his clothes back on and leaves."

He threw his hands in the air and walked around me. "I don't have time for this. I'm leaving. If you want to see me again, Teresa, you have my number."

He snatched his shirt from the floor, and as my mother got off the bed with a sheet wrapped around her, trying to stop him from leaving, I grabbed one of her arms. She reached up to slap me, but I blocked it.

"Sit down and let that fool go," I said. "You're acting like some kind of desperate woman who don't have nothing else to do with her time. Your foolishness stops today, Mama, and I do mean today!"

"I've had enough of your insults. You are going to make me do something to you I may regret. You act like a man can't be attracted to me, but the last time I checked, I can have any man I want, no matter how old he is. This isn't about Malik, is it? It's about your black ass always trying to control everyone and everything around you. You had no right to speak to him that way, and you damn sure have no right to come in here and act like you're my man."

"Who I'm acting like is your son. You need to get it together. It makes no sense for you to be out there clowning like you are." I paused when I heard the front door shut. Apparently, Malik had finally left. I continued my conversation with my mother. "You know people are watching, you know they're going to put you on the news, and to be frank with you, the shit you do is embarrassing. I'm trying to get things in order, but every time I turn around, I have to answer questions about your ridiculous actions. You've got to do better. If you need some help with your drinking problem, I suggest you go back to rehab. Stay there for as long as it takes and stop giving those damn reporters something to talk about."

She walked away from me, and after tying the sheet over her breasts, she went right over to a nightstand where there was another bottle of alcohol and a glass next to it. She poured Gin to the rim of the glass, then put it up to her lips while peering at me. After taking several sips, she smiled.

"Just so you know, there are times when I've felt embarrassed by your actions too. Times when I've been so proud of you; after all, you are my son. You may not approve of some of the things I do, but I will make no adjustments to my life to appease you. Learn to accept me for who I am, and if you don't, there will be no loss here."

"So, in other words, you're not going back to rehab, right?"

"When you go, I'll go. You have a lot of problems too. Sweeping your messy shit underneath the rug won't make it go away."

"The only problem I have right now is you."

She laughed and sipped from the glass again. I was so frustrated with her that I rushed up to her and snatched the glass from her hand. I threw it against the wall, causing the glass to shatter and alcohol to spill on the wall.

"Hell yes I have problems, Mama! But this ain't about me. It's about you fucking up! Do you even realize what you're doing to yourself? It's beyond making a fool of yourself, and I thought we were over this. After all that happened in the past, I thought you would never, ever want to drink again."

"You're the one who caused me problems. That's why I started drinking to begin with, so don't you dare talk about I'm the one fucking up."

172

My past flashed before me, but it was her intentions to throw me off and make me feel responsible for her actions. Not this time. She was on her own. I told her just that.

"When you hit rock bottom, don't you come to me, begging me to help you. I'm done with you, with all of it. I'm not going to save you from yourself again, and the next time you invite your young puppet over here again, tell him to wash his damn feet. It stinks in here, and a man with funky ass feet speaks volumes."

I pivoted to walk away.

"And a boy who kills his own father isn't shit either. That's just a little something to think about while our relationship is on hiatus."

Her comment caused me to stop in my tracks. I didn't bother to turn around—just took a deep breath, then released it. My mind traveled back to that horrific day, but as I had done for many years, I shook it off and kept moving.

First Lady,
Raynetta Jefferson

Unfortunately, love didn't live in my heart anymore. How I knew this was true, I was no longer excited when I saw Stephen. No matter how handsome he was, I wasn't moved. I hated to be in his presence, and every time I saw him speaking to people, I cringed. He seemed so fake to me. He definitely wasn't the man I had married many years ago. I didn't sweat it anymore, nor did I worry about Mr. McNeil being my grandfather. Emme provided me with just enough information I needed to put this book together. When she put me in touch with a literary agent, it didn't take long for publishers to bite. So far, five publishers were interested in my tell-all story and the price to purchase it was steep. My agent, Beth Ann, said she would contact me later to let me know who the first bidder was. In her opinion, I could probably get more than what I had asked for. Everything was done behind the scenes, and even the publishers knew this had to be done in secrecy. The only thing I'd provided, thus far, was minimal juicy details about Stephen's past and present, about some of Mr. McNeil's dealings, and about his son, my biological father, being a rapist. I even intended to include damaging information about Teresa. For the right price, people would know she was capable of murder. For the right price, I planned to tell it all. Stephen should've thought long and hard about what he'd done to me. Mr. McNeil should've done so too.

As Stephen was at the U.N., I watched him deliver his speech while I was in the hotel suite getting some writing done. His message to world leaders was inspiring, and even though another war had been the topic for many months, Stephen and his administration had taken a diplomatic approach that prevented further wars from happening. The last thing this country needed was to go to war with another country. We had our own problems right here. The racial war that had been brewing required Stephen's attention, more than anything. People were getting killed on the streets, just because. It had been quiet for a few days, but no one could predict when another unfortunate incident would happen.

I couldn't concentrate on writing, so I tuned in to Stephen's speech again. The television always made him appear more handsome than what he was and his confidence was such a turn on. I understood why so many women loved my husband, but they didn't know him like I did. He had turned into a monster, and one of these days, Michelle Peoples would get a taste of who he was. I didn't wish harm on anyone, but as far as she was concerned, I wanted her to get what she deserved. I truly believed she had fallen in love with him and probably couldn't stop herself from wanting to be with him. I knew she had come to the White House that night, and while I didn't know the specifics of what had happened, I could only imagine. As I thought about what could've occurred, I started to write again, embellishing a few things here and there.

Tears poured from my eyes as I peeked through the east side doors to the Oval Office and witnessed another woman with her legs wrapped around my husband's waist. No woman should ever feel the gut-wrenching pain I'd felt in that moment, and even though I wanted to run away that night and cry myself to sleep, I couldn't. I was numb from head to toe and couldn't move. The way they feverishly kissed, the way he touched her and caressed her entire body made me more jealous than I had ever been. This was the first time I had witnessed Stephen in action, and even though he'd had multiples affairs before, this one hurt more. This woman was in love with my husband, and the passion in his eyes, as he gazed into hers, proved to me that he loved her too. Maybe even more than he claimed to love me. I wasn't sure, but I continued to watch. I watched for hours, and after each loud grunt, I sunk to a new low. I couldn't fulfill my duties as the first lady, and I surely didn't feel like one. I finally realized our marriage meant nothing to the president and that was a hard pill for me to swallow, especially since I had given my marriage my all. In no way was I perfect, but I would give Stephen the world. I had been his rock, and to see him, time and time again, dishonor his vows was more disappointing than anyone would ever know. We argued on a regular basis, and if I got too loud or threatened to leave him, he would make me pay. The physical and mental abuse went on for years, and I found myself sleeping alone for many nights. Sometimes, my eyes would be black and blue. I covered my bruises with makeup, and when I couldn't hide my bruises, I had to cancel scheduled events. I wanted to tell someone, but so many people in the White House loved the president. He could do no wrong in their eyes, so I had to keep my secret, in hopes that he would one day snap out of it and be the man I knew I deserved.

As the world leaders applauded Stephen's speech, I looked at the TV and smiled. A small part of me didn't want to do this to him, but for sixty or maybe even seventy million dollars, what woman in my situation wouldn't do it? Maybe some wouldn't, but this was the decision I'd made. I flipped the page to my notebook and started to write again.

Maybe I had been too hard on my husband. Or maybe I should've gotten him the help he needed, instead of encouraging him to run for president. A wise first lady once said that the presidency doesn't change who you are, it only reveals who you are. It will be revealed that Stephen is a murderer, a manipulator and he was a very troubled child. A child who was abused by both of his parents, more so his father whom Stephen tried to wash from his memory. He was often afraid to sleep because sleeping brought about nightmares. Nightmares that left him waking up in cold sweats and regretting that he had killed his father one day. Stephen always said he didn't want to do it, but his mother was evil. She'd made him do it, and she stood by Stephen's side when he pulled the trigger. No matter how anyone looked at it, it was murder. Stephen never told me where his father's body was; he also said he doesn't remember. I kept his secret because I didn't want anyone to know. In order for my husband, president of the United States, to heal himself, he must deal with it and the world must know the truth.

I released a deep sigh then closed the notebook. I didn't feel like writing anymore, and since Stephen told me to be ready by six o'clock, I decided to shower, do my hair and get totally beautified for the night.

A few hours later, I was dolled up and ready to go. My hair had been brushed to one shoulder and was full of loose curls. The navy strapless dress I wore had sequins around the breasts area, and diamonds added glam to my fit. With teardrop earrings on, and an expensive diamond-filled bracelet, I felt like royalty. I reached for my purse, sprayed on a dash of sweet perfume, and then I went to Stephen's room to see if he was ready to go. With Secret Service waiting outside the door to his suite, Stephen opened it with his shirt off, slacks unbuttoned and a toothbrush in his mouth.

"Come inside," he mumbled. "I'm running a little late."

I entered his suite, examining everything I saw. It was rather messy. Papers were on the table, his clothes were on the sofa, several pairs of shoes were here and there and a box of KFC was on the table too.

I looked at him as he stood near the bathroom's doorway, still brushing his teeth. "You're already living like a bachelor," I teased. "And work that toothbrush good. I surely don't want to smell her goodies all on your breath."

He cut his eyes at me and closed the door to the bathroom. I walked around, being nosy. His cell phone vibrated, and even though I didn't care who was calling him, I still looked at the screen to see who it was. Andrew's name flashed on the screen. I didn't bother to answer.

Minutes later, Stephen came from the bathroom while buttoning his white shirt. He also had on navy slacks. I didn't intend to coordinate with him.

"I would've been ready, but I had to take some important calls." His eyes scanned me from head to toe. "You look nice. I know you're not excited about doing this, but thanks anyway."

"I'm not doing this for you. I'm doing this for me, just so you know."

While trying to put his cufflinks on, he stepped forward and stood in front of me.

"It really doesn't matter who you're doing this for, but going forward, let's try to talk to each other with respect. We both know where things stand, so there's no need to keep on being bitter about this. What's done is done. At least we can both say we tried." He extended his arm to me. "Put on my cufflinks for me. I can't do it."

I hesitated to assist him, but I did it anyway. After I was done, he asked me to attach his bowtie to his shirt.

"This is the last thing I'm going to do. Get your girlfriend to do it."

He winked at me and smiled. "I would, but I'm sure she's somewhere busy, getting ready for tonight too."

I hated that my attitude didn't seem to annoy him. And with all the money I'd soon be getting, I guess I needed to change my attitude too. I intended to, after this last little jab.

"So, if she's going to be here, why do you need me to go with you? I guess she's not as pretty as I am, and the only time you really want to be seen with her is in private."

I nearly choked him as I put on his bowtie. He licked out his tongue and gagged.

"Shit," he said. "Does it take all that to put on a bowtie?"

"Your neck shouldn't be so fat. Don't blame me."

"Whatever. My neck isn't fat. You're just trying to hurt me, that's all."

"Maybe so; after all, I'm dying to hurt you."

Stephen ignored my comment. He walked off, and after putting on his jewelry, jacket and shoes, we left the suite together with Secret Service leading the way. The Presidential Motorcade was waiting for us, but before we could get to it, we were swarmed with crowds of people who had been waiting to take pictures and get a glimpse of us. We were rushed to the motorcade by Secret Service, and once we were inside we waved at people.

"How long are we going to be here tonight?" I asked.

"I hope not long because I'm kind of tired. Unfortunately, sometimes, these events can go on forever."

"If it lingers on after eleven, I'm going to give you a signal. I'm kind of tired, too, and I haven't been resting well lately."

"I guess I don't have to ask why. Did you ever get a chance to chat with Mr. McNeil?"

"Yes, but I don't want to talk about it. I'm still not sure about a whole lot of things. Changing the subject, have you spoken to your mother lately?"

"I spoke to her, but that's something I don't want to discuss. I'm going to try and enjoy myself tonight. I hope you do too."

I wasn't so sure if I would, but after we arrived at the fundraising event and I started conversing with so many interesting people, I did enjoy myself. There were numerous speakers, including Stephen, and several others who entertained the crowd. The dinner plates cost five thousand dollars; I was sure the Democrats had raised millions tonight. Speaking of dinner, it was delicious. They served lobster tails, steamed vegetables, risotto and stuffed mushrooms. I also ate a salad and the chocolate rum cake had me full as ever. I wanted to crawl in my bed and sleep the night away. But people kept talking and the band kept playing. Stephen asked me to dance, and as we paraded around on the dance floor like a happy couple, many people watched. Several other people were on the dancefloor too, and with a variety of alcoholic beverages being served, many people were tipsy.

"Didn't I say you would enjoy yourself tonight?" Stephen asked with one arm secured around my waist and his other hand clenched with mine. I tried to keep a little space between us, but he was real close.

"You did and I'm glad I came. It helped me relieve some of the stress I've been under."

He didn't respond. He looked into my eyes, and then spun me around, before holding my waist again.

"For someone who says she's been under a lot of stress, I must say that you did your thing tonight. You look very nice."

Any other time I would've appreciated his compliment. I pretended as if I did. "Thanks for the compliment, but where is this going, Stephen? Are you horny or something? Is your girlfriend not treating you right or are you having some regrets?"

He spun me around again, before answering. "No regrets. None at all."

For the next few minutes, we danced without saying anything to each other. I saw his head turn in another direction, and as I shifted my head to the left, Michelle was dancing several feet away with a white man. I figured she would be in attendance tonight, especially since the media basically followed Stephen nearly everywhere he went. She couldn't keep her eyes focused on her dance partner. I saw her taking glances at Stephen; I also saw him looking in her direction too. He even nudged his head in one direction, and a few minutes later, she exited the floor. Shortly thereafter, he cleared his throat and backed away from me.

"I need to go to the men's room. I shouldn't be long, but after I say goodnight to a few people we can go."

I nodded and watched Stephen make his way through the crowd. He stopped a few times to chat with several people, but when his eyes searched the room and he nudged his head again, I saw Michelle follow his lead.

At first, I wasn't going to follow them. I wasn't really mad about it, but then I changed my mind and decided to go see what else I could find out. I wanted to include photos in my tell-all book too, and it was my chance to get a clear photo of the two of them together. I saw Stephen go up the arched staircase; Michelle went up them too. I waited before I went up the stairs, and when I did, I went up on the opposite side, just in case someone else was paying attention. From a distance, I saw Stephen and Michelle standing face-to-face while talking. He said something and she laughed. She then straightened his bowtie and said something to him that made him blush. Minutes later, she reached for his hand and he followed her. She led him into one of the empty ballrooms, but as I hurried down the hallway to follow them, Senator Dressel jumped right in front of me, halting my steps.

"I'm so happy to see you tonight, Raynetta. I had planned to call you, and I would love for you to join me on the campaign trail next month. You mentioned your support before, and I think my constituents would be delighted to see you. Will you join me at a rally next month?"

"I'll have to check my schedule and let you know. Can I give you a call sometime next week?"

"Sure you can. I look forward to hearing from you. I hope that. . ."

She kept rambling on. I looked over her shoulder to see if Stephen and Michelle had left the room. They hadn't.

"Uh, Senator Dressel, do you mind if I cut this short? I really need to go to the restroom."

"Oh, I'm sorry," she said, stepping aside. "Don't forget to call me."

I walked off and made my way down the hall. As I stood outside of the room where Stephen and Michelle were, I sucked in a deep breath. I didn't know what to expect—what would I do if I saw them having sex? I told myself nothing, but then again, I was still his wife. I reached for the knob, cracking the door just a little. Immediately, I saw them in an embrace. There was no breathing room between them, and he was saying something to her that made her nod. He kissed her forehead, then pecked her lips. She softly rubbed the back of his head and pursued a lengthier kiss. Right then, I lifted my phone and snapped a picture. I couldn't stand to watch anymore. My anger had taken over; I decided to leave without him. I stopped by the restroom to wash my hands and put on some more lipstick. Even chatted with a woman inside for a few minutes. As I exited the restroom, I saw Michelle and Stephen at the top of the staircase. They were getting ready to boldly go down together, so instead of going down on the side they were on, I went to the opposite side to walk down. Stephen had one hand touching the small of her back; his other hand was in his pocket while he searched the lower level. I figured he was searching for me. It didn't take long for him to see me on the other side of the double staircase, and the evil stare I gave him let him know exactly what I was thinking. He nudged his head toward the exit door, but I turned my head in another direction. Seconds later, I heard several popping sounds that sounded like firecrackers. It wasn't until I saw people scattering like roaches, when I realized the sounds were gunfire. Things appeared to move in slow motion. I saw numerous Secret Service agents rushing up the stairs, but Stephen was running in my direction. I made my way toward him too, and as I jetted up the stairs, I twisted my damn ankle and fell.

"Stay down," Stephen yelled at me. "Stay down on the floor!"

"Mr. President, get down!" Secret Service hollered.

Bullets were flying everywhere. Glass was shattered, people were screaming and many cries rang out. I rolled my way over to Stephen with my hands shielding my ears from the loud gunfire. By then, Secret Service had covered us and rushed us through a concrete staircase that led to the parking garage. My body trembled all over; hands were shaking badly. My legs felt so weak that I could barely make it down the stairs. My twisted ankle didn't help. Stephen held my hand, and with a scrunched face and sweat beads dotting his forehead, he didn't say anything. He seemed slightly out of breath; I could feel his palm sweating. Secret Service busted through the exit door, examining our surroundings. There was a car waiting for us with the doors wide open.

"Go!" One of the agents said to the driver, after we were shoved inside. "Now!"

The car skidded off, and as we sat on the backseat, Stephen finally let go of my hand.

"You alright?" he asked as he removed his suit jacket.

I was still nervous. "No, I'm not. Wha . . . What in the hell is going on? Were those men shooting at you?"

"I don't know anything yet. I'll soon find out."

It wasn't long before Stephen's phone rang. While he was in the midst of a long conversation with Andrew, I sat there shaking and wondering if this was just another set up. It couldn't have been because there were real bullets flying. People were on the floor severely injured. I saw a few bodies, and unfortunately, one of the bodies was Senator Dressel. I felt so bad for her. I couldn't stop thinking . . . *what if it was me?* Stephen's actions surprised me. He didn't run for Michelle, he came for me. He rushed in my direction to protect me. I wasn't happy about seeing the two of them together, but I was relieved he wasn't hit. It wasn't that I wanted him dead or anything like that. I just wanted him to hurt like I was. I also wanted as much money as I could get to make up for my heartache.

Stephen still hadn't said much. At least, not until we got to the hotel, where more Secret Service agents and police were at. They took Stephen and me to my suite first. And after he was briefed about the situation, he found out it wasn't a hit on him. There was a hit, however, on several senators who had angered four men. The men were able to make their way into the event and cause major damage. Three people had been killed, five in critical condition and eleven people seriously injured. Three of the four people involved had been arrested; one man had been shot and killed by police. This time, it was real and I felt horrible.

"Once things settle down," Stephen said, sitting on the sofa with the bottom of his leather shoe pressed against the table in front of him. "We need to get back to the White House. I know you're tired, but we have to leave tonight."

"That's fine with me. I hate this happened, and is one of the people dead Senator Dressel? I had just spoken to her about campaigning with her."

"Unfortunately, she is one of the deceased."

Stephen's phone vibrated. He looked down at it, then quickly glanced at me. Without saying a word, he got off the sofa, walked toward the TV and started texting. I wasn't sure if he was texting Michelle or not, but I assumed it was her. Feeling frustrated about all of this, I went to the bathroom and splashed water on my face. My clothes were wrinkled, I had also scraped my knee when I fell and my ankle was still tender. I dabbed a wet towel against it, and covered the scar on my knee with a Band-Aid. After I was done, I returned to the bedroom to remove my clothes. I changed into a T-shirt and jeans, and while I rummaging through my suitcase to look for my tennis shoes, I heard Stephen's loud voice behind me.

"What in the fuck is this?" he shouted.

I quickly turned around, only to see my notebook in his hand. The damn notebook that I'd forgotten was on the table.

From the dreadful look on his face, I could tell he had read enough of the content to know what I had been up to. Still, I lied.

"It's just a notebook I was writing my thoughts in, Stephen. Calm down."

"Your thoughts, huh? Don't lie to me, Raynetta! Your notes and these lies tell me exactly what you've been up to!"

"I haven't been up to anything. Calm down and give it here."

I extended my hand, but Stephen ripped the notebook to shreds and threw what was left of the notebook at me.

"I can't believe you wrote that shit for a book deal! How much are they paying you, Raynetta? How much are you willing to sell our fucking secrets for and tell your gotdamn lies?"

"All of it isn't lies, and why are you assuming I'm pursuing a book deal?"

He reached in his pocket and flicked a business card at my face. "Because that's your agent's business card. It was in the notebook too, along with a bunch of figures. What you wrote tells me everything I need to know!"

I rolled my eyes, and as I proceeded to move to the other side of the room, Stephen rushed up from behind and put me in a chokehold. I was caught off guard. His hold was so tight on my neck that I couldn't move it.

"I hate you, Raynetta! But I'm not going to do a damn thing to you, because you're going to hang your fucking self. Write your story, tell your lies and make all the money you can get. In the end, I hope you get what you always wanted. This just proves that greed is the only thing you love, just like your sucka-ass grandfather."

He released me and pushed me hard on the floor. I skidded and banged my knee. As he stormed toward the door, I yelled after him.

"Call it whatever you want! I call it getting what I deserve!"

He swung around and pointed his finger at me. "If you sell that shit, you're going to get what you deserve. I promise you that, so think real hard. The choice is yours!"

He punched the bedroom's door on his way out, and after I heard the other door slam, I snatched some of the papers off the floor. I couldn't piece anything back together, so I got off the floor and searched for a pen in my purse. Another notebook was on the nightstand, and instead of going back to the White House tonight, I stayed at the hotel, writing until nearly four o'clock in the morning.

President of the United States, Stephen C. Jefferson

The situation at the fundraising event had everyone on pins and needles. Yet again, people were upset because security that was put in place hadn't worked. We had recently left a massive meeting in the Roosevelt Room, with several agencies who were tasked with keeping everyone safe. The sad thing was, not much was accomplished. The blame was transferred from one person to the next. I was tired of firing people, and there wasn't much hiring going on. We still had numerous positions to fill, but I was in no rush to fill them. The minimal amount of people working at the White House, the better it was for me. Some people took on multiple duties—mainly people I had started to trust. Those people were Andrew, Sam and also General Stiles.

I'd found out more details about Raynetta and her book deal. Her agent had been shopping it around and numerous publishers were biting. I had the power to shut it all down, but I didn't do it. I wanted to see if she was brave enough to go through with it; it appeared she was. I saw her writing here and there. I knew she had gone to several meetings to discuss the details. The last thing Andrew told me was, she was close to a decision and would get an advancement in the millions. This was why trusting the person you intended to spend your life with was so important. I'd shared all of my secrets with Raynetta, and no matter how bad things had gotten between us, I never thought she would tell the world what had actually happened to my father. I stood in the Oval Office, gazing out at the Rose Garden, while thinking about a day that had haunted me for years.

I was eleven years old and had just come home from school. It was already a bad day, because every time I'd gone to school, kids made fun of me. My hair was too nappy, the clothes I wore looked like hand-me-downs, and they teased me about being too skinny. I had fights nearly every day and the boy I'd fought with that day had busted my lip. I rushed into our one bedroom apartment where the living room was my room. My mother always kept everything as tidy as she could, but on that particular day, dishes were in the sink. I had forgotten to wash them after dinner last night. And after I wiped my bloody mouth, I intended to take care of the dishes. I ran to the bathroom and grabbed a towel from the linen closet. As I looked in the mirror while wiping my lips, my father appeared in the doorway. He was a mean-ass man and his gaze was very intimidating. Standing six-feet-four and three-hundred pounds, I definitely feared him. He never had anything nice to say, and if he wasn't beating my ass for something, he was fussing and hitting on my mother.

"What happened to yo damn lip, boy?"

"Nothing. I tripped and fell."

"You need to trip and fall yo ass out of this bathroom and get in there on those dishes. Didn't yo Mama tell you to do those dishes last night?"

"Yes, Sir, she did, but I had homework to do and a test to study for. I fell asleep doing my homework and didn't have time to do the dishes."

He grabbed me by my shirt, and yanked me out of the bathroom. We stood in the hallway as he continued to chastise me.

"You got plenty of time now, so get the fuck in there and get busy. And for lying to me about falling, you know I'mma hurt you, right? I saw Li'l James outside kicking yo ass. All his daddy gon' do is brag to me about it and laugh at me for having a punk-ass kid like you. You ain't shit. I'mma teach you, again, how to stand up for yourself."

"I did stand up for myself. I hit him back and punched him in his stomach. He may have busted my lip, but I won the fight. You can ask the kids who watched."

"A winner doesn't have a busted lip. How in the hell can you call yourself a winner and yo lip looking like that?"

He pushed me again and slapped me upside my head. With tears in my eyes, I ran to the kitchen and started on the dishes. My whole face was scrunched. I pouted as I listened to him ramble on about what a loser I was.

"Stupid ass motherfucker. You ain't nothing but a Mama's boy, a bitch and a little faggot. Those good grades you make don't mean shit, and all that studying you do ain't gon' get you nowhere in a white man's world. You need to know how the streets operate. How to beat a nigga's ass when he come for you. Turn yo ass around and let me show you what to do when a nigga comes for you."

I was in no mood for this, but I turned around with tears streaming down my face. Trying to appear tough, I smacked my tears away and held up my fists. My father had his up too.

"Come on, son, hit me. Show me what you got and hit me in my face."

I gritted my teeth and swung out at him. He blocked my punch and landed a hard blow to my chest that made me fall to the floor.

"Get up! Get up and try it again!"

I got up with more tears streaming down my face. Snot drizzled from my nose and my head was starting to hurt.

"If you stop all that gotdamn crying, maybe you can focus and hit me like you supposed to."

I growled as I swung out at him again. This time, I punched him in his ear. My punch angered him; he reached up to hold his ear.

"I said punch me in my face, fool. Like this!"

He started punching me in my face, on the back of my head and in my chest. I crouched down on the floor, feeling dizzier after each blow. Li'l James' punches from earlier felt nothing like my father's punches. They felt like hard bricks being thrown at me, and it wasn't long before he drew blood. I could taste it in my mouth; my left eye started to close.

"Fight back, nigga! Don't you know how to fight back?"

"I can't!" I cried out. "It hurts, Daddy, please stop! It hurts!"

He didn't stop until my mother came in. She could barely stand and was drunk as hell. After she saw my bloody face and trembling body, she sobered up a little. Her eyes grew wide and she staggered into the kitchen where I sat on the floor in so much pain. Daddy stood over me with tightened fists.

"What have you done?" she shouted. "What have you done to my baby?"

"He ain't no damn baby! That's why he fucked up now. I'm teaching him how to be a man!"

Mama rushed over to us and shoved him away from me. She then pulled me up from the floor and held me in her arms. I sobbed as I squeezed my arms around her waist.

"I'm sorry, baby," she said, kissing the top of my head. "He shouldn't have done this to you. How could you do this to your own son?"

She started to cry, too, and while holding me close to her chest, the stench of alcohol was real strong.

"Shut up, you drunk bitch. You mean, how can you do that to him. How can you make him such a wimp and not want him to be like these other boys around here?"

While rocking me in her arms, she defended me to him. "You're damn right he's not like these other boys around here. He's smart as hell and he's going to make something out of himself. He can learn how to fight later. You can't teach him how to fight like this, and shame on you for beating him Reggie!" Mama released her arms from around me, then looked at my battered face. "Go wash your face and put on some clean clothes. You don't have to cry. Crying isn't going to solve a damn thing so wipe those tears."

I wiped my tears, but as I walked away from her, my father smashed his fist into the side of my face again. This time, I saw darkness. My weak body hit the floor hard. My head was spinning. I could hear the two of them going at it. I crawled on the floor and made my way over to a drawer where he'd kept two guns. I was sick of this shit, and I didn't want to hurt anymore. I didn't want Mama to hurt anymore either, so I removed the gun and aimed it at my father who had Mama in a chokehold. When he saw the gun aimed at him, he released Mama and laughed.

"It's about damn time, boy! About time you want to be a man and stand up for yourself. But if you gon' aim a gun at somebody, you damn well better use it. Shoot that drunk bitch and let's go get something to eat!"

As the heavy gun trembled in my hand, I looked at my mother. She, too, had a busted lip but a stern look was on her face.

"Kill that nigga, Stephen! Shoot him! I'll dump his body in the trash where it belongs!"

When he reached out and backslapped her, it prompted me to pull the trigger. I fired once, then again and again. Daddy's body dropped to the floor; he was gone. Mama ran up to me and snatched the gun from my hand.

"Go to my room, shut the door and don't let nobody in here. I'll be back. I'm so sorry about all of this, baby. So sorry."

She held me in her arms, before pushing me toward her room. I had stopped crying, and as I looked at my father's dead body, I didn't regret a thing. I went to the bedroom like Mama had told me to. While peeking through the cracked door, I saw her cover Daddy's body with a sheet. She made a phone call, paced the floor and poured herself several drinks. A few minutes later, I saw a man I had never seen before come inside and drag Daddy's body out of the apartment. Mama returned a few hours later and told me to never tell anyone our secret. The only person I had ever told was Raynetta.

I continued to look out at the Rose Garden. I wondered what Raynetta would ultimately decide. The more I'd thought about it, my answer became clearer. Not only would she tell about my past, she also knew who was behind her assistant Claire's death. The American people wouldn't understand. They would want me and my mother arrested. We had come too far to go down like this. It would be hell for me; I just couldn't let that happen.

Several hours later, I went to Camp David to get my thoughts together. I knew what had to be done, but this was one time that I didn't have the courage to do it. I was waiting for General Stiles to come; after all, she said she wanted to talk. She didn't know about my plans, but I was sure they wouldn't surprise her.

With jeans hanging at my waist and no shirt on, I walked across the wooden floors and stood in front of the fireplace. The cabin-like house was chilly, but always cozy. I hadn't come to Camp David since the incident with Claire, but I needed some privacy. Secret Service was nearby, but no one was in the cabin with me. I stoked the fire and then I sat on the leather sectional to chill until General Stiles arrived. She said she would be here in about fifteen minutes—that was nearly ten minutes ago. When my phone vibrated, I thought it was her. Instead, it was Michelle. I hadn't spoken to her since the fundraising event, but she'd sent me a text message, asking if I was okay and telling me she was fine too. She'd told me to call her, but I'd been so busy that I hadn't had time. I answered the phone and propped my feet on an ottoman in front of me.

"I know you're busy, and I know you have a lot on your mind," she said. "But I need to share with you how I'm feeling about something. I'm bothered by what happened at the fundraising event. Maybe I shouldn't be all in my feelings about this, but the way you ran over to Raynetta truly hurt me. I was right in front of you, Stephen. And when those bullets started flying, you didn't do anything to protect me. You didn't ask if I was okay, and you didn't even bother to pick up the phone and call me. I was the one who reached out to you, to make sure you were okay. I know she's your wife, but in the moment, you could've made sure I was okay too."

I rubbed my waves and cocked my tense neck from side-to-side. "In the moment, I was trying to save my life too. I didn't know who the target was, and I assumed those bullets were for me and Raynetta. We are targeted, you know, and I'm sorry if you felt like I didn't do enough. Maybe I wasn't thinking clearly, and right after that incident, I didn't have time to call anyone. I'm sure you know many people were trying to reach me."

"I get that, but . . ."

"But my ass, Michelle. I got a lot of shit going on. The last thing I need is you calling me about some petty mess I don't have time for. If you—"

As my tone went up a notch, she hung up on me. I didn't call her back because there was a knock at the door. I hurdled over the ottoman and rushed to the door to open it. General Stiles came in looking pristine with a general's cap on and a navy colored suit. Numerous proficiency badges were on the flap of her pocket; she had earned a substantial amount of ribbons for her heroic actions. I was used to seeing her in camouflage, but no matter what she wore, she represented strength.

"Sorry I'm late," she said, walking inside. "I tried to get here as soon as I could."

"I know being on time is important to you, but I'm not upset with you for being five minutes late."

She sat on the sectional and removed her cap. After placing it on the table, she leaned forward and clenched her hands together. She looked at me as I sat next to her, leaning back on the sectional with my arms resting on top of it.

"I have to say a couple of things," she said. "And I don't want you to think I'm some kind of ungrateful bitch who don't appreciate my job. But I work my butt off, okay? I step up when I have to and I don't ask anybody for anything. I barely ever complain, but I need you to help me with some problems I'm dealing with. Because I'm a woman, I'm not paid as much as the other generals are. Some of the things they say to me are very inappropriate, and I'm trying my best not to call anybody out for sexual harassment. Lastly, as our president, I need you to do more for the military. Too many of us suffer from PTSD, and there isn't enough being done to help us. This shit isn't easy, and I'll be the first to say that our government is failing us. I haven't been privy to speak to presidents like this in the past. If I could have, I would've said the same thing to them, so don't take it personal. My question to you is, are you capable of doing more?"

"Of course I am, and I understand that many members of the military never complain. I'll call a meeting with Congress when I get back, so we can go over the budget and see what we can do to increase military spending and tackle some of the things you mentioned. I'll make sure you get more money, and I want you to give me the names of anyone you personally know who is sexually harassing women in the military. I know that is an issue too, but more women need to speak up."

"They're afraid to. I'm afraid because I've worked so hard and I don't want to lose my status. But I'll give you some names. Just promise me you won't tell anyone the information came from me."

"You have my word. I'm real proud of you, you know. Remember that I have your back, just like you have mine. On another note, I need you to make me a promise too."

"What's that?"

"Promise me that this conversation stays between us and you won't tell anyone about what I'm getting ready to ask you to do."

She smiled and crossed her fingers. "If I haven't said anything before, I won't say anything now. Who's going down this time?"

I didn't hesitate to answer. "Raynetta. She's planning to publish a damaging book about me and my mother. I can't let that happen. Even though I have the capabilities of shutting it down, the fact that she is even considering it bothers me."

General Stiles stood and cracked her knuckles. "The first lady? Wow. This could, uh, backfire, you know? What if we make her just . . . just disappear? Are you sure you want her out of here?"

I hesitated to answer, but under the circumstances, I had to nod my head. "Unfortunately, I do. I know it won't be easy, but it has to be done. Sooner, rather than later."

General Stiles nodded. She paced the floor by the table and then halted her steps.

"I know you were trying to scare her last time, but have things gotten that bad? And why don't you just shut the book deal down and divorce her? It may be easier to do that. That way you won't have any regrets. Have you really thought this through?"

"I have and I came to the conclusion that it must be done."

General Stiles sighed and stayed silent for a while. She stared at me, as if she was puzzled. "You must really trust me. Why do you trust me so much? You know I could—"

"I know you could betray me, but something in my heart tells me you wouldn't. Am I wrong?"

She plopped back down and looked straight ahead. "No, you're not wrong. I'm loyal to you, Mr. President, but I want you to be loyal to me and very honest when I ask you this question. This doesn't have anything to do with you wanting to be with Michelle Peoples, does it? Do you want the first lady out of the way so you can be with your mistress?"

"Trust me, it's not that serious between me and Michelle. And I would never lie to you."

"It looked pretty serious to me. I can't get the thoughts of seeing the two of you together out of my head. Going out like that in the Oval Office was a risky move."

I shrugged and removed my arms from the couch. "I love taking risks. Nothing wrong with that. Besides, I haven't taken a risk that hasn't paid off yet."

Her response was very blunt. "I love taking risks too, but what are you prepared to do for me, Mr. President? I've done a lot for you. When am I going to be rewarded?"

"How do you want to be rewarded? And don't limit yourself, because, for you, the sky is the limit."

She sat silent, and minutes later, she got up and stood behind me as I remained on the couch. She started to unbutton her jacket, and after she finished, she tossed it in a chair.

"I definitely won't limit myself," she said. "If you say the sky is the limit, I'm shooting for the stars. Are you prepared to make me see stars?"

I didn't respond as she took off the rest of her clothes and put them in the chair. She stood naked behind me while massaging my chest. I dropped my head back to look at her firm breasts and muscular frame that was sexy as fuck. The swelling of my steel made my jeans rise, and when she reached down to touch it, it grew to great heights. She bent over to kiss me, and as we tasted each other's tongues, my chest heaved in and out. She was stroking my muscle fast—so fast that I was about to explode in her hand. Unable to control myself, I reached for her waist and flipped her over the couch. With her back facing me, she straddled my lap and spread her legs. I rubbed my fingers between her moist folds, stirring her juices. The sound of her tearful moans sounded off in the room, and instead of my fingers dancing inside of her, she cried out for so much more.

"I'm reaching for the sky," she said, inserting my oversized muscle into her super tight, warm hole. I removed my sticky fingers, then placed my hands over her breasts to massage them.

She began to ride me at a speedy pace. It was a rough ride that forced me to beat her pussy and make her come multiple times that night. It was imperative that I took her to that level; after all, I was counting on her to come through for me in a major way.

President's Mother, Teresa Jefferson

I stood in church, clapping my hands and stomping my feet as the choir sung so beautifully. After all the shenanigans that had been going on between me and Malik, I felt like I needed to hit up the church and pray for forgiveness. It had been a long time since I'd been to church. Now seemed like the appropriate time. Unfortunately for me, though, after the choir got finished singing, I found myself dozing off during Pastor Haynes' sermon. I had been up all night with Malik. He had come to church with me, looking handsome as ever in a brown suit and white shirt with no tie. Nearly everybody kept looking and smiling at us. I figured I'd get hit with questions when church was over, and as soon as it was, Sister Lorraine came running up to me before I could exit the pew.

"Sister Teresa, where have you been? It's been a long time. I'm surprised to see you here."

She looked me up and down with jealousy in her eyes. The black and off-white hat I wore was tilted just enough where you could see my feathered hair. My makeup was flawless and the off-white linen dress I wore had a thick black belt around my waist. I topped off everything with yellow accessories and pointed-toe, high-heeled shoes.

"I'm surprised to still see you here too," I said. "Especially since Pastor Haynes' wife, the first lady, found out the two of you were sleeping together?"

I guess she thought I didn't know about her drama, since I hadn't been here. That surely made her rush away and not ask me anymore questions. Malik laughed, but as we took a few more steps forward, many more people came over to greet me.

"Teresa, how is the president doing?" Sister Payne asked. "He and Raynetta looked awesome the other night. It's a doggone shame what happened at that fundraising event. I hope they're okay."

I frowned and had no idea what she was talking about.

"What fundraising event?"

Another lady, Vetta, spoke up. "Girl, you didn't hear about it? It was all over the news. Some white men shot up the place. I heard the president was okay, and I've been praying for your family every day since then."

I pursed my lips and rolled my eyes at Vetta. "God doesn't like liars, Vetta. I doubt that you've been praying for my family every day, so please don't say it if you haven't been."

She put her hands on her hips, ready to attack me. Before she could say anything, Malik reached for my hand and pulled me in his direction.

"Can we please go?" he asked. "Let's go before things turn real ugly in here."

"Is that your boyfriend or do you have another son?" Vetta asked. "I'm just asking because he looks kind of young to be your man."

I had to respond to this nosy fool, so I pulled my hand away from Malik's and answered her question. I didn't care that several other people were listening.

"For the record, I don't do boys or boyfriends. I only mess around with men who know how to get this old woman's juices flowing, so call him what you wish. I got my special name for him too, but I'll save it for later when the bed starts rocking again."

I left them all with their mouths hanging open and walked off. Malik just shook his head. When we got to his car, he opened the door for me.

"I don't know what to say about you." A smile was on his face. He got in the car and drove off. "You are something else."

"I just don't like nosy people. They are too nosy for me, so I gave them an earful." I looked up and closed my eyes. "Please forgive me, Lord. I had no other choice."

Malik added his two-cents to my prayer. "Yes, forgive her. She doesn't mean any harm. Amen."

I opened my eyes and finally asked if he'd heard anything about a shooting. I surely hadn't, but what Vetta said had me worried.

"I haven't even watched the news," I admitted. "Barely even looked at my phone."

"I haven't heard anything about a shooting either. Been too busy running back and forth from my place to yours. Maybe you should call your son to see what's up."

I thought about our last conversation—Stephen was so doggone nasty towards me. I didn't want to call him, but I did want to know more about what had happened. Instead of calling him, I charged my phone and searched it on Google to see what I could find out. As I read about the incident, it angered me. I gave Malik the details. He advised me to contact Stephen.

"I know things didn't go well that day, but don't hold a grudge against him. I'm sure he wants to hear from you. I really do think you should reach out to him."

Malik drove his car to a gas station. I wasn't sure if I would call Stephen or not. Maybe when I got home.

I watched as Malik felt his pockets, then he turned off the car. "Dang, I don't know what happened to my wallet. I had it earlier, but I must've left it at your place."

I looked at my manicured nails and straightened the diamond ring on my finger. "No, you didn't leave your wallet at my place. You may want to check all of your pockets or look up underneath the seats for it."

He got out of the car, checking his pockets again. He then looked underneath the seat, and realizing it wasn't there, he snapped his finger.

"I bet it fell out of my pocket while we were at church. I kept standing up and sitting down when the choir was singing. I bet I left it on the pew."

"That could be the case too, but without any gas in your car, you don't have enough gas to make it back to the church and look."

He sighed and got back in the car. "Unfortunately, I don't have enough gas to make it there. Let me hold twenty dollars so I can get some gas. I'll give it back when I find my wallet."

I removed my hat and laid it across my lap. "Let me be very clear about one thing, Malik. And that is, I do not give men my money. I don't care what the situation is, don't you ever ask me for one dime."

His forehead lined with wrinkles as he looked at me. "That's cool and everything, but I need to put some gas in my car. I don't know where my wallet is, and I know you have some money in your purse. I only asked for twenty dollars. I said I would give it back to you."

See, he messed up and got on my bad side already. "How in the hell do you know what I have in my purse? You don't know, but I will confirm that I have, at least, two hundred dollars on me. I also have multiple credit cards, but I will not and cannot let you hold twenty dollars to put gas in your car. When you came to pick me up, your car should've been on full. I don't play these kinds of games, Malik. You'd better call somebody, anybody to loan you some money. That twenty dollars will turn into fifty dollars. Fifty dollars will turn into a hundred. I'm letting you know in advance I'm not that kind of fool. With that being said, my question to you is, who are you going to call for some gas money?"

His mouth was dropped open; he appeared stunned as he looked at me. "I can't believe you're serious. You couldn't be serious, are you?"

I opened the car door to show him how serious I was. "I'm calling an Uber. Call me when you get your gas tank taken care of."

I got out of the car and strutted toward the convenience store so I could go inside and call an Uber. Malik started the car and drove next to me.

"This is real fucked up. I've been nothing but nice to you, and I thought we were cool. I can't believe you got an attitude over twenty dollars. After all I've done to you, the least you can do is loan me twenty dollars so I don't have to drive all the way back to the church."

"You'd better stop talking and keep moving before you run out of gas. And what exactly have you done to me? Your penis wasn't worth twenty dollars. Even though your head-game was, you should've told me I had to pay for it. Had I known, I would've opted out."

Malik mumbled something underneath his breath and drove off. A few minutes later, an Uber driver showed up. She knew I was the president's mother, and all the way to my place, I had to listen to how amazing and fine Stephen was. I was glad when she pulled in front of my apartment building. I paid her for the ride and gave her a hundred dollar tip.

"Thank you," she said with glee in her eyes. "You're so sweet. Tell the president I said hello, and wait a minute so I can give you my card. If you or him ever need a ride somewhere, be sure to call me. Tell him to call me anyway."

I thanked the woman, took her card, but threw it in the trashcan when I walked into the lobby area. The security guard spoke to me, and after I swiped my card, the elevator opened. I took it up to my apartment, feeling a little bad about Malik. I just didn't like for men to ask me for money. If they did, let it be five or ten years into the relationship.

I removed my clothes, showered and then went to the kitchen to prepare a quick dinner. Just as I took some chicken out of the fridge, my cell phone rang. I looked to see who the caller was. To my surprise, it was Stephen calling me from his private phone. Whenever he called me from that phone, I knew it was something serious.

"I thought you were done with me," I said even though I was glad to hear from him. "Why are you calling?"

"Because I want you to know about something, before it happens."

His tone was real soft and calm.

"Before what happens?"

"Raynetta. She's been plotting to do something real foolish behind my back. I found out that she's been writing a tell-all book, and one publisher is willing to pay her sixty-five million for it."

"Hell, maybe I should write a book too. But what does she have to tell? She doesn't have anything to tell that's worth that kind of money."

"Yes she does, Mama. I told her about, you know. About what," he paused and didn't want to say it. "About *him*. I know I wasn't supposed to say anything, but at the time, I thought I could trust her."

I stood silent as I thought back to that horrific day, many years ago. Stephen didn't have a choice. I was sick of Reggie abusing us, and I buried his ass good. I didn't think his body would ever be found, but if Raynetta put something out there, maybe people would start looking. My thoughts of that day caused tears to form at the rims of my eyes.

"Stephen, you knew damn well you couldn't trust her. I told you not to ever say anything to anyone. Why would you tell her, and what are you going to do now?"

There was a long silence on the other end, before he finally spoke up. "I don't want to say it, but you already know what I have to do. I have to because she's going to include what happened to Claire too. She's embellishing so much shit, and I honestly feel people will believe her."

"Maybe so, maybe not. I don't like this, Stephen, and I am so upset with you right now for telling that heifer anything."

"I fucked up for sure. But after tonight, General Stiles is going to take care of everything. It'll all be over and done with. Just wanted to let you know, before you heard about it on the news."

Stephen hung up. My mind was racing a mile a minute. I was sick and tired of this crap, and even though I was mad about Raynetta putting us out there, I couldn't let Stephen go out like this. I didn't think he would do anything to her while she was at the White House—she probably wasn't there. I quickly punched in her number and was relieved when she answered her phone.

"Where are you?" I shouted.

"What? Why are you yelling in my ear?"

"Don't worry about it. Where are you? We need to talk. It's urgent. I need to come see you now."

"Teresa, not today. I'm real busy. I don't feel like talking to you about anything right now."

"Listen, you got five seconds to tell me where you are or else you will find yourself sniffing dirt tomorrow. Where are you?"

Raynetta finally told me what hotel she was at in the downtown area. I rushed out of my apartment to get to where she was. I drove like a bat out of hell on the way there, and while I was in the car, Malik had the audacity to call me. I hit the talk button on the navigation screen to see what he wanted.

"I'm real busy right now, Malik. What's good?"

"Not us. I got my gas, but I want you to know that you don't have to worry about me calling you anymore. I . . ."

"Listen, that's fine with me. You don't have to announce it. I'm glad you got your gas. Bye and thank you for the good time. It was fun while it lasted."

I hit the end button and sped up to get to the hotel. When I got there, Secret Service was by the bar area. Both agents were watching a football game, and without them seeing me, I was able to go up to Raynetta's suite that took up the entire top floor. She opened the door with her brows scrunched inward.

"What's this all about, Teresa?"

I responded in a panicky voice. "You have to listen to me, okay? I know you don't like me, but I overheard something today that troubled me. I'm so upset with Stephen for involving himself with that crazy woman. I knew she would one day come after you."

"Who are you talking about? Michelle? Why is she coming after me? She has Stephen wrapped around her finger, so there's no need for her to come after me."

"No, not Michelle. General Stiles," I said, lying. Stephen would never be involved with her, but I pretended that something was going on between them. "She's a lunatic and she's out to get you, Raynetta. You have to stop her. When she comes here tonight, you have to stop her."

"What do you mean by stop her?"

We sat on the couch and I concocted a plan to deal with General Stiles. I knew she was coming tonight, but I wasn't so sure when it would be. Raynetta had turned down all the lights and the two of us sat in a closet, waiting. She seemed real nervous; I pretended that I was too.

"Why don't we just call Stephen and let him deal with this," Raynetta suggested.

"No. Stephen doesn't need to know about this. You know how he is Raynetta. He and I have fallen out again. I don't know what's gotten into him, and since he's involved with General Stiles, he may very well take her side."

Raynetta shook her head, displaying disgust. "This is a mess. If he won't deal with her, maybe the police or Secret Service can. I'm not staying in this closet any longer. I'm going to call the police and let them deal with this, in case she decides to show up."

Raynetta rushed out of the closet and hurried into the living room area. I followed behind her, but before I could open my mouth, I could see the doorknob wiggling. Seconds later, the door squeaked open. In walked General Stiles, dressed in camouflage and black combat boots. A cap was on her head—she looked ready to handle her business. The room was dim, but she saw Raynetta and Raynetta saw her.

"Excuse me," Raynetta said. "Why are you coming in here like you live here?"

It didn't take General Stiles long to fess up to why she was there.

"I'm here because I have some business to take care of for the president."

Before she said too much, I walked further into the room so she could see me. I had to distract her, so I stood in front of her to block her access to Raynetta.

"I don't know what kind of business you came here to take care of, but I think you'd better leave. Nothing is going down in here tonight, okay? Because at the end of the day, Stephen loves his wife and he doesn't want you."

General Stiles stood with confusion on her face. She intended to follow through with her plan, and when she attempted to move me aside, I pushed her several inches away from me. She shoved me, and putting on a very good act, I fell to the floor and reached for my gun. General Stiles raised the one in her hand and aimed it at Raynetta. All her wimpy self did was scream, and as she ducked, a bullet whistled from General Stiles' silencer and pierced the wall.

"My gun," I shouted to Raynetta. "Pick up my gun and shoot!"

General Stiles looked at me again. She was so caught off guard by my involvement and she couldn't figure out what to do. I'm sure she knew there would be a price to pay for shooting me.

Her delayed actions allowed Raynetta to pick up the gun I had slid across the floor in her direction.

"Now, Raynetta!" I yelled. "Do it now before she kills you!"

To save her own life, Raynetta snatched up the gun and fired it twice. General Stiles fired back, but because she was hit first, her aim was off and the bullet hit the wall again. The shots Raynetta fired hit General Stiles twice in the stomach. She fell to her knees, and with wide eyes, she looked at me before crashing to the floor. Raynetta panicked while breathing hard. Tears ran down her face; she appeared to be in shock. I slowly got off the floor, and after I walked over to her, I grabbed her sweaty face and squeezed her cheeks in my hand.

"Secret Service is in the bar area bullshitting around. You have ten or maybe fifteen minutes before they show up. That is plenty of time for you to get rid of her damn body. If you need my help, it'll cost you sixty-five million dollars. If you don't want my help, I'm going to write a tell-all book and start it off with the events that occurred here tonight. The choice is yours. Just tell me what you want to do."

Raynetta knew she had screwed up. She was speechless, and as she stood there in a daze, pondering what to do, I stepped away from her to call Stephen's private phone.

"I can't talk right now, Mama," he said. "Is this important?"

"Very. Like always, I fixed your little problem for you again. General S. came to where Raynetta was to follow through with everything. Thanks to me letting Raynetta know what was up, General S. is no more. Raynetta's hands are as dirty as yours. There will be no tell-all book, unless I decide to write it."

There was silence on the other end of the phone.

"Hello," I said.

"Are you telling me that Raynetta shot and killed General Stiles? Please tell me that's not what you just said."

"I don't want to repeat myself, but—"

"Damn-it, Mama! Why do you always have to fuck shit up! I can't believe you went there and," he paused and I could hear his heavy breathing through the phone. "I can't believe this shit! Fuck!"

I heard him pounding on something, and I didn't understand why he was so upset. There would be no book, and he would be off the hook for doing anything stupid to Raynetta. General Stiles was nobody to him. Nobody. Then again, my mind started to wander.

"You were screwing her too, weren't you? That's why you're so upset, because you were involved with General Stiles too. Weren't you, Stephen? Tell the truth and don't lie to me."

It took him at least a minute to speak up. "The truth is, you and Raynetta need to get the hell out of there now. I'll send somebody over there to take care," he paused as if he didn't want to mention General Stiles. "To take care of that, but get out of there now. Lock the door and get to the White House. Now, Mama, and don't you dare ask me another fucking question."

I ended the call and shoved the phone into my pocket. When I moved back into the living room area, Raynetta was still standing there with her arms across her chest, back against the wall. She stared at General Stiles who was lying there in a pool of blood.

"Come on," I said. "We need to get out of here. Stephen is going to send somebody here to clean this up. He wants us to come to the White House."

"I . . . I don't want to go there," she said tearfully. "You two are very bad people, and I don't want to be a part of this anymore."

I put my hand on my hip, looking at her like she was crazy. "We're bad people, but you're the one who just shot that bitch. You need to snap out of it and let's get out of here before the police come to arrest us. Mainly you, because I didn't kill nobody."

Raynetta moved slow as she made her way to the car with me. I made her reach out to the Secret Service agents who had been at the hotel with her. She told them she'd been looking for them, but couldn't find them. She also mentioned she was on her way to the White House with me. They informed her that they were on their way back to the White House too. When Raynetta and I arrived, we went straight to the Oval Office. Several people asked if Raynetta was okay; she was walking like a zombie and didn't say much to anyone. I knocked on the door to the Oval Office, and when I entered with Raynetta, Stephen was sitting in his chair with his head on the desk.

"Make sure the door is locked," he said softly. "I don't want anyone to come in here."

I locked the door, but when I turned back around, Stephen's head was up. His eyes were fire red; it looked like he had been crying—hard. I hated to see him this way; I couldn't believe he was so torn like this over General Stiles. While Raynetta stood there with a blank expression on her face, I moved around her and walked up to his desk.

"Did she really mean that much to you? I'm confused, Stephen, please tell me what I am missing here."

"It doesn't matter what she meant to me. This is over with, Mama. I'm done."

"Done? Done with who and what?"

"With all of this. I want out, and I don't deserve to hold my position any longer. I can't keep living like this. I need to get away from you, and I have to free Raynetta and move the hell on. All I ask is that nobody speaks about what happened today. Just let it go and—"

Stephen paused and swallowed hard. He covered his face with one hand; I witnessed many tears fall from his eyes. He was crushed, so was I. My eyes filled with tears too, and when I turned to look at Raynetta, her hand was over her chest.

"Stephen, don't do this, okay?" I pleaded. "We can work it all out. We've come too far to give up everything. Like you said, this stays between us. Just the three of us and no one will know a thing."

He removed his hand from his face and shook his head from side-to-side. "No, Mama. I've heard it all before. We can't work it out. I need to step down. I have to get out of this place. It is making me so fucking crazy."

He stood and reached for a piece of paper that was on his desk. I snatched it up before he did, and saw that it was his resignation letter. I pleaded with him again.

"No, Stephen. Don't do this, please. This is a sign of weakness and I always taught you to be strong. If you walk away, you will walk away from so many people who have faith in you and who believe you are the one president who can bring about real change. Please think about this. Take a few more days to think about this, but don't resign today. Please, I'm begging you."

Raynetta finally spoke up. "She's right. Don't do it."

He looked at her, wiped his tears and swallowed hard again. "Don't do it, huh? I sent General Stiles over there to kill you tonight. That's how bad things have gotten, and when I'm here, I feel so damn invincible. Like I can do anything I want and get away with it. I don't want this anymore, and I'm sorry for making the two of you experience this with me. Free yourselves. Free yourselves now, before it's too late."

Stephen took the paper from my hand and walked toward the door. I called after him, but he ignored me. Raynetta called out to him; he ignored her too. He walked out, and the two of us looked at each other with tears in our eyes.

"What are we going to do now?" Raynetta asked.

Unfortunately, this time I didn't have an answer. And the sad thing was, when Stephen's mind was made up, no one could change it. The media would have a field day with this. By ten o'clock that night, they surely did.

"We are awaiting the president's speech in the Oval Office," a news anchor said while sitting behind a desk with multiple other newsroom contributors. *"Our sources are telling us that the president is expected to resign. We have no idea why. We'll have to wait and see what he says."*

I sat on my bed and watched the TV in my bedroom, while trying to control my flowing tears. This was gut-wrenching. I held my stomach tight as I waited to see if my son would really give up on his dreams. Even folks in the media were in a somber mood, and I figured that nearly every household in America was tuned in.

"Here we go, people," the news anchor said, before taking a deep breath. *"President of the United States, Stephen C. Jefferson."*

Black President: Going out with a Bang
Season 2, Finale

President of the United States
Stephen C. Jefferson

Call my term as president messy or whatever, it was. I had gotten myself in a bind and this was the only route I could take to get out of it. Instead of plotting to have Raynetta killed for spilling my horrific past to the American people, I had to put her in a predicament to cause someone else harm. And instead of cussing out my mother for the one-hundredth time and disowning her, she too had to suffer. I had to do things my way, no matter who liked it or not. More than anything, I was grateful to General Stiles for helping me pull this off. Her loyalty to me meant everything. After this task was completed, I intended to extend my gratitude to her in any way she wished. Until then, nearly everyone in the country eyes was glued to the TV, waiting on me to deliver my speech tonight. I was ready, and after I sucked in a deep breath, I eased into my chair behind the Resolute desk and looked straight ahead at the bright white lights and camera. A saddened look was displayed on my face. It was clean shaven and my waves were sharply lined. My attire for the night consisted of black slacks and a burgundy, V-neck Cashmere sweater which showed the definition of my muscles. A platinum watch was on my wrist, and even though Raynetta's and my marriage was barely hanging on, my silver wedding band was still there. I clenched my hands together, feeling somewhat relaxed.

"Good evening everyone. There's been much speculation about what I intended to say tonight, and even though some of you have heard I was going to resign, that is not the case. Unfortunately, there was an explosion in Syria today that killed hundreds of civilians and six American soldiers. Our intelligence agencies are in the process of gathering more information about this tragedy and I assure everyone that a thorough investigation is already underway. At this point, we don't know if this was an act of terror or something else. We do, however, know that we lost some brave Americans, including General Brooks and General Stiles whom I had the pleasure of working closely with to secure the safety of our nation. My heart is heavy tonight and I offer my condolences to the families of our soldiers. I had recently spoken to General Stiles about the ill treatment of women in the military and about how much women deserve the same benefits as men, no matter what position they hold. In honor of her, I will continue to fight for some of the issues that mattered to her the most and after a complete investigation, any individuals sexually harassing or abusing another will be relieved from their duties. That is something we won't tolerate, and I invite Congress to work with me on drafting legislation that delivers stronger punishments which fall into that category and immediate termination in some cases. As your president, this is my way of paying tribute to a woman who gave so much to this country. Creating legislation, in her name, is the least I can do. Please know that I'm not politicizing this tragedy. I'm only seeking to do what someone asked me to do, and to do what the American people deserve. Some changes will be made through executive orders and I expect Congress to act soon. More specifics about the explosion will follow in the coming days. Until then, may God continue to bless us all."

The lights to the camera were turned off. That was when Andrew walked up to my desk. Knowing exactly why I had fabricated this story, he gave me a few pats on my back.

"All done," he said, straightening his nerdy glasses. "Now go and get closure with this situation regarding General Stiles so we can move on."

I nodded and stood. My private line started to ring, but I ignored it. It kept ringing back-to-back, but I didn't answer because I already knew it was my mother who, on purpose, I wanted to feel guilty. I'd put on a darn good act earlier and she, along with Raynetta, were devastated because they thought I was going to resign. They didn't want me to resign, because being at the White House and enjoying all the perks meant more to them than it actually meant to me. That, indeed, was a fact.

Secret Service pulled out the black Suburban. They drove me to a vacant building where I had scheduled a quick meeting. I went inside carrying a briefcase in my hand, and as I exited the squeaking elevator on the top floor, I saw General Stiles standing by a row of tinted windows. Some of the windows were broken and there were red bricks stacked high that would be used for upcoming renovations. General Stiles' back faced me as she gazed outside. Her sexy, petite frame was muscle packed and her tight jeans melted on every curve. The black ankle boots she wore elevated her height and her leather jacket had Biker Bitch in bold letters on the back. Trying to disguise herself, mostly all of her hair had been cut off and sharply lined. Dark shades sat on top of her head, and as I moved closer to her, I could see part of the Glock 9 she always carried, tucked behind her. I cleared my throat to get her attention. That was when she turned around and smiled.

"You did well on TV tonight," she said, before the direction of her eyes moved to the briefcase. "Looked good too, and I hope you continue to follow through on your promises to me. This sexual harassment shit needs to stop and the military needs to be the first place to start."

"I promise not to let you down, and I can see many members of Congress already drafting legislation in your name and in honor of you."

I extended my arm and gave the briefcase to her. She reached for it and held it.

"I don't know if they'll act that fast, but let's just keep our fingers crossed," she said. "Meanwhile, thanks for the money. You really didn't have to give me this much. Your request was rather easy, and even though I'm a little sore from when that bullet hit my vest, and from falling hard to the ground, I'm glad everything worked out."

With her jacket opened, she lifted her shirt to show me where Raynetta had fired two bullets at her stomach. Her six-pack was impressive.

"She got me right here. I dropped to the floor and squeezed those blood packets while my hands were underneath me. Both of them thought I was dead. They argued and it was difficult for me not to get up and laugh my ass off. All I can say is, your mother is quite a character."

"You don't have to convince me that she is and I'm thankful for bulletproof vests. Raynetta thinks she killed you and that's what she needs to think. I don't know what to say about my mother. I guess she thought she did good by poking her nose where it didn't belong."

General Stiles laughed and moved away from the window. "She is a mess, and I have to give her credit for trying to have your back. That woman is willing to do anything whatsoever for you. That's not good."

"No, it's not and I can only hope and pray that this is the last straw."

General Stiles laid the briefcase on the floor and squatted to open it. The inside was filled with stacks of hundred dollar bills with a rose on top of them. She lifted the rose, sniffing it.

"This is real sweet, Mr. President. I didn't expect a rose and I can't tell you the last time I've gotten one from a man."

"I just wanted to give you a little something extra to let you know how much I appreciate you. Your loyalty means everything to me, and wherever you decide to go outside of the country, I hope you find a man who will shower you with gifts and roses every single day."

"Maybe I will, maybe I won't. No matter what, though, I'm sure with all this money in my possession, I'll have my happily ever after and then some. More than anything, I'm looking forward to retirement and living in peace."

She closed the briefcase and stood. As I moved closer to her, she opened her arms to embrace me.

"Take care handsome. I don't know what you're going to do without me, and trust me when I say finding a replacement for me won't be easy."

"I already know, so I won't start looking for a replacement for a long time. Besides, I'm going to do my best to stay out of trouble. That way I won't need anyone like you to rescue me."

She backed away from our embrace and laughed. "Good luck with that. I'll be rooting for you, but I don't know if I have a lot of confidence in you staying out of trouble."

Before I responded, she lifted the briefcase and moved towards the elevator. "My transportation is waiting for me," she said. "My phone has been turned off and it's been a pleasure working for you and serving this country. Aside from some of the bull I discussed with you about being treated unfairly at times, I've had fun."

I stood with my arms folded across my chest and eyes narrowed while admiring one of the most beautiful and bravest women who had ever crossed my path. I surely hated to see her go for good, but this was exactly how we'd planned it.

As I was in deep thought, she snapped her finger to get my attention.

"Come on," she said, waiting for the elevator to open. "Let's go. What are you waiting for?"

I shrugged and sucked in my bottom lips. "I was hoping you had a little more time on your hands. Wondered if you would be willing to do me one more favor before you go."

She looked at the watch on her wrist then shrugged too. "I may be fresh out of favors, but it depends on what you have in mind."

"Why don't you swing back in this direction so I can tell you? I don't want to say anything with you being all the way over there."

Right then, the elevator opened. General Stiles winked at me and stepped forward to get on it. I rushed to the elevator, holding the door so it wouldn't close.

"Sorry, but I have to go," she said. "I told you my transportation is waiting for me."

"Your transportation can wait. As your commander-in-chief, I'm requesting your assistance."

"Assistance with what?"

I looked down at the swelling hump in my slacks that caused the fabric to stretch. She examined the hump and commented.

"Now I see what you need assistance with. Why didn't you just be more specific and clarify a few things for me? For *that*, yes, my transportation can wait."

She sauntered by me and placed the briefcase on the floor. While I remained by the elevator, she removed her jacket and tossed it at me. It landed on my shoulder. Her jeans landed near my feet and her panties landed on top of my head.

"There," she said, carefully placing her Glock 9 on the floor. She then opened her arms wide so I could see every bit of her nakedness. "Ready to assist, whenever you are too."

She strutted her super-sexy self up to me and hiked up on the tips of her toes. After licking across my lips with her tongue, I pulled my sweater over my head. She unbuttoned my slacks then lowered them and my briefs to the floor. I stepped out of them, barely able to stand still as her mouth started to excite my steel. Right as the deepness of her throat made my knees buckle, I lifted her from her knees, carried her over to a work station in the center of the floor and laid her back on it. Her legs curved over my broad shoulders; I thanked her well for all she'd done. My tongue was in so deep inside of her that she squirmed around and scratched my back with her manicured nails. The arch in her back grew to great heights.

"I . . . I'm going to miss this," she confessed. "Too bad it has to end like this."

My mouth was full of her goodness, so I couldn't respond. And even though I was sad about it ending like this too, I granted her a perfect ending we would never forget.

First Lady
Raynetta Jefferson

The book deal was off. Sixty-something million dollars disappeared just like that and my agent was livid with me. She begged me to reconsider, but under the circumstances I just couldn't go through with it. The way I saw it, it wasn't worth it. I didn't want to bring Stephen down, especially after the lie he'd told to the American people to prevent me from being arrested. He knew I was the one who had killed General Stiles, and even though I was only defending myself, America would have taken the side of a woman like her, before taking mine. I felt horrible about the whole situation. Couldn't believe it had come to this, and I was so grateful to Andrew for talking Stephen out of resigning. Somehow or someway he'd done it. I couldn't do it and his mother definitely couldn't. We were so sure he was going to throw in the towel, and as I watched him on TV while in the Executive Residence, my heart went out to him. I didn't know how he would handle resigning, but I was relieved when he spoke about an explosion and mentioned General Stiles had been killed. Brilliant. That cleared my name for sure, but then, in the back of my mind, I kept sensing something fishy. Had I not seen General Stiles dead with my own eyes, maybe I would doubt what had happened. But there was no question she was dead and I had killed her. I was on edge after learning Stephen had actually put a hit out on me and ordered her to kill me. I never thought he would ever consider something like that, but I figured sharing his past secrets with the world caused him to cross that line. I could only imagine what would've happened had Teresa not shown up. In a sense, she'd saved my life. I didn't know if I should've thanked her or been upset with her for setting me up to shoot General Stiles.

In a nutshell, this whole situation was crazy. Whenever Stephen had time, he and I needed to discuss so many things that were lingering. He seemed to be avoiding me. Hadn't been to the bedroom, hadn't eaten breakfast or dinner with me, hadn't come to my office . . . nothing. He'd been busy working with VP Bass and several members of Congress, pertaining to issues with women's rights. The previous administration had done some idiotic things that snatched away the rights of women. Stephen was trying to make things right again. He also had to deal with ongoing issues with racism. The verdict regarding another cop killing an unarmed black man and his son was expected to come down soon. Many Americans were on pins and needles; they were prepared to protest and or riot. Things had been calm since Stephen had taken a stand with the protestors, but this verdict was capable of changing everything.

While in my office with my assistant, Emme, I reworked my weekly schedule. When the phone rang, she answered and told me it was my agent calling again to see if I would reconsider about the book. I reached for the phone to speak to her.

"Libby, I already told you it's not going to happen," I said. "I know the publisher is upset, but I never signed the contract."

"No, you didn't, but how can you afford to wash your hands to that kind of money? I really need you to rethink this, Mrs. Jefferson, especially since the publisher is willing to offer you more. Just tell me what I need to do to get that manuscript to them. You have them right where you want them, just don't fold. Please."

I released a deep sigh and repeated what I'd said earlier. "Sorry, but it's not going to happen. I thank you for trying to work out this deal, but I don't think releasing a book like this one will be in my best interest right now."

"You said, right now. Is there a chance you will . . ."

When I looked up and saw Stephen standing in the doorway, I abruptly ended the conversation.

"I'll speak to you later. Thanks again."

After hanging up the phone, I looked at Emme who had already stood to leave. She was cool to work with, and what I appreciated about her the most was she dressed very conservative. She wasn't trying to bring attention to herself by dressing sleazy, like some of the other women around here did to get Stephen's attention. And she was reliable. She was polite and had the fluffiest and prettiest long red hair I had ever seen.

"Go make some copies of these schedules and deliver them to the people who need them," I said. "You and I will catch up later, okay?"

"Sure," she said then spoke to Stephen as she exited my office. He spoke, before closing the door behind her.

"It's good to see you make your way to my office just to converse with little ole me," I said sarcastically. "Seems like you've been avoiding me, but I could be wrong. Then again, you may be concerned about having a wife who's a killer. Is that why you're avoiding me?"

With a navy tailored suit on, Stephen sat in a chair in front of my desk, crossing one leg over the other.

"I'm not concerned about you being a killer; after all, it was self-defense, correct? And the last thing I'm trying to do is avoid you. There's been a lot going on and I'm working hard to get certain things done around here. We're on the brink of passing sweeping legislation, pertaining to women's rights. I could really use your help, and I need you out there on the front lines, speaking out and helping us get this across the finish line. You've been too quiet. Too many people are starting to ask questions about your silence."

I sat silent for a few seconds, before getting up and moving closer to Stephen. He checked me out in my red skirt and silk yellow blouse. My high heels had a four-inch heel, and like always, my long hair was full of loose curls that hung several inches past my shoulders. My makeup was on like art, brows were arched perfectly and lips were painted a sexy red. I stood in front of Stephen with my arms crossed and expressed exactly what was on my mind.

"Just so you know, I don't mind getting involved with what's going on, but I've been so out of it. It's not like I go around killing people every day, and I can't stop thinking about all that has happened. I keep seeing General Stiles dead on that floor, and I can't stop wondering how involved you were with her. Not to mention that you wanted her to kill me, Stephen. That's a hard pill to swallow. It's hard for me to walk around here and pretend everything is kosher when it's not."

"My suggestion to you is to get over it. What's done is done. I fixed it, so let's move on. I regret asking her to cause you harm, but I didn't want all of my secrets put in a book for the world to see. There are certain things that must stay between us, Raynetta, and my past is one of those things. I felt so betrayed by you, and no matter how bad things are between us, I would never share your secrets, well, your past with anyone. I don't care how much money a publisher offered you. You should've turned them down. But, like I said, it's over. We both know where we stand with each other and we now have closure."

"So, this is what closure feels like to you? Are you still upset with me about threatening to tell your secrets and how do you know I still may not do it? I know you don't trust me, but to be honest, that's a lot of money to turn down. I really could use the money, and, what if I reworked the story? I could write it without sharing details about your past."

Stephen leaned back in the chair and rubbed his waves. He sighed, before responding. "I don't trust you as far as I can see you, but like I said, Raynetta, what's done is done. If you could really use the money, go ahead and tell your story. I may even tell mine too. I can guarantee you it will be worth way more money than yours."

I had to laugh. "I doubt it. Your story would be full of lies. Mine would speak the truth. The truth about living in the White House, about my experience as the first lady, about your multiple affairs, the presidential playbook, the ongoing lies and about your reckless mother. I would tell it all, and I do believe the American people would be very interested in knowing what *really* happens in, around and outside of the White House."

"They would be very interested, but if you go that route, be sure to tell them about your multiple affairs, your ongoing lies, your lack of support, your numerous betrayals and about your stupid ass grandfather. Don't sugarcoat anything to spare your reputation, and please do not include anything about my past. And don't go into too much detail about my mother. All that other mess, I don't care about."

I walked away from him, and he had the nerve to stare at my ass like it never belonged to him. "You should care, because first of all, I haven't had multiple affairs. Only one, so get your facts straight."

"As much as you fucked around with Alex, I'm counting that as multiple affairs. And since you're so good at keeping secrets from me, I'm sure there could be more."

I cut my eyes at him and sat behind my desk. With a notepad and pencil in my hand, I started to jot down a few things.

"Okay, since you're giving me the go ahead on this book, and you say you don't care about all that other mess, tell me how many affairs you would like for me to include in my story. I know of, at least, seven or eight. Are there more, and if so, do you care to share? I want to make sure this book is as juicy, scandalous and salacious as it needs to be. My one affair won't move people like your multiple affairs will."

Stephen stood and snatched the pen and notepad from my hand. He started to jot down a few words and paused for a few seconds to think.

"If you only write a book about my multiple affairs, it could get pretty boring. Be sure to include what really matters like how ambitious I am, how I want the best for all Americans, how I haven't had one full night of sleep since I've been here, how I work my ass off to get things done, how I've made peace with many of our enemies, strengthened America's relationship with our allies, cleaned up our reputation . . . you know, all that other stuff you ignore. And don't forget to tell everyone how good I was to you when you weren't telling lies, keeping secrets and stabbing me in my back. That there will be some damn good reading."

He shoved the notepad in my direction. I read what he'd written with my mouth dropped open.

"Who are all these women? And why didn't I know about all of them?"

He shrugged and slipped his hands into his pockets. "Don't know, but maybe you should've been paying attention."

"I was paying attention, but I hadn't a clue you'd been with more than fourteen women. I am so done with you, and I thought General Stiles was just obsessed with you. I should've known you still had a thing for ghetto girls."

It didn't surprise me that he defended her. "Yeah, some of those ghetto girls are the best ones to be with. She's not what I consider ghetto and my opinion is the only one that matters." He reached for the notepad and wrote down one more name. "Almost forgot about her too. You definitely want to include her."

I looked at the name he'd written. It was Claire. "Claire, as in my previous assistant, Claire? You didn't do anything with her, did you?"

He shrugged with a smirk on his face. "Hey, as you said, make it as salacious as possible. And since she was kind enough to give me head, why not tell it all?"

He turned to leave. I yelled after him. "Stop lying, okay? I'm trying to be truthful and you're taking this as a joke."

He faced me with seriousness in his eyes. "It is a joke. A big joke, because not one woman on that list can tell you I was in love with her. That I actually spent quality time with her and the short-term relationship revolved around more than sex. If you need specifics for the book, go interview them. I've said all I'm going to say about it and you can take it from there."

He moved closer to the door, but halted his steps after my next question.

"If you never loved any of the women on this list, do you still love me? And since Michelle Peoples' name isn't on the list, does that mean you love her? We don't spend quality time together anymore, and after all that has happened, I have a feeling that you hate me."

Stephen answered without turning around to face me. "I can't answer your question about loving you. Ask me when you can tell me how much you still love me and when you're willing to be everything I want and need you to be. You aren't quite there yet, are you?"

He turned to face me, awaiting an answer. I swallowed the lump in my throat and moved my head from side-to-side. In a low tone, I answered truthfully. "No, I'm not ready. Too much—"

Stephen shot me a stern gaze and cut me off. "That's what I thought. And just so you know, you don't have to explain because I've felt it for a long time."

He walked out and left me in deep thought. I wondered why he ignored my question about being in love with Michelle. He skipped right over it—interesting. Minutes later, I picked up the phone to call my agent. She was happy to hear from me.

"I think I may have to revise my previous manuscript. If so, are you still interested?"

She responded with two words. "Hell yes."

President's Mother
Teresa Jefferson

I hated funny acting people, especially a son who I had given birth to. I had been calling him every day, trying to find out why he'd changed his mind about resigning and why was he willing to lie to the American people about General Stiles being killed in an explosion. He should've told them what Raynetta had done, especially since he couldn't trust her not to tell his story. I still didn't trust her, but I was glad things had settled down. He seemed to be focused more on the important things like running this country. I tried to let him handle his business, but after not hearing from him for almost a week, I marched right over to the White House to see him. Secret Service had the audacity to tell me he was in a meeting and didn't want to be interrupted. And when I refused to leave, they went and got that nerd Andrew, as if he was really going to stop me from seeing my son.

"Teresa, we're going to wrap up everything in about an hour or so. Why don't I ask the president to meet you somewhere for lunch? Now isn't a good time. We're so close to finalizing major legislation."

"That's fine, but what does that have to do with me speaking to my son? Does he know I'm here?"

"He does, but he's unable to exit the meeting." Andrew looked at his watch. "Listen, I'll have the president meet you at Barkley's around one o'clock. We should be all done by then and the two of you can have a nice and quiet lunch together."

I wasn't happy about this, but lunch with Stephen did sound good. I told Andrew to make sure Stephen came to the restaurant. If he didn't, well, I didn't want to say what would happen.

I left the White House and stopped by a strip mall to purchase hair products. As soon as I got out of my car, I was surprised to see a young man I'd been *playing* with, Malik, park his car next to mine. Obviously, he had been following me. I didn't appreciate it one bit. Besides, I'd told him it was fun while it lasted, but I wasn't interested in having any more fun. Feeling frustrated, I got out of my car displaying a tight face. Hated to be so ugly, especially when I was so pretty. He got out of his car with a wide smile.

"You are one lady who is hard to catch up with. I've been calling you, leaving you messages, doing everything to reach out to you."

"Everything like following me too? I don't know what else you want, Malik, but I already told you this wasn't going to work out between us. I don't like men who ask me for money and you made a big mistake that day."

"I only asked because I'd lost my wallet and I didn't have gas in my car. And, I only asked for twenty bucks. You act like I asked you for a million dollars or something. I didn't and you have my word that I will never ask you for another dime."

I tucked my Michael Kors purse underneath my arm and stood with an attitude. "Good. Please don't and please stop following me. I don't know what else you want from me. Don't you know when a woman is no longer interested?"

He nodded and leaned against his car. "I do know, but I'm persistent. We had fun while we were together, and in addition to that, I enjoyed having you on the front lines with me, fighting for the cause. You also caused the media to bring attention to some of our issues and I wanted to know if you would attend a rally with me and several members from my organization later tonight. We just want to energize young people and encourage more of them to take a stand for our future. A person like you could be really helpful to us, so give it some thought and let me know if you can make it. I'll be more than happy to come pick you up with a full tank."

"I don't know if I'll have time, but if I do, I don't need you picking me up. A man riding on empty speaks volumes and I'm still bitter about the money thing. As for us, we're done. I do, however, like what your organization is doing, so I may come out and support it."

"I hope so, even though I'm disappointed about you saying we're done. You need to give it more thought, and I promise you I won't ever ride on empty again."

Malik laughed, showing his dimples. I had been real hard on him, but the truth was, I just didn't have time to entertain him anymore. I told him I would reach out to him later. Truthfully, I didn't think that would happen.

I was able to grab a few items from the beauty supply store, but like always, I felt like someone was watching me. That included an Asian woman who kept browsing the aisles, looking to see what I had in my hand.

"Can I help you with something?" she asked.

"No you may not. What you can do is get out of my face, before I put this shit down and walk out of here. Black folks spend too much money in places like this for you to be following us around and watching us. Go watch that blond head woman over there. She walked in two months pregnant, now it looks like she's eight months pregnant. So bye."

"No, no, I not watch you. I was only trying to help."

"I'm the president of the United States' mother. Do I look like I need help to you?"

She rolled her eyes at me and walked away. Some other people in the store knew who I was and they kept bugging me while I shopped. I had a feeling that Stephen had Secret Service keeping an eye on me too. I hated to have them anywhere near me, and I'd made it clear to Stephen that I didn't need them following me around all the time. After I left the store, I got in my car and headed to Barkley's to meet Stephen. I wasn't even sure if he would show up, but twenty-or-so minutes after I was seated, Secret Service came to examine the restaurant. The owners were very excited about Stephen's visit and they offered to clear out the place so we could have some privacy. I heard Stephen from a distance, telling the owners it wasn't necessary. They all shook hands and he also shook hands with several people who were there having lunch. My handsome son was very likeable; then again, some of the people in the restaurant seemed fake. I could tell by their forced smiles and half-ass handshakes. I guessed Stephen was used to those kinds of reactions; he finally made his way over to the table where I was. Before saying anything to me, he sent someone a text message then pulled back a chair. His purple crisp shirt with a white collar was tightened on his muscles and black suspenders were attached to his pants. I loved his attire, but he'd already gotten enough compliments from several people inside of the restaurant. I was sure his ego was up there.

"I already ordered for us," he said. "I can't stay long, but you do have my attention."

"It's about time because I've been trying to reach you. I don't know why you're ignoring my calls. What did I do this time to upset you?"

"Do you really have to ask? You keep doing the same things over and over again. I wish you would get some business so you can stay out of mine."

"I tried to get some business, but in case you forgot, you messed it up by throwing Malik out of my place that day. I haven't heard from him since."

"Yeah, well, keep it that way. He's nothing but trouble, and if you're that lonely or bored, why don't you take a vacation?"

"I'm not lonely or bored, but I'm sick and tired of you suggesting what I need to do. I haven't forgotten about your little tirade while you were at my place that day. You need to learn how to have more respect for me. I've done a lot for you, Stephen. I continue to do a lot and I keep telling you that you do not want me to become your enemy."

"The problem is you do too much. In no way do I want to be disrespectful to you, but you're working my nerves, Mama. Your interference got General Stiles killed. Had you just—"

I waved my hand around to cut him off. "No, correction, my dear son. My interference saved your wife's life. I would think you'd be happy about that, but maybe you're not happy about her being alive. Do you hate her that much? If you do, then man up and do away with her yourself. It was a cowardly act to send another woman over there to do your dirty work. You should feel horrible about what happened, but you don't seem bothered at all."

Stephen looked across the table at me with a blank expression on his face. I could sense something with him wasn't right. I saw it the night he'd spoken to the American people, but now that he was in front of me, something strange was written all over his face.

"Out with it, Stephen. Out with it right now. I need to hear the truth and nothing but the truth. Is General Stiles dead? I saw Raynetta shoot her, and I saw her lying on the floor in a pool of blood. Still, I know how *creative* you, along with people affiliated with the government can get when need be. I also remember what I was told about Joshua. Something fishy is going on and you need to come clean."

He sat calm as ever, looking rather annoyed by what I'd said. "Mama, you know what happened. You were there, so stop trying to make something out of nothing."

The direction of his eyes shifted to the right and his nose flared a bit. My mouth dropped open, voice went up a notch.

"No, you, didn't, did you? Why, Stephen? Tell me why you would lie about something like this, fake cry and make us believe you were going to resign? I can't believe one word that comes out of your mouth these days. Instead of being the president, you should've been an actor."

"I just told you to stop trying to make something out of nothing. You can believe what you want, but what's done is done. I handled everything and General Stiles is deceased. I wish it didn't have to be that way, and I do feel responsible for what happened. Unfortunately, there's nothing I can do about it. Nothing you can do about it either."

"I can and will do something about it, if I find out you're lying to me. You know how good I am at finding out things, so you may as well tell me the truth."

He couldn't even look at me; he was anxious to change the subject.

"I wish you would spend more time on your life than on mine. We would get along so much better if you did, and I just don't know why you can't understand that."

As Stephen spoke, he kept looking over my shoulder. I wasn't sure why, until I turned around and saw Michelle Peoples sitting at a table with another news reporter. He was a nice-looking black man I'd seen numerous times on TV. They laughed and seemed to be enjoying each other's company. I looked back at Stephen and smiled.

"Looks like she's finally moved on. And every time I try to stay out of your business, something like this comes up and I can't resist. She's probably trying to get pregnant by him so she can blame the baby on you. It wouldn't surprise me one bit, especially since you're not that skilled at picking side-tricks."

"You're pretty lousy when it comes to picking men, but that's just my opinion. And if Michelle wanted to get pregnant by me, all she had to do was accept the money you were willing to pay her and convince me to stop using a condom. You did offer her some money to have my child, didn't you? Just another example of you crossing the line, in case you want to keep denying it."

I threw my hand back and pursed my lips. "If she told you I offered her some money to have your child, she lied. I would never choose a woman like her to have my grandchildren. You're better off having children with Raynetta. Then again, I take that back because I do not and cannot have any grandchildren related to Mr. McNeil. That's a hard pill to swallow, and I know damn well you have some issues with that too."

Stephen peered over my shoulder again. I could tell that seeing Michelle with another man upset him. He would never admit it, but the look on his face said it all.

"I've made no decisions about me and Raynetta, but after what happened with Joshua, children are the last thing on my mind. You haven't heard anything from him or Ina, have you?"

"Not one word. Called a few times, but they never answer their cell phones. I'm upset about it, but this is one situation we both have to wash our hands to."

Stephen agreed. And after our food and drinks came, the remainder of our lunch together was pleasant. He continued to keep his eyes on Michelle. The second she left the restaurant with the reporter, Stephen seemed to be in a rush to go.

"I need to get back to the White House and finalize a few things. I'm also going to leave you with some solid advice, so listen up. Slack up on the drinking, Mama. Don't think I haven't noticed you've had three drinks already and I'm sure you're not done for the day."

"For the last time, I have my drinking under control so there is no need for you to offer me your solid advice. Besides, I'm heading home to relax and catch up on some of my favorite TV shows. I'll check in with you in a few days. By then, maybe you'll be willing to tell me the truth about General Stiles and you'll be over Michelle going to her place to get laid by that handsome reporter. He is very attractive, but he seems a bit too old for her, doesn't he?"

The way Stephen cut his eyes at me I could tell my words had gotten underneath his skin.

"I don't know how old he is and it's not my business. As for General Stiles, it's a wrap. Allow her to rest in peace."

He got up from the table, and after giving me a quick hug, he left the restaurant with Secret Service in tow. In no way was it a wrap when it came to General Stiles. My gut told me to ask around and check out a few things. And even though I didn't give a care if she was dead or alive, I truly wanted to know if Stephen had put on an act the day Raynetta and me went to his office, after she'd shot General Stiles. I felt so sorry for him that day; he made me feel guilty as hell for interfering. All I was seeking was the truth. As for Michelle, I sensed that she'd had a slight hold on Stephen. I assumed the White House wasn't his final destination today and I hoped he wouldn't find himself in a heap of trouble messing with her. It was time for him to turn her loose. That was my opinion, only because I knew how upset he could get when things didn't always go his way.

I returned home around four o'clock that afternoon. Had me a few more drinks and I found myself dancing around my living room while listening to R&B music. I'd thought about meeting up with Malik tonight, but I was too tipsy to drive. The peach, long silk nightgown I wore was sexy and elegant at the same time. He would be delighted to see me in it—his horny ass would be pleased to see me in anything. I plopped on the plush sofa, propped my feet on the ottoman and reached for my cell phone. Just as I got ready to call Malik, I heard a knock at the door. I placed my glass of Martel on the table then straightened my short, layered hair as I made my way to the door, asking who was there.

"It's me," Malik said. "I got your call."

My brows scrunched inward. I didn't know what he was talking about—I hadn't called him. I opened the door, immediately examining him from head to toe. He had on well-pressed denim jeans, a leather jacket and his dreads were gathered in a ponytail. Chocolate skin appeared smooth, teeth were bright white and dimples were always in full effect.

"Sorry, I don't know what you're talking about," I said. "I didn't call you. You must have mistaken someone else's number for mine."

Malik pulled out his cell phone then looked at it. "Nope. This is your number and definitely your name. I figured you weren't going to show up tonight, so I decided to come here in case you needed me."

The direction of his eyes traveled to my breasts which were clearly visible through the upper section of my nightgown. I held out my hand and asked to see his phone.

"Show me my telephone number. I want to see where I called you and what time I supposedly did so."

Malik didn't hesitate to show me. And sure enough, my name and number was displayed on his phone. Maybe I'd called him by accident. The alcohol kind of had me tripping, so who knows what I did.

"I don't recall making a phone call, but since you're here, you may as well come in and have a few drinks with me. I was getting ready to catch up on *The Haves and the Have Nots*, and just so you know, I don't wish to be interrupted with wasteful conversation."

Malik strutted inside. "I wouldn't dare distract you with wasteful conversation." He reached out for my waist and pulled me closer to him. "But I do intend to distract you with a little something else."

After his lips touched mine, I melted like butter in his strong arms. It didn't take long for things to get heated, and within a matter of minutes, I was laid back on the sofa, drunk as hell while he'd had his way with me. Somewhere in the midst of it all I passed out. I woke up with a severe headache, and as I squinted to look around the room, Malik was gone. I didn't see him anywhere, nor did I see my purse I had left on the table or my diamond watch that was right next to it. I hurried off the sofa to look for my cell phone. It was gone too.

President of the United States
Stephen C. Jefferson

It had been a long day, but when all was said and done, the House had passed a bill that tackled women's issues pertaining to stricter punishments for sexual harassment/abuse, equal pay, affordable childcare . . . to rights referencing their own bodies and healthcare. I was ecstatic about the good news and the bill was on its way to the Senate for a vote. It was expected to pass there too, and as I sat in the Roosevelt Room with several members of my staff, mostly women, they were overcome with joy. Tears were in many of their eyes, because many had protested, rallied and fought like hell for this day to come. Some had suffered from the unnecessary changes the previous administration had made, and based on opinions of the women in the room, things were starting to feel normal again. Vice President Bass had finally admitted the same thing.

"The President and I have been working on these issues for a long time with Congress," she said while standing at the head of the table. "We've had plenty of disagreements, but I always knew we could find common ground and get this pushed through. It wasn't easy, but yet again we did it!"

She shook her fist in the air and caused every person in the room to cheer with her. I definitely didn't want to spoil the moment or steal her shine, but I stood there thinking about how much she had rejected all of my proposals. The fight was worth it, and as long as we got to the finish line, I was good.

"Today is our day," she continued. "After the Senate votes and the president signs the bill into law, we're going to party like rock stars!" Everyone cheered again. "So, thank you, Mr. President. Thank you for your hard work and for staying so committed to this, even though I know there were times when you wanted to give up."

I nodded and clapped my hands. But just as I got ready to speak, Andrew came into the room and signaled that he needed to speak to me.

"Just for a few minutes," he said. "In the Oval Office, if you don't mind."

He and I went to the Oval Office. My Press Secretary, Sam, was there too. He had been gathering information so he could address the press within the hour.

"I hate to tell you this," Andrew said, pacing the floor. He wiped sweat from his forehead then looked at me as I sat against the desk stroking my chin. "But a vote is not happening in the Senate today. It might not happen at all, because five senators changed their votes to no. Four Republicans, one Democrat. I thought the Republicans were on board, but I'm not sure what made them change their minds."

Sam spoke up before I had a chance to weigh in. "That's ridiculous. I thought we had way more votes in the Senate than needed. Has the media been made aware of the count yet? If so, that's a problem. Not only that, but it's embarrassing because we've been reporting that we have the votes."

I was pissed, but for now I remained calm. "Yeah, I kind of have a feeling this was done to embarrass me. It makes no sense for the Majority Leader to tell us the votes are there, and then all of a sudden we're down by five. They know we're over here celebrating. This is their way of trying to shut us down. I don't care what the media knows or what they've been told. Andrew, set up a meeting with me and those five senators. I want to know what in the hell is going on and I need to know now."

Andrew made a suggestion. "Why don't you go to Capitol Hill and make it appear that you're there to congratulate the Senate and witness them cross the finish line. I can then set up a meeting with you and the five senators and, hopefully, we can find out what caused them to stall on this and fix it."

I looked at Sam who sat on the sofa, disgusted.

"Hold off on your press conference," I said. "I have a feeling this may take some time, and if those suckers are making this all about me, shit is about to turn real ugly. There is no way in hell I'm going to tell the women in this country we couldn't get this done. No way and I promise you that, no matter what you say, Andrew, I won't be able to maintain my composure, if they don't get on board."

"I know how you feel, sir, but try very hard to work this out with them. The ball is in their court. If you want to get this done, it is imperative that you approach them in the right way. Meaning, a respectable manner."

"There is no right way." I grabbed my suit jacket and put it on. Just as we were about to leave the Oval Office, I saw Raynetta walking down the hallway with Emme. They were talking to each other with smiles on their faces. I had to admit that seeing them smile made me feel good.

"We were just coming to see you," Raynetta said, standing in front of me. "Congrats on getting the House to pass that bill. People are really excited about it. I guess you haven't been watching the news."

"I haven't had time yet, but thanks. It was long overdue. I'm glad we were able to get it done."

Raynetta pushed. She sensed that I wasn't as excited as I should have been. "Are you okay? What . . . Where are you going?"

"I'm fine. On my way to Capitol Hill to make sure the Senate votes today. I'll talk to you later when I get back."

"Okay. Have fun and don't hurt yourself over there."

She smiled and they walked away. I made my way to Capitol Hill with Andrew right by my side. There was always a big deal when I walked the halls at the Capitol, and to no surprise the media was there in large numbers. I had just passed through the Rotunda with the central dome above it, when several reporters yelled out to me. I ignored them and glanced up at the *Apotheosis of Washington* surrounded by maidens and painted Greek and Roman gods and goddesses. Couldn't help but to think about the many slaves, some free, who cut logs, laid stones and baked bricks to build this place.

"Mr. President, how does it feel to get a bill like this one through the House?" a reporter asked.

Another questioned me too. "Do you know for sure it will pass the Senate? Rumors are starting to circulate and some are saying numerous senators aren't on board with the House bill. Do you know why?"

I just smiled and proceeded down the Senate Wing with a number of friendly politicians surrounding me and Andrew. No question they were there for the photo op. We all waved as if everything was in motion. My demeanor changed when I entered the Majority Leader's suite on the second floor, and he gave me some insight on why those five senators had backed out. I stood by the door, frustrated, while listening to him speak.

"For one," Senator Madison said. "We were told there were a few changes in the House bill. None of us have had a chance to re-read it, but we were willing to take a vote on it. In addition to that, some senators feel like the bill is too generous to women. I totally disagree with that assessment, but you know how some of the senators are."

"I do know. That's why I'm here. Andrew is getting those senators together now, and I really want to know specific details about why they've changed their minds. As it pertains to re-reading the bill, how long does it take to read less than five hundred pages? Let's find out what those changes were to the House bill and discuss it. No one communicated any changes to me, and I'd like to hear about them too. Maybe the House Leadership needs to join us."

"Maybe so," Senator Madison said. "I think we can get this done, but some senators may need more clarification."

I had calmed down, until I moved to a hideaway office on the third floor with the five senators who had issues with the bill. There was one change to the bill. It revolved around more money allocated to fund Planned Parenthood. We had previously discussed what the additional funds would be used for, but some senators complained about the amount that would be utilized for women's health.

"That's a big problem for me," Senator Phillips said. "And to be quite honest, Mr. President, I think this bill covers too much. We need to break it up into several pieces, and then vote on it. You may get a yes from me on part of the bill, but certainly not all of it in its current form."

"I concur with Senator Phillips," Senator Charleston added. "The bill includes too much and we have other issues that are priority, other than women's rights."

"I must say that I agree with both senators," Senator Stewart said. "I can't vote yes for this bill, and even though I was considering it, giving more money to Planned Parenthood isn't something I'm willing to do. Besides, my constituents are totally against it."

Senator Blaylock added his two-cents next. "I think we can all get around to voting for this bill, but I haven't heard VP Bass or you, Mr. President, mention how you intend to meet us halfway on this. My state could really use some extra funding for local projects, and I'm sure you could get some of the other senators to move quickly, if you agree to funding some additional projects in their states too."

I released a deep sigh while sitting next to two senators who had already addressed their concerns. As I looked around the round table, each of them waited for a response from me. Many words were at the tip of my tongue; I just had to make sure those words flowed out correctly.

"The hypocrisy here is unbelievable. And one minute you all are deficit hawks, the next minute everyone wants to spend money on pork barrel projects that cost this country billions of dollars each year. Instead of spending the money for women's health, you all prefer to contribute to wasteful government spending that continues to dig a ditch for taxpayers. I'll meet everyone halfway by reading half of this bill out loud, and you all can take turns reading the rest. We're not going to keep building bridges to nowhere anymore. Those days are over. This bill needs to get passed today and on my desk for a signature by midnight. Tell me how we're going to make that happen. If it's not going to happen, go out there right now and tell the women in this country that you all have failed them, once again."

"Mr. President," Senator Phillips said. "I'm not sure if you understand how this works. We have every right to ask for additional money for projects in our states and . . . "

I hated to cut him off, but I did. "No, that's how it used to work. And to be honest, it didn't work then and it's not going to work now. In case you haven't noticed, some of the rules around here have changed. And whether we get this done today or next year, it will get done. Simply because I will work hard, very hard, to find replacements for all of you. No one will thwart my agenda, and I regret that it has to be this way. Remember, as I sit here today with a sixty-two percent approval rating, the ball is not in your court. Realistically, it's in mine."

All of the old white men sat calm while looking around the table at each other. Senator Charleston cleared his throat, before speaking up.

"I don't think you understand, Mr. President, that your threats continue to make matters worse. If you . . ."

Unfortunately, I had to cut him off too. "Let's stop talking about what I don't understand. I comprehend things very well, so stop utilizing that term. I'm not going to waste much more time with this and I'm looking forward to a vote before midnight. If the bill goes down on the Senate floor, so be it. You all know where I stand, and if any of you think taking a vote on women's rights issues is difficult, just wait until I start tackling issues pertaining to racism again. I know many of you will stall on that, but be prepared because my proposals are coming soon."

I stood and without saying another word, I left the room. Andrew rushed after me, and from a distance, I could see the media quickly gathering to speak to me near several press galleries. I buttoned my suit jacket while moving at a speedy pace. Andrew could barely keep up with me.

"Mr. President, wait," he said. "Slow down and let's talk about this."

"There's nothing to talk about, Andrew. This is a game that Congress has played for too many years. Everybody looking for something, but they aren't willing to give a damn thing. The American people are suffering and I'm not going to keep sending them a tax bill for these ridiculous pork barrel projects that keep get added to bills. There is no reason for me to agree to add any of those projects, so forget it. The only way forward is to re-read the bill, vote yes or be prepared to pack it up in their fancy, hideaway suites, where all they do is negotiate with lobbyists, and go home at election time."

Andrew appeared frustrated with me. Surely, he didn't think I was going to come to Capitol Hill and cave in, did he? Maybe so, and like always, he tried to convince me to go against my gut and change my mind.

"If agreeing to add some of those pork barrel projects gets us across the finish line, why not include them in the bill? In your position, you have to listen to others, Mr. President. I think this was a big mistake."

I swung around to address him. "No offense, but I don't give a damn what you think. I came to Capitol Hill like you asked me to, but never, ever will I operate like a gotdamn puppet. Now, I've said all I'm going to say, and if you don't want to be threatening to resign by this evening, please back off and do not share anymore of your ass-kissing thoughts with me."

Andrew shot me a dirty look. He quickly pivoted to walk in another direction. I, however, made my way towards the press with several more senators who were on board with the House bill.

"We're going to get this done," Senator Morris said, patting me on my back. "No worries. Just wait and see."

I was willing to do just that, and after I gave thumbs up to the press, I went back to the Oval Office and waited. Andrew was there with me, but he hadn't said much. Sam was there too and so was VP Bass. Even she was upset about the five senators changing their minds. She kept rambling on and on about what a disappointment it was.

"My stomach is in knots," she said while sitting on the sofa. Her cheeks were flushed and her hair was in a messy bun. The polka-dot, black and white dress she wore made her look wider and her purple shoes didn't match a thing. Then again, maybe it matched her bracelet and earrings. "What are we going to say to the American people if this bill goes down on the Senate floor? It's going to be highly embarrassing and the backlash won't be pretty."

"No it won't be," Andrew said in a snippy tone. "We had a chance to secure this, but that didn't happen. We blew it."

I was nervous too and Andrew's attitude didn't help one bit. "And I had a chance to put my foot in your ass, but that didn't happen either."

To no surprise, he got up and stormed out of the Oval Office. Sam, VP Bass and me waited. We waited to hear from Senator Madison; his call didn't come until almost nine o'clock that night. I put the phone on speakerphone so everyone in the Oval Office could hear.

"Mr. President, this is your call. I don't think we have the votes to pass the House bill, but this is one of those times when I just don't know what will happen if I put it up for a vote. Personally, I think we should wait. At least until we know for a fact the votes are there. Maybe we should give it another month or two."

"No," I rushed to say. "Proceed right now and take the vote tonight."

"Hell no," VP Bass said as she stood by my desk. "If you don't have the votes for sure, don't do it. We'll embarrass ourselves and many of us are already disappointed about this whole thing. How could you let something like this happen, Senator Madison? You were confident the numbers were there. Why wait until the House passes the damn bill to tell us the votes aren't there?"

"My hands are tied. I can't seem to get those senators to change their minds, and I've done my best this evening to try and convince them to vote for this bill. Mr. President, are you sure you don't want to reconsider when it comes to meeting them halfway on those projects? I'm sure that getting this done is just as important to you, as it is to others."

I made myself clear by raising my voice. "I will not reconsider. Take the vote and let's get this over with tonight."

"But the vice president thinks we should wait too. She's . . ."

"The vice president isn't the president!" I yelled and slammed my hand on the desk. "I am! Vote now, get everyone's vote recorded and let's be done with this!"

I could hear Senator Madison sigh over the speakerphone. "Your call, sir, not mine."

He ended the call, and as VP Bass made her way to the door to exit, she turned to bark at me.

"I'm not taking the blame for this. You will have to tell the American people how and why this happened. And if you think those congressmen are afraid of your threats, you are sadly

244

mistaken. Your threats give them good reason to turn against you and leave you in limbo at times like this."

I opened my arms and shrugged. "They're already against me so what do I have to lose? And people have turned against me and left me in limbo for years. Nothing new, so goodbye and I'll see you in the morning."

She left and it was just me and Sam. Sweat was building on his forehead, wet spots stained the armpits of his white shirt and there was no smile on his face. He sat on the sofa with his eyes glued to the TV above the fireplace. Several news anchors had already reported the votes weren't there. They were anxious to see what would happen and the cameras were locked on what was transpiring on the Senate floor.

"What is your gut telling you, Mr. President?" Sam asked as he looked at me sitting on the sofa across from him. My palms were sweating; the knot in my stomach had tightened too.

"I can't even feel my gut. My stomach is hurting too bad, but I hope like hell they get this right."

We both took deep breaths at the same time. Our eyes were zoned in on the TV, where breaking news scrolled at the bottom of the screen. SENATE VOTE EXPECTED SOON was displayed. According to my count, we could only afford to lose two of the five senators who said they wouldn't vote for the bill.

"They'd better get it right," Sam said. "I can't bear to watch this, and if you don't mind, I need to go to my office and get some more work done."

"I don't mind," I said. "Not at all. And thanks, Sam, for everything."

He stood and reached out to shake my hand. "No, thank you, Mr. President. No matter how this turns out tonight, I appreciate your efforts."

I nodded, and after Sam left, I was so damn nervous that I had to go over to the cabinet and pour myself a drink. There was a bottle of Hennessy I offered to my guests, and after I poured the liquid in a glass, I guzzled some of it down and cleared my throat. My cell phone rang before I could take another swig. I looked to see who it was, it was Raynetta.

"What's up?" I asked while keeping my eyes on the TV.

"Just checking on you. You said you would reach out to me later, but you didn't. I just wanted to find out what's taking this vote so long? I know you asked me to go out there and support your efforts, but I didn't think a vote was coming this soon. Had I known, I would've gotten ahead of this and conducted a few rallies to energize more people. When the American people take a stand, Congress will do the right thing. You know what I mean?"

"Yeah, I do, but we've been talking about these issues for a long time. Maybe you've been focused on other things."

"I'm not really focused on anything else, but I probably won't get back to the White House until late. Emme and I attended a healthcare function for kids diagnosed with diabetes. We're still waiting on two or three more people to speak. It's been a long day. I can't wait to get back to the White House and get some sleep. Keep me posted on the final vote, and congrats, again, on a big accomplishment."

I thanked Raynetta, before ending the call. I was a little salty about her not stepping up to the plate as first lady and doing more, especially in regards to this issue. By now, though, I knew what and what not to expect from her. She was, indeed, focused on something. That something was trying to figure out a way to rewrite her story, without insulting or angering me.

Nearly fifteen minutes later, the Senate started to vote. I was back on the sofa with the glass of alcohol tightened in my hand. I kept taking sips, and after each NO vote, my sips turned into swallows. Two of the five senators I'd met with had already voted NO. The other three hadn't voted yet and I needed all of them to vote YES. Unfortunately, that included Senators Phillips, Charleston and Blaylock. I was sick to my stomach about this and not many people knew, other than other presidents, how tense these moments were. With all the work that went on behind the scenes, it was tough to watch it come to this. Maybe I shouldn't have ordered Senator Madison to take the vote. And shame on me for thinking they would come around and do the right thing. As the clock ticked away, there was a mixture of YES and NO votes. I got up and paced the floor while counting every single vote. When Senator Blaylock was called on to enter his vote again, a sigh of relief came over me, after he signaled YES. Senator Charleston was a YES vote too, and by the time Senator Phillips was called on, I was on my feet with my hands clenched behind my head. Felt like I was watching the last seconds of a football game, where the kicker had to make the kick in order to win the game. I held my breath and my eyes stared at the TV without a blink. I could feel my heart slamming against my chest; my shirt sleeves were rolled up to my elbows.

"Come on," I whispered through gritted teeth. "Do this, damn, get it done."

I held my breath again and stood with wide eyes as Senator Phillips vote came in at YES. As I stood on the Presidential rug with a seal, I dropped to my knees, bent over and press my forehead on the floor. "Yes, yes, yes," I shouted while trying to control myself. Almost immediately, my phones started ringing. I ignored every last call, and I didn't get off my knees until I'd heard the news anchor confirm the bill had passed.

"Thank you," I said, looking up. I got off the floor and while my phones were still ringing off the hook, I ignored them. I quickly told my secretary I was heading upstairs to the Executive Residence.

"As soon as the bill arrives, bring it upstairs to the Yellow Room so I can sign it."

"Will do, sir. What about your phone calls? And you know everyone is heading this way to speak to you."

"Don't let anyone in the Oval Office. I don't feel like being bothered. Tell them I'll see them tomorrow. Don't forget about the bill. It's imperative I sign it tonight."

She nodded, and as soon as I entered the master suite, I took a lengthy shower, changed into a comfortable Nike sweat suit and put on my white tennis shoes. I grabbed a bottle of champagne from a bar in the Yellow Room, and after I placed a cap on my head to hide my identity, I relaxed and waited for my secretary to bring me the bill. Nearly ten minutes later, she did. I didn't need any cameras, nor did I need the media present to take notes. I signed the bill, making it law.

"Thanks," I said, handing the leather binder back to my secretary. I also gave her the pen I'd used as a keepsake; she smiled and thanked me repeatedly. After she left, I asked one member from my Secret Service detail to take me to my destination. To no surprise, that was to Michelle's place. Yes, I was disturbed after seeing her with that reporter. She hadn't called me since I'd raised my voice at her about being upset with me for protecting Raynetta the day of that shooting. I felt like there was no need for me to explain myself, and since General Stiles was on her way to see me that day, I just didn't have time to deal with Michelle's concerns. Obviously, she'd been keeping herself busy with another man. And when I stuck the key in her door and opened it, my assumption was correct. He was chilling on her sofa with his shirt off, while watching the news. A bowl of popcorn was in his hand; he almost dropped it on the floor when he snapped his head to the side and saw me enter Michelle's condo. His eyes shifted to the champagne bottle in my hand then back to my face.

"I, uh, hello, Mr. President," he said, standing with his mouth wide open. "I'm, uh, are you sure you're at the right place?"

"Positive. Where is Michelle?"

My confirmation shocked him. He stumbled back and looked down the hallway.

"She's, uh, in the shower. But I'm a little confused here. Did she know you were coming? Had I known I wouldn't even be here."

"Well, now you know. And she's the only one who can ask you to leave, unless you choose to exit on your own free will."

He appeared stunned. He didn't know what else to say or what to do. I, however, went into the kitchen and removed two champagne glasses from the shelf. I popped the cap on the bottle and carefully poured the champagne to the rim of the glasses. The reporter stood near the doorway, putting his shirt on, along with his shoes.

"If you wouldn't mind, please tell Michelle I'll call her some other time. I apologize for this and I'm shocked that the two of you," he paused and waited for me to respond.

I placed the bottle on the counter and picked up both wineglasses. "No need to apologize, because Michelle and I are just good friends. I'll be sure to tell her what you said, and if you wouldn't mind locking the door on your way out, I would appreciate it. I would lock it, but my hands are full."

He stood for a moment, still stunned by my reaction. And as I walked past him and made my way down the hallway, I heard the front door shut. I also heard the shower running in the bathroom. I entered the dim room that had two flaming candles lit on the counter and soft music was playing. Michelle's backside faced me as she washed her body with a soapy, white towel. With my clothes still on, I entered the shower and reached over her shoulder to give her the glass of champagne.

"Awww, this is so sweet of you." She slowly turned around. Her eyes grew wide when she saw me, and the champagne glass slipped from her hand and hit the floor. Glass shattered and caused me to step back. She tiptoed over the broken glass and quickly exited the shower.

"Excuse me, but what are you doing here?" she asked with a frown on her face. "Where is William and why in the hell do you keep showing up like this?"

She snatched a towel from the rack to cover herself with it. I turned off the water in the shower, before stepping out too.

"William chose to leave. I came here to celebrate my good news with a friend, but had I known he would be here I would've opted to celebrate elsewhere."

"Well, you should have." She rushed out of the bathroom and went into the living room area to see if William had left. I used a towel to dry part of my clothes that had gotten wet, then I followed behind her with the glass of champagne in my hand.

"I told you he left," I said.

"Fine. And you need to leave too, Stephen. I have tried my best to remain calm about all of this, but this is too much. You're too much and there is no way I'm going to let you control my life and show up like this, whenever you choose to."

I sipped from the glass of champagne then placed it on a credenza next to me.

"Calm down and stop talking all that mess about control. I'm not trying to control anything. All I wanted to do was come see you tonight so we could celebrate the passing of major legislation."

"Congrats on that, but you are trying to control things. And I'm sorry, but I have to get this off my chest tonight. The only reason you're here is because you saw me with William. You haven't called me, you haven't said anything to me while I've been at the White House and the way you ran after Raynetta that day truly broke my heart. Not to mention there are rumors swirling around about you being involved with General Stiles before she was killed. Whether I believe that or not, I've had enough of this. I can't do this with you anymore, and Lord knows I have tried to keep my mouth shut and just let it be, considering the circumstances."

I sighed because I really didn't want to hear this tonight.

"I'm not going to explain to you again why I rushed to cover Raynetta that day. Nor am I going to apologize to you for doing so. I take offense to you saying I'm trying to control things. If I was, I would've made demands about who can and can't come here. I would've demanded that you see no one but me, and the only reason I haven't called you is because, as your president, I've been busy."

She cut her eyes at me. "Yeah, that's what you always say. And I see you touched on everything else, except for what I said about you and General Stiles. Is what I heard true or not?"

Feeling irritated by her question, I shrugged. "What difference does it make? If I don't answer to my wife, I really don't have to answer to you."

Michelle stared at me with fury in her eyes. Her chest heaved in and out; I could tell she was livid.

"No, you don't have to answer to me and you don't have to lie to me either. Therefore, when I ask you a question, it should be easy for you to answer. I never thought I would say this to you, but you are one disrespectful asshole. You are so full of shit and I hate like hell that I ever got involved with you."

I had never seen Michelle like this—I was disappointed. While she felt it was necessary to attack me, I still remained calm.

"If it helps you to know the truth, then yes, I was involved with General Stiles, and no, I'm not being disrespectful. I just refuse to argue with you, Michelle. Calling me names is what's disrespectful and saying you hate me doesn't help."

"Never said I hated you, but I do hate that I got in so deep with you. You are a complete mess and tell me this. How long had you been involved with General Stiles?"

"Probably around the same amount of time you've been involved with William. I told you not to keep questioning me, because you're not going to appreciate my answers, if you continue to push."

She shook her head, displaying disgust. As I moved closer to her, she darted her finger at me. "Don't touch me, Stephen, I mean it. If I haven't been enough woman for you, why do you keep coming here? I guess I can answer that for you, because no matter what you say, we both know you're here for this, aren't you?" She dropped the towel and exposed her nakedness to me. My eyes didn't drop below her face. "All you want to do is come here and fuck me," she said. "For so long I've shown you that's okay and you would never, ever hear me gripe about your bullshit. I don't know what you expect from me, but have it your way, Mr. President. Take what you want and I promise to keep my mouth shut like the timid and passive woman you want me to be."

The direction of my eyes finally traveled below her neck. Brown and beautiful. Everything about her was flawless . . . from her natural hair, doe-shaped eyes, to her firm breasts and chocolate nipples. As I searched further, she turned in a circle so I could see what she was offering in the moment. I had to admit her round, perfect P-shaped ass was everything.

"Go for it," she said. "Why are you still standing there? This is what you want, isn't it?"

"Are you trying to serve me leftovers? You did just have sex with William, didn't you?"

"I damn sure was getting ready to, but thanks to you it didn't happen."

"Well, call him to come back here so it can happen. Leftovers aren't that good to me, so I'm going to bow out until he's done. Done, meaning, for good. When you've had enough of him, you know how to reach me."

I glanced at her one last time, before opening the door to leave. On my way out, she continued to lash out at me.

"You have no idea what I've been through. No idea and this struggle is so real because I screwed up and fell in love with you. All I wanted was the same in return, yet all I've gotten is this. I feel so empty. You make me feel so empty."

I stood on the other side of the door and responded. "Don't stay on empty. Fill yourself up with everything William has to offer. I'm not mad about it, but what I'm not going to do is keep having these moments with you. I could've stayed at home for this segment, and tonight, this is something I don't care to hear. Not even your love story has moved me."

"Then maybe my door will."

She slammed the door in my face, and after I took the elevator to the ground level, I climbed into the backseat of the Suburban with tinted windows. A Secret Service agent was behind the wheel. He looked at me through the rearview mirror.

"Where to, Mr. President? Back to the White House?"

"No," I said as I reached for a glass to pour myself a glass of wine. "Just go park somewhere. Anywhere, where I can't be disturbed."

He drove off, and as he searched for a private place to park, I celebrated my accomplishments alone. I drank two glasses of wine and dropped the seat back to chill. Even before Secret Service stopped to park the truck, my eyelids faded and I was out like a light.

First Lady
Raynetta Jefferson

I didn't get to the White House until almost midnight. I was dead tired and I figured Stephen must've been in his normal spot on the sofa in the Oval Office. We'd gotten used to not sleeping together anymore, yet I was shocked when he came into the bedroom at two-thirty in the morning to get some rest. I was tired, but I had gotten tied up with trying to rework the story. Several notebooks were on the bed; I even had a copy of the unsigned contract my agent had given to me on the nightstand. Stephen glanced at my mess and didn't say anything about it. He removed the jacket to his sweat suit, took off his tennis shoes and lay across the far end of the bed.

"What's wrong with the sofas in the Oval Office?" I questioned. "Are they starting to get too uncomfortable?"

"Not really, but I have a headache tonight. Call myself tossing back a few drinks and now I'm paying for it."

"I knew it was something. Why don't get some aspirin and lay straight on the bed. I will move my things to the floor or on the nightstand so you can get comfortable."

"Really? You want me to be comfortable? I'm surprised."

"I don't know why you're surprised by that. I do still care about you, no matter what we've been through."

He didn't respond. Just got off the bed and went into the bathroom to get some aspirin. After he changed into his pajama pants, he got in bed next to me. This felt kind of awkward for me; I wondered how he was feeling.

"This bed feels good," he said then stretched his arms "I forgot how comfortable it was."

With my notebooks now on the floor, I turned to my side and looked at him. "I know you may not feel like talking about

254

this, but what happened to us? How did we get here, Stephen, and did you ever think it would be like this between us?"

He turned sideways to face me too. "Actually, yes, I knew we were headed down this path. I'm surprised you didn't see it coming. I did and I do regret that we are unable to fix this."

"I have some regrets too, and at times, it hurts to know that one day we're going to have to walk away from each other for good. I want you to know that while I'm no longer in love with you, I do still love you. I will always support you, and I will do anything to help you get through your first term. I'm sure you'll be seeking a second term too, but I don't know if I'll be able to hang around that long. I just wanted to let you know that so you can prepare for it."

My admission didn't seem to surprise him one bit.

"I'm shocked that you're going to hang on for the remainder of my first term. You really don't have to, and even though some Americans may be upset about us separating and or divorcing, we have to do what is best for us. I do plan to seek another term, but if I win, it will be up to the American people. I'm sure many questions will be asked about us and I'm prepared to explain that some marriages just don't work out. While we're no longer in love with each other, we do still care for each other. I want the best for you too, and if there is anything I can do to make your time here feel more rewarding, just let me know."

I figured Stephen had fallen out of love with me too, but it was strange to hear him finally say it. In our case, we had tried but failed. Maybe not tried hard enough, but I was tired of all the finger-pointing. The most difficult thing for me to get over was knowing that he had been angry enough to ask someone to kill me. And while I had definitely made plans to cause him harm, having me killed seemed evil. I guess he felt I was evil too—there was really no way to balance all the harm we had done to each other.

"There's not much else you can do," I said. "And whether you know it or not, I'm okay with living in the White House. I've gotten used to all the special treatment, so it may be a while before I start looking for my own place. Meanwhile, I'm going to continue to write my story and carry on my duties as the first lady. That's unless you decide to replace me. If so, let me know so I can make some different arrangements."

"I have no intentions to replace you and I doubt I will ever get married again. I'm not that good at it, and quite frankly, I suck at being a husband."

He laughed and so did I. "No, you're not that good at being a husband, but you're so good at other things. I promise to point out those things in my book and once it's finished, you're going to be so proud of how it all comes together."

"Do you have a title for it yet? And promise me, Raynetta, that you won't go putting all my personal business out there."

"I promise I won't get too specific, but I do need to share some things so people will know what it's like to live here and walk in my shoes. Some people may believe me, others will dispute what I write. There's really no way to tell what's true and what's not, so you won't have to worry about a thing. In reference to the title, I'm still thinking about it. Do you have any suggestions?"

Stephen lay silent then he turned on his back and stretched his arms again. "Why don't you call it exactly what it is, or should I say, who it is going to be about. Title it Black President. This world will never be the same after my term is over and I have so many more things I want to accomplish."

I snapped my finger and smiled. "I kind of like that title, but we'll see. In the meantime, you can stay up all night thinking about all the things you want to accomplish. I'm tired and I need to get some sleep. I have another busy day tomorrow, and believe it or not, McNeil called earlier and asked me to meet with him. I don't know what he wants. The last time I saw him, things didn't go well."

"I'll let you decide how to handle your racist-ass grandfather, and I'm sure he's upset about me signing that bill into law. He probably wants to talk to you about that, and if he says anything to you about causing me harm, I want to know about it, Raynetta. Don't keep anything like that from me again and do not accept any money he offers you."

"I won't and trust me when I say I've learned my lesson. That man is pure evil, but when the enemy calls, sometimes, you have to find out what they're up to. I would appreciate if you wouldn't refer to him as my grandfather. He, along with his family has disowned me for many years. There is no love within me either. I will say that it hurts not to have a close family and the way he treated me the last time I was at his house stung. But, I still have you and I'll always be grateful for whatever way you fit into my life."

Stephen yawned and opened his arms for me to lay my head on his chest. I snuggled close to him, and as we both lay silent, no question we were in deep thought about many things.

The following day, I woke up only to see Stephen was gone. I was sure he'd had a busy day ahead of him too, so after my shower and breakfast, I decided to stop in at McNeil's office, where he'd asked me to meet him. A Secret Service agent was with me, and as we made our way through the lavish lobby in the office building, many people reached out to me.

"I'm so pleased to have you as our first lady," one woman said to me. "You and the president are so awesome. Keep up the good work."

I shook her hand and told her I would. The Secret Service agent was so close that I barely had time to simply say hello to all the people who confronted me. All I'd heard were nice things, until I made my way to the 20th floor where McNeil's office was.

As I stood inside of the tinted glass doors, he sat behind a cherry-wood desk that stretched, at least, 12 feet long. Elegance defined the office, and it was decked out with gold accessories. A breathtaking view of Washington D.C. could be seen through the windows, and pictures of his privileged and wealthy family covered the walls, in addition to his numerous awards.

"I would ask you to sit," he said, raking his snow white hair with his fingers. His bushy brows were scrunched inward and his evil eyes were like looking into the devil's eyes. "But this shouldn't take long. I'm glad you came, and for the last time, I need your help."

A cigar dangled from the corner of his mouth, and as smoke infused the air, I just stood there staring at him.

"What's the matter, gal?" he asked. "Cat got your tongue or did that nigger tell you to come here and not speak?"

His words got a quick reaction from me. "That nigger, as you insist on calling him, is my husband. My loving husband whom I don't appreciate you speaking ill of. If you need my help pertaining to anything relating to him, you won't get it. You're wasting your time, and as I'm sure you already know, he's on cloud nine these days. He's been getting so many things done by rolling over any and everyone who stands in his way. I know that's frustrating for you, but deal with it."

He grunted and blew smoke in the air from his cigar. "He may be sitting sky high for now, but what goes up will come down. We're behind the scenes doing lots of things to make sure he will not see a second term. There are also certain things he's done which may be cause for impeachment. You'll hear about those things in the near future, sweetheart, you just wait and see how we gon' get him good. You can pretend all you want that your marriage is peaches and cream. Your nigger husband is in love with another woman and you's just a prop he's using to keep the American people on his side."

I didn't want to stand there and keep listening to him disrespect Stephen, so I interrupted him. "Get to the point. Tell me why I'm here again and make it quick."

He chuckled and leaned far back in his chair. "I wish you would wake up and smell the coffee. If you did, I would be happy to put your name in my Will and leave you something special, provided the unthinkable happens to me. Unfortunately, the president's cock has your mind twisted. You can't see him for who he truly is, and all I want you to do is one thing. Divorce him and leave the White House now. Speak from your heart and tell the American people what a shitty husband he has been. You are an abused woman. He has used you, and I have watched him degrade you time and time again. The one thing America won't do is support a bachelor president who disrespects women. I don't care how good he is or what he has accomplished, there are certain values a president must uphold. After all the heartache he has caused you, this task should be the simplest thing. Wouldn't you agree?"

"No, I don't. And just so you know, the president and I will never get divorced. You can plan his demise all you want to, but Stephen is a very smart man. He's already twenty steps ahead of you and a second term he will have. Now, if that's all you wanted to speak to me about, I'm out of here."

"Yes, that is all, but I'm so disappointed in you granddaughter. I wish I could drain every ounce of my blood from your veins because your stupidity and loyalty to that nigger frustrates the heck out of me. How could you be so stupid and stay with a man who doesn't even love you? I don't quite understand this ride-or-die chick terminology, and it's so sad that you intend to ride with that sloppy nigger until the wheels fall off. I'm warning you that when he goes down, you'll go down with him. Save your reputation and get out now. If you do, there will be great rewards. This is my last and final call to you. I hope you's listening and take action."

I walked closer to his desk to look straight in his eyes. "I wish like hell I could drain every ounce of your blood too, because you are one sick, old racist bastard who I look forward to dying and rotting in hell. Take your rewards and shove them up your wrinkled ass. Don't you ever call me to come here again, and the only other thing I have to say to you is this."

I gathered spit in my mouth and released it right at his face. He jumped from his chair and reached out to grab me. I quickly backed up. The Secret Service agent who brought me there rushed into the room. He must've been watching us while standing outside the door.

"Get her out of here before I break her fucking neck," Mr. McNeil shouted. He wiped my spit from his face with a handkerchief he'd pulled from his pocket.

I smiled wickedly at him as I backed out of his office. I also pushed over one of his gold statues by the door. It hit the ground and broke into multiple tiny pieces. The loud boom caused several members of his staff who worked in cubicles to stand up and see what was going on.

"Leave now!" he shouted and charged towards me. "Get this nigger lover out of here!"

I was already on my way out with Secret Service. He rushed me down the elevator and into the car. Without saying one word to me, he sped off. I sat on the backseat thinking about Mr. McNeil, shaking my head. Like always, his words cut deep, but I would never let him see how much damage they'd caused. I wiped a tear that had fallen down my face, and as I'd thought about what he had said about Stephen, my cell phone rang. It was him.

"How did your meeting go?" he asked. "What did Massa want?"

I swallowed the lump in my throat and told Stephen everything Mr. McNeil had said. He could tell I was bothered by all of it.

"Listen, okay?" he said. "Don't let him upset you. You can't let an ignorant fool like him get underneath your skin. Why do you allow him to have that kind of effect on you?"

I sniffed and wiped my runny nose with a tissue. "I don't know. Maybe because I want him to be better than he is and it pisses me off that I'm related to someone like him. I wish you had never told me. I hate him, Stephen, and I wish he would choke on his own spit and die."

"Maybe one day he will, but until then, calm down. Everything will be okay and trust me when I say I'm not worried about him. I used to let him get to me too, but when I ignore him he is powerless. Don't give him the satisfaction of hurting you and go have some fun today. I heard you and Emme are heading to New York today for an uplifting college fair revolving around new technology. That sounds interesting. I know you're looking forward to it."

"I am. Been thinking about it all week and I can't wait to get involved. You should join us too."

"I would, but you already know my schedule is locked in for the next two weeks or so. I have lots of things to get done before my seven day trip out of the country. I mean, wish me luck. I can only hope and pray that nothing serious happens in between."

"Good luck with that, but you already know."

We both chucked, and after speaking to him, I felt better. Much better, even though some Mr. McNeil's words rang true.

President's Mother
Teresa Jefferson

I had pursued another mission and came up empty. I couldn't find Malik for nothing in the world, and after driving around looking for him for many days and nights, I'd wasted my time. I'd gone to his apartment, called his phone . . . everything. I even called my phone that he'd taken, but every time I'd called it went to voicemail. As for my purse, I was so lucky I'd changed my purse earlier that day and left my important things in the other purse. Yes, he'd gotten one of my credit cards and some money, but I was able to report the card as stolen so he wouldn't be able to use it. He'd probably pawned my diamond watch. Unfortunately, it was one Stephen had purchased for me. It was definitely sentimental to me; I swore to God that whenever I saw Malik again, I would make him pay for this.

The sad thing was, Stephen had warned me. I was too embarrassed to tell him what had happened, so I avoided reaching out to him. He must've suspected something was wrong, because after not hearing a peep from me, he showed up at my penthouse on a Sunday morning with flowers in his hands. I looked around as he stood in the doorway, dressed in gray slacks and a money-green shirt with a smirk on his face.

"What are the flowers for?" I asked. "Did somebody else die?"

"No, but I thought by giving them to you, I could brighten your day, especially since you've been down in the dumps lately. Usually, that's what happens when you drink too much, and allow a young punk to come into your home and steal from you."

"You must have some kind of hidden cameras around here. I told you I don't appreciate being watched, Stephen, and just so you know, I can handle Malik."

Stephen walked further into the room, laid the flowers on a table then picked up a red juicy apple that was in a bowl. He bit into the apple and chewed while looking at me.

"I'm sure you can handle him, but you have to find him first. After all, you have been looking for him, haven't you? I don't think you've had much success."

"I've asked around. I'm waiting on a few people to call me back and give me the scoop on where he is. I don't need your help, so you can mosey on back out of here with those cheap flowers that aren't even pretty."

Stephen bit into the apple again and picked up the flowers. He put them in a vase and filled it with water. After he sat the vase in the center of the table, he looked at me again.

"Have you learned your lesson about drinking too much yet? The only reason he was able to take advantage of you was because you were highly intoxicated. And yes, Secret Service has been watching you. Thankfully, they were watching Malik too."

"What is so wrong with me drinking alcohol in the privacy of my own home? Nothing at all and it's good to know they were watching Malik. Where is he?"

"Do you really want to know or would you prefer to see him for yourself?"

I wasn't sure if Stephen knew where he was or not, but he sure as hell pretended like he did know.

"Of course I want to see him. I also want my stuff back, but I'm sure my money is long gone."

Stephen walked casually to the door and opened it. He walked out; a few minutes later he returned with two Secret Service agents and Malik. I almost couldn't believe it was him. I gasped at the sight of the right side of his swollen face and one of his eyes was nearly shut. His two front teeth had been knocked out and the T-shirt he wore had been ripped.

I held my chest with my mouth wide open. "Oh my God, Stephen, what did you do to him? Don't you know it's Sunday? You didn't have to beat him like this. The items he took weren't even worth it."

"Come on, Mama. You know I wouldn't do anything like this to anybody. He's the one who slipped, fell and bumped his head. You can thank my agents for saving his life and for getting your items back."

One of the agents reached out to give me my purse and watch. I didn't even get a chance to look inside and see if my money was still there, before Malik spoke up. His words didn't come out right with missing teeth.

"I apolothize for thaking your thuff, but you pissed me off about that thwenty bucks. I never wouldt've done this, had you not thisrespected me that day I ran out of gas."

I rolled my eyes and fired back at his explanation. "Yes you would have and you got what you deserved. I have no sympathy for you. You are lucky that you lived to see another day."

With his mouth in the condition it was in, he had the audacity to talk slick.

"Everythody in here lucky thoo, because I could go to the police and thell them what these jokers did to me. The prez is gangstha and you don't have no business running this country with a menthality like the one you got."

Stephen chucked and raised his hands in the air. "One of the qualifications for being president is to make gangsta moves, you idiot. And for the record, I didn't lay one hand on you. You're too petty for me to waste my time on, and if you feel a need to call the police, please do. Just call them after I do this."

Catching me off guard, I was shocked when I saw Stephen swing his fists around and slam it into the right side of Malik's face. The punch was so hard it caused the side of my face to sting.

Malik's head snapped so fast to the side, I thought his neck was broken. He hit the floor, hard, and while lying flat on his stomach, he struggled to get up.

"Stephen, that's enough," I said, pushing him away from Malik. Secret Service stood there unfazed by all of this. Then again, I wasn't even sure if the two men were Secret Service. All of this made me nervous—I didn't want this fool to die on my living room floor.

Malik groaned and moaned as he struggled to get on his knees. He shot Stephen an evil glare and had the nerve to threaten him.

"You'd better kill me now, because you know I'm thuming for you later. For you and for your bitch-thass mother. None of this would've happened if it wasn't for her."

His words touched a nerve. And this time when Stephen stepped forward, I didn't even stop him. I stood behind him and reached out to smack Malik across the back of his head with my purse.

"Get him, baby," I said to Stephen. "Go ahead and finish him off. We don't need this mess. I tried to spare this fool from getting what he clearly deserves, but he thinks this is a joke."

Stephen grabbed Malik by the back of his neck and lifted him from the ground. He shoved Malik towards the two men who held him up b his arms.

"Get this punk out of here. I don't care what the two of you decide to do to him, the choice is yours. Malik, I never want to see your face again. If you're lucky enough to live, you'd better not ever bring your ass to my mother's place again. Secret Service will be watching her, and if you come anywhere near her again, you and your family will be dealt with. As your president, I don't make threats. I only make promises."

Malik could barely stand as the two men drug him out of my penthouse. I wasn't sure what else they would do to him, but I figured after that ass kicking, I would never see him again. I held my chest and released a deep breath.

"I thank you for looking out for me, but you do owe me for all—"

"Yeah, yeah, yeah, Mama. I don't owe you anything, but what he did was wrong. I don't like to get involved in mess like this and I've been trying to stay on a straight and narrow path lately. Shit like this gets me off track, and the next time I warn you about someone, please listen. Now, I have to go. I thought we might have time for breakfast, but unfortunately, I need to go deal with another headache."

"I'm not even going to ask who that may be, but be careful. I'm proud of you, you know and I apologize for putting you in a predicament like this. Next time, just let me handle it."

Stephen said goodbye, and after I shut the door behind him, I said a little prayer, thanking God things with Malik didn't turn out any worse.

President of the United States
Stephen C. Jefferson

I wasn't lying when I'd told my mother I was trying to stay on a straight and narrow path, but certain things irked the hell out of me. One of those things was Mr. McNeil. It troubled me he'd had Raynetta so upset; I pondered what I would ultimately do to him. I had to do something because he was still coming for me. After all this time, he still had it out for me and I had just about had enough. Dealing with him took careful planning though. Sooner, rather than later, he would be no more.

Since Sam wasn't feeling well, I decided to take over his position for the day and answer questions for the press. I had only dedicated fifteen minutes to it, simply because Andrew had scheduled another meeting with me and several members from my administration. It was on to drafting the next legislation which was infrastructure and dealing with racism in this country. We needed to correct our unjust judicial system and increase the punishments for hate crimes. I was sure this subject would make a lot of people uncomfortable, but it was time for us all to be honest with ourselves and start holding people accountable for their actions.

Ever since the other day when I'd signed off on the new bill regarding women's rights, Andrew and nearly everyone else around the White House who'd doubted me, they had been sucking up to me. I got tired of Andrew telling me how sorry he was for disagreeing with me and he'd even purchased a gift card from one of my favorite restaurants. I laughed and tossed the card in the trash.

"Sir," he said as we sat in the Oval Office, getting ready for my press conference today. "Don't take too long and remember your meeting is at two o'clock. That gives you roughly twenty or so minutes to answer questions for the press and get out of there."

"I'll do my best to wrap it up quickly, but you know how much I like to talk. The press will be surprised to see me, and I didn't want Sam to go out there hacking his head off today."

"Yes, he has a pretty bad cold. I hope neither of us gets sick and I would hate for you to get sick on or before you head out of the country in a few days."

"I would hate that too, that's why I told Sam to stay far away from here. I hope he listens."

Andrew agreed. Minutes later, we headed to the Press Briefing Room. As soon as I entered, plenty of smiles could be seen. The press was ready to dive right in with questions, and after I provided an update about what my administration had been working on, I started to take questions. I pointed to a reporter who had his hand up in the front row.

"Good afternoon, Mr. President. It's always good to have you in the Press Briefing Room with us and we wish you would come here more often. Since you can't, I wanted to ask you about your detailed plans for infrastructure. We've been talking about building up our nation for years, but it seems like many of the infrastructure projects are always put on the backburner. Are you sure it's going to happen this time and are there any states in particular you intend to focus on first?"

"I agree we have put off fixing our roads and bridges for way too long. I'm not going to necessarily focus on certain states in particular, but a more detailed plan will be coming, after my meeting this afternoon. I can tell you the bill we're going to push for will be unlike anything you've ever seen. We're going to find a way to pay for it and we're hoping to generate a massive amount of jobs."

I pointed to a female reporter in the second row. "Thank you, Mr. President," she said. "My question to you pertains to the verdict we're still waiting on relating to the cop who killed an unarmed black man and his son. Do you know what is taking the jury so long to come back with a verdict and have you been given details about what actually happened that day?"

"Yes, I was given detailed information by the DOJ and I hope and pray the jury gets it right. We can't afford to keep going down this path where cops are not being held accountable for their actions. And if they're innocent, we certainly don't want them to go to jail. But let me allow the jury time to review all of the evidence, before I speak further."

"But you already said you hope they get it right. That means, you think the cop should be convicted. Are you willing to say you are hoping for a conviction?"

"What I'm willing to say is what I said. You can spin it how you wish, and the way I see it, no further clarification from me is needed."

I pointed to another reporter in the far back. "Sir, thank you for being here, but how's your mother? Has she been able to get her drinking under control? If she hasn't been able to, have you thought about putting her in rehab again?"

I had gotten to the point where I knew dumb ass questions would come out of certain reporters' mouths, particularly from reporters who worked for the conservative side of the media. This time, I was ready.

"My mother is doing well, Randy, and thank you for asking. Her drinking is very much under control, but if it wasn't, I would definitely send her to the same rehab facility your father is in. He's been there for quite some time, hasn't he? I feel bad about how abusive he was to you and your mother, but, hey, shit happens sometimes, doesn't it?"

His expression fell flat. He shot me a look like he wanted to rush up to the podium and beat my ass. Obviously, some of the reporters could dish it out, but they damn sure couldn't take it. I was ready to move on, so I called on Michelle who'd had her hand up. She stood when she asked her question and she looked at me without a blink.

"Mr. President, since you were so eager to push for more women's rights in this country, why do you attempt to silence us? Several women from your administration have complained, including VP Bass who said, and I quote, that you do not listen to her advice and when she offers it, you ignore her. She went on to say you have no issue with listening to or following the advice of men. She once stated you referred to her by using the "B" word and are you willing to admit you have gone that far and utilized the "B" word in her presence?"

I gazed at Michelle for a few seconds and did exactly what she tried to accuse me of. I ignored her and pointed to another reporter to question me. Before he did, I made it clear that if the questions didn't pertain to vital issues which were happening in or outside of our country, I wasn't going to answer. The next several questions did, and after I answered, I waved and told everyone to enjoy their day. I knew Michelle was still upset; she'd tried her best to get underneath my skin. It didn't surprise me one bit when she came after me and asked me to follow her to a meeting room we always went to. After I went inside, she slammed the door behind me. She had something in her hand, and when I looked to see what it was, it was duct tape. She tore off a big piece and slammed the rest of it on the table.

"Why didn't you answer my question?" she asked. "You knew exactly where I was going with it and the least you could've done was answer it."

"I didn't answer because you made it more about VP Bass than you did about you. I'm shocked that you're still upset with me. I honestly don't know why."

"I can't tell you why because you don't want to hear me. You don't want to hear anything I have to say and all you want to do is silence me. If my silence pleases you, then fine. I'll stay silent just to . . . just to be with you and you will never hear me complain again."

She slapped the tape over her mouth and rolled her eyes at me. I hated she was so upset with me; the last thing I was trying to do was silence her.

"Michelle, stop this nonsense, alright? You are leading us down a path you don't want to go. If you're that upset with me, tell me why and be done with it. I think I heard all your gripes the other night, unless there is more."

She stood while mean mugging me with the tape over her mouth. When I reached out to remove it, she smacked my hand away. I certainly didn't have time for this, so I stepped around her and reached for the knob on the door to open it. She aggressively pulled the back of my suit jacket and grabbed my arm to turn me around. Her head moved from side-to-side as she yanked my shirt apart, ripping it down the middle. My buttons popped off and rolled on the floor. With my chest exposed, she reached for the zipper on my slacks. I grabbed her hand to stop her.

"No," I said adamantly. "This isn't what you want. You made it clear that you wanted William, not me. Do you still want him?"

She moved her head from side-to-side.

"Are you still seeing him?"

Her head moved from side-to-side again.

"Do you want me and only me?"

She slowly nodded and her pretty brown eyes staring into mine while confessing her need for me had me hooked.

"Are you saying it's over between the two of you?"

She nodded and reached for my zipper again. I reached for the tape over her mouth and carefully removed it. Her first soft words to me were, "Nothing ever got started between us, because I need you so badly. I want only you, and I didn't mean to be a pain in—"

I silenced her when I covered her mouth with mine. We exchanged sloppy wet kisses, and as she literally ripped off my clothes, I hit the lights and leaned her back on the table. Our mouths stayed attached and while rubbing the back of my head, she passionately sucked on my lips.

"I can't hold back anymore," she said as I lifted her skirt and massaged her cheeks. "I want this. I want us to be together and I want to take care of your every need."

She covered my mouth with hers again, and between juicy wet kisses, and heavy breathing, she continued to express her thoughts.

"I will take care of you. I will make you so happy and celebrate all of your accomplishments with you. I need you, Stephen, and I want you to need me too."

Everything she'd said caused our kissing to get more intense, and by now, my hard head was knocking at her door. I moved the wet crotch section of her panties aside and steered my muscle right in. The warmth and tightness caused me to shut my eyes and as I started to stroke her insides, she pulled me closer to her and planted her soft lips close to my ear.

"Allow me to satisfy you in every way. I want more than just sex. We can have so much more and we deserve it. Just say the word and I will give you everything. I will cook for you, bathe you and be there for you every step of the way. I want you to meet my children and I want all of us to be together always."

Her lips returned to mine, and I had to admit I was sold on a lot of what she had said. It sounded damn good to me; so good that I was in a trance as our bodies rocked fiercely together in sync. Her wetness was all over me, and the sexual aroma filling the room made me feel high.

"Give me more, Stephen, please give me more. Go away with me for a few days and let's enjoy life. I want to see the world with you, give you more children, if that's what you want, and just . . . just love you like you've never been loved before."

By now, I felt heavily sedated. Michelle had put it out there and laid it all on the line for me. I couldn't get enough of her and when she eased off the table, ready for me to enter her from another position, she stood with her back facing me. My steel rested between her healthy cheeks and with my arms wrapped around her, I squeezed her nipples and massaged her breasts together. Her head was turned sideways so her lips could continue to tangle with mine. We could barely catch our breaths, and as soon as she fell forward and bent over the table, I got back to work and hit it hard. Michelle hollered out after each thrust forward—she started to express herself once again.

"Let's go, baby, please let's go," she whined. "Two days, three days, whatever. I need to show you we can have even more than this. I hope you already know we can."

I wanted to respond, but couldn't. I just kept pushing my goodness into her while watching her mountains clap and waiting for her juices to overflow. In the midst of her orgasm, she forced me back and quickly turned to face me. She placed my hand over her slit and as I softly rubbed against it, she threw her arms around my neck.

"I love the hell out of you, and I want you to love me back. Do you love me, Stephen, please be honest. Now is the time. Or are we going to just keep screwing each other until one of us get tired?"

I pulled my glazed finger out of her insides and tightly wrapped my arms around her. Her soft breasts were smashed against my chest while I searched deep into her eyes.

"I'm afraid to love you," I answered. "Afraid to give us a chance and I continue to ignore my feelings because I don't want to hurt Raynetta. I'm disappointed about my failed marriage and I feel guilty about the feelings I have for you. It's easier for me to suppress my feelings and I keep telling myself that this can never be more than just sex."

"It is so much more than sex. So much more and I know you feel it. All I ask is that you give me a chance to show you. Let's go somewhere private for a few days. Just you and me, and Secret Service if need be. Please think about it, and if you can make that happen, call me and let me know. I'll be waiting on your phone call."

Michelle had put some serious shit on my mind. I was so messed up that I couldn't even attend my two o'clock meeting. My clothes were ripped, body was wet and sticky, and if anyone saw me, they would instantly be able to tell what I had been up to. Michelle straightened her clothes and left the room before I did. I waited before exiting, and as I made my way down the corridor, that was when I saw Andrew standing near the Rose Garden.

"You missed the meeting," he said. "After you didn't show up within the first ten minutes, I cancelled and rescheduled for tomorrow."

"Thanks," I said as we entered the Oval Office through the glass doors. "Something came up. I just couldn't get away."

"From the way you're looking, that's pretty obvious. Maybe you should head up to the Executive Residence and get yourself together."

"That's what I plan on doing, but I need you to stay right here, until I come back. I need to speak to you about something important."

Andrew nodded and I hurried to the Executive Residence to shower and change clothes. I returned to the Oval Office in a pair of navy sweats and a soft cotton T-shirt that rested on my muscles. Andrew questioned my laxed attire.

"Obviously, you're not going anywhere else important for the rest of the day," he said, jokingly. "And what is it that you want to speak to me about?"

"About a quick vacation and Raynetta."

"Yes, please take a quick vacation. You've been working your ass off and you and the first lady should get away. Are you going to Camp David or somewhere else? I can handle things while you're away, but you have to get back here and prepare for your trip out of the country. The first lady can join you on that trip too. You may not have much time to spend with her, because that trip will be more about business than anything."

"Raynetta and I won't be vacationing together. As a matter of fact, we've been talking about getting a divorce. I think it's time and I want to know how severe you think the backlash will be from the American people. I do plan to run for a second term, but do you think I'll be successful without Raynetta by my side? We're not in love anymore, and I don't think it is fair for her to remain here with me, under the circumstances."

Andrew wiped down his face and leaned forward as he sat on the sofa. "I know you've been seeing Michelle Peoples for quite a while now, but does this have anything to do with her? Is that who you want to vacation with and do you have plans to divorce Raynetta and marry her? I don't know if that's a good idea, Stephen. It doesn't look good, and for you to divorce your wife and be with your mistress is—"

He was getting too far ahead of himself; I had to make a few things clear to him.

"First of all, I never mentioned anything about getting married again. That's not happening and stop with the mistress bullshit. I don't have a mistress. I am involved with a beautiful woman who loves and treats me better than my wife. I have strong feelings for her and I would be a fool to keep ignoring a woman who I know can bring some happiness to my life. She's not the reason I want a divorce, and as you know, Raynetta and I have had problems for a very long time. There is no way for me to be all I can be with a woman I do not trust. Not now, not ever."

"I get that, and since you asked for my opinion, here it is. Finish your term and don't run for a second term. The American people won't stand by you, Stephen, especially women who will not be happy about you separating from the first lady. They love her too. They love the both of you and they root for the two of you together. It's a shame to see two beautiful people fall out of love with each other, but it happens all the time. Neither of you should live your lives being unhappy, and if Michelle Peoples is capable of making you a better man, I'll root for the two of you as well. Take a vacation, but only for a few days. Be sure to have your phone with you at all times, and before you go, tell Raynetta. Just tell her what you really want, Stephen, and if she decides to stay, fine. If not, let her go and try your best not to have any regrets."

"I can't tell her everything right now. Soon I will, but I need for you to cover for me for the next couple of days. Can you do that for me?"

Andrew nodded. "Of course I will. For three days I will, but after that, Mr. President, I need you to get back here so we can prepare for your trip. You have multiple meetings scheduled and when you leave the country, we always like to update you and keep you informed on specific world issues."

"That's fine. I'll be back, but first I have to figure out where I'm going."

Andrew told me about a private farmhouse his cousin owned near the beach in Long Island. He even showed me some photos of the place, and after arranging everything for me I called Michelle to confirm.

"Be ready tomorrow morning," I said. "And prepare yourself to have a good time."

"You too. Thank you for agreeing to do this. I'll see you in the morning. Rest well."

I was excited about going away with Michelle for a few days. It was exactly what I needed and I was sure everyone in the White House could manage without me for a few days.

The 7.5 million dollar farmhouse mansion we stayed in, in Long Island, was less than 4,000 square feet. The house sat on nearly 35 acres of well-manicured land and the sandy beach was less than a half mile away. More than anything, the whole place offered us nothing but privacy and serenity. It felt so good to be here, and this place was ten times better than Camp David. A wine vineyard was on the property and the thick green grass and willow trees added much beauty. Michelle and I sat on a cozy porch that wrapped around the house with our wineglasses full. She had on a strapless sundress with no shoes, looking sexy as ever. A checkerboard game was on a small table between us and we had just started to play. Because of the soothing, slightly breezy temperature, my shirt was off but a cap was on my head. I had on sweatpants, socks and sandals. I was very comfortable, and if I could live in a place like this for the rest of my life, I wouldn't have any complaints.

"Your move," she said as I stared at the checkerboard. "What's taking you so long to make a move?"

By looking at the board, I had already planned the next ten moves in my head. I didn't even know what her moves would be, but there was no way I would lose.

"I'm just thinking about my moves, before I make them. Be quiet and give me a minute."

"Sorry, but that would be called cheating. How can you strategize, before the game is played?"

"That's how you do it, if you want to win. Don't you know how to win?"

Michelle got up and came to sit on my lap. She wrapped my arms around her and held her hands with mine.

"How can you ask me a question like that?" she said. "I'm always a winner, especially when I'm with you."

She turned her head to give me a kiss. I knew she was trying to distract me; I teased her about it.

"Distract you how?" she asked. "I'm just sitting on your lap, trying to look at the board from a different angle."

"No, you're sitting on my lap with no bra or panties on, kissing on me and trying to get me focused on other things so I don't win this game. I'm already hip to what you're doing."

"If I wanted to distract you, trust me I know so many other ways to do it. It has nothing to do with me not wearing a bra or panties, and everything to do with what I'm planning to cook. They say the way to a man's heart is through his stomach, so I got plans, baby. Big plans and I hope you like fish."

"I do, so why don't you go ahead and hook me up. I'm starving and those pancakes you made earlier could've been a little bit bigger."

She cocked her head back. "Are you complaining? I hope not, because you sure weren't complaining while you were eating them."

"That's because I knew how sweet the *syrup* would be."

Michelle laughed, knowing I was referring to her *syrup*. She went inside and started on dinner. That gave me a chance to check-in with Andrew. He'd called earlier, but I didn't answer the phone because Michelle and I were busy. He followed up with a text message, telling me it wasn't important but to call him when I had time.

"What's good?" I asked him.

"Hopefully, you are. Are you enjoying yourself?"

"As a matter of fact, I am. This place is real nice, quiet and peaceful. Been a minute since I've heard nothing but birds chirping."

"I understand how that is and you won't hear many of them chirping in this environment. I called to let you know the verdict came in a few hours ago on that cop case. He was found guilty. Can you believe the jury got it right? I know you're glad about that and so am I."

"Very glad. I was told about most of the evidence against him and I'm so grateful to the jury for getting it right this time. Maybe things are starting to change? I guess we'll soon see."

"Yes, we will. I won't keep you, sir. Be sure to tell Michelle I said hello."

I told Andrew I would, and after tossing back more wine, I went inside to check on Michelle. She was in the kitchen, seasoning the fish and rinsing some vegetables. I eased up from behind her and secured my arms around her waist. As I placed delicate kisses along the side of her neck, she tilted her head.

"We're never going to eat, if you keep interrupting me to do this. At least let me get the fish into the oven."

"The fish can wait." I lowered the top part of her sundress underneath her firm breasts, exposing them. She turned to face me and as we kissed again, I lifted her on top of the sink. My mouth dropped to her left breast that I squeezed and gently sucked. She squirmed while wrapping her legs around me to hold on.

"Ju . . . Just take me to the bedroom," she said. "Like I said before, we're never going to eat."

We ate and then some. Made love, watched TV, danced to soft music, played board games, chilled by the fireplace, bathed together, walked down to the beach and raced each other in the yard. I had the time of my life with Michelle, and after three long days together, I knew exactly what my next move had to be.

President of the United States
Stephen C. Jefferson

Michelle and I returned to Washington on a high note. She had to go pick up her kids from her sister's place and I was already back in the Oval Office getting an update on what had been happening for the past three days. Nothing real severe, but there were a few storms that caused damage on the East Coast, some people were upset about the guilty verdict and a couple of fights had ensued when a group of White Supremacists gathered in the streets in support of the cop. Worldwide, a terrorist organization had been making threats about attacking the United States, but that was nothing new. We had very good intelligence, and it was nearly impossible for anything like 9/11 to occur in the United States again. Another bridge had collapsed, but there were no injuries. I had to get busy on infrastructure and I also had to finalize what I'd decided about Mr. McNeil. After that, it was all about me and Raynetta. I picked up the phone and dialed out on my private line.

"What time should I meet you?" I asked.

"I should have him with me around six, no later than seven," he said.

"Your time needs to be precise, because I don't have time to waste."

"Six thirty, Mr. President. See you then."

I ended the call, but I was almost late as I sat in my office, trying to catch up on everything. Raynetta was nowhere to be found, and when I went to her office earlier, I was told her and Emme wouldn't be back until eight. I needed to hurry up and get this over with, so I left the Oval Office and had one of my Secret Service agents take me to my special hideout—the bunker. I hoped this was the last time I had to go there, and after Mr. McNeil was out of the picture, I expected many things to change. The grip around many members of Congress would loosen; no question it would be easier for me to get things done. I wondered what had taken me so long to do this, and at this point, I knew this was something Raynetta wanted too. She had said so, and when she'd mentioned how much she wished he was dead, I knew she meant it.

With a new tailored suit on, I strutted down the long, concrete hallway that was partially dark. All I could hear was dripping water and laughter. I recognized the laugh, and when I opened the door to the muggy room where Mr. McNeil was being held, that was when I saw Alex standing next to him with his arms folded. Reminding me of 007, he had on an olive green T-shirt, camouflage pants and black combat boots that were unlaced. His white skin was so tanned it looked baked and there was a quirky smirk on his face. No question he got a kick out of doing shit like this. That's why it was imperative for me to keep him on my team, no matter what had happened between him and Raynetta. I didn't blame him for pursuing her; she should have rejected him. I'd told her he was dead, but deep down, I suspected she always knew there was more to his abrupt disappearance.

"This guy is hilarious," Alex said. "I don't ever think I've seen an old man cry this much. I don't know if the tears are real or fake."

I looked at Mr. McNeil who sat in the chair in his white, dingy drawers and socks. He had urinated on himself and the stench was prominent. His whole face was red; I wasn't sure if that was due to Alex punching him or from him sobbing so much.

"Listen, for once in your life listen to me," he said. "My family won't like this and you can bet your last dollar they will seek you out and come after you. You won't get away with this, boy, and how is killing me going to help you?"

I sighed and contracted my eyes as I looked at his pathetic self.

"You remind me so much of your grandson, Tyler, as he sat in the same chair attacking me and trying to pretend how brave he was. Killing you is going to feel like the best piece of pussy I've had, and trust me when I say I've had some darn good pussy. Your family won't miss you and let's be realistic here. As soon as your body is discovered, they're all going to rush to their lawyers, and your lawyers too, to figure out how to divvy up your good fortune. You should've left me alone, Mr. McNeil. And continuously hurting Raynetta's feelings was the last straw. Say your prayers, old man. You do have a little more time to repent."

"Not much time," Alex said, before lifting his Glock 9 and circling it on Mr. McNeil's temple. The second he opened his mouth to speak, Alex pulled back on the trigger and blew his damn brains out. His body hit the floor; I looked at him and thought . . . problem solved.

"This was too easy," Alex said. "How many days do you want to pass before the word gets out about this?"

I shrugged. "A day, maybe two. Or you can wait until I leave the country. Just make it look like a robbery. I assume you already know the criminals who can go down for this. If not, I know a young man, Malik, who would be a good candidate. Just let me know and we can work something out."

"I'll let you know, but I have two other idiots in mind. You'll appreciate them much more, because they just joined one of those racists groups that's been stirring up trouble across the country. They already have several robbery charges against them, and one of the idiots went to prison for beating his wife and kid."

"Sounds like you may want to move in that direction then. Thanks for your help with this and be sure to clean up real good down here."

Alex saluted me. As I made my way towards the door, he cleared his throat. "Don't forget to tell Raynetta I said hello. Does she still ask about me?"

"Hell no," I said and turned to cut my eyes at him. "It's over and you should've been ashamed of yourself for falling for her. She's good, but not that good."

"That's your opinion, not mine."

Alex winked and as I walked out the door, I told him to tell General Stiles hello for me. He laughed again and promised he would.

Nearly an hour later, I returned to the White House. Raynetta was back, and when I peeked into her office, she was sitting behind her desk, typing on her computer.

"Come in," she said. "And close the door behind you. I don't want to be interrupted by Emme. She knows she runs her mouth too much. Sometimes, I can't get anything done."

"A person like that is right up your alley. You run your mouth too, so I don't know what you're complaining for."

"You may be right about that, but have a seat. I've been looking for you. Where were you?"

I sat on the sofa and placed my hands behind my head. "I disappeared for a few days. Needed to get away from here and relax."

"You did need to get away from the White House, because you've been wearing yourself out. Where did you go and did you go alone?"

I swallowed then answered her question. "I went to a quiet place in Long Island. I didn't go alone. Michelle was with me."

Raynetta had finally stopped typing to give me her full attention. She swooped her long hair behind her ears and sat up straight.

"Soooo, why did you take her with you? Is your relationship with her getting serious?"

"More serious than I thought it would ever get, but that doesn't mean I want to marry her."

"Well, what does it mean, Stephen? Are you in love with her and are you here to ask me for a divorce?"

It pained me to say it, but I had to. "Yes, I am in love with her, and eventually, I want you to divorce me. I don't want you to stay here, unless you want to. I do intend to spend more of my down time with Michelle. I know that's going to make you uncomfortable and I don't want you to feel embarrassed by media reports or any other reporting that may occur when the two of us are together. I hope you understand the two of us can't go on like this, and no matter what, I will always care about you."

Raynetta slowly closed her eyes. She remained quiet while gathering her thoughts. Finally, she opened her eyes and stood. After walking my way, she sat on the sofa next to me. A glassy film covered her eyes and her lips quivered as she spoke.

"Do whatever makes you happy, Stephen. I can't fight with a woman who has your heart, but I wish she would've let us work through this without interfering. She's had a hold on you for a long time. I predicted a while back your feelings would change about her. I don't want to be here while the two of you spend time together, so expect me to make my exit soon. I haven't a clue how to break the news to everyone, but I guess you have that all figured out too."

I slowly nodded and reached for her hands that were clenched together. I brought her hand to my mouth and kissed the back of it. "Thanks for understanding. We'll discuss later how to finalize everything, and if you want to talk more about this, let out your frustrations or whatever, I'm here to listen."

Raynetta stood and walked to the door. She opened it, signaling for me to go. I stood and as soon as I got to the door, she reached for my hand. She leaned in to plant a soft kiss on my lips. I didn't back away from it—it was short and sweet.

"I'll have my lawyer get the divorce papers to you soon," she said. "Be sure to check your desk, and just so you know, this hurts, but I'm okay with bringing closure to this too."

I nodded, and after I walked off, Raynetta closed the door. I heard her crying. It wasn't a good feeling, but we both knew this day was destined.

President's Mother
Teresa Jefferson

After the incident with Malik, Stephen had been conducting himself like a changed man. He was gearing up for a long trip out of the country; I surely was going to miss him. I'd spoken to him last night and he broke the news to me about him and Raynetta getting a divorce. I wanted to call her and offer my condolences, but I was so sure the last person she wanted to hear from was me.

Unfortunately, sometimes, marriages just didn't work out. Neither Stephen nor Raynetta put forth the effort to really change things around and this was the end result. I'd seen this day coming many years ago. Yes, Stephen was an asshole, but he needed a stronger woman by his side. Not only that, but a trustworthy one too. Raynetta had never been loyal to him and being pretty wasn't enough. I wasn't so sure if Michelle would be any better, and as a matter of fact, I didn't have much faith in her. Nonetheless, I wanted to wipe the slate clean and give her a chance. I'd called her earlier to patch things up with her, especially since she and Stephen planned on spending more time together. He seemed to adore her, and even though he admitted to being in love, I wasn't sold on that either. What I did know was, as a woman myself, she really loved him. I could tell by her actions and by how happy she'd sounded over the phone. I managed to persuade her to have dinner with me this evening so we could patch up our mistakes from the past and try to get along better for the sake of making Stephen's life a whole lot more peaceful. Maybe it would be easier for me to get along better with her than I'd gotten along with Raynetta. Lord knows I'd butted heads with her a lot, but that was because I never thought she was Stephen's soulmate. I couldn't stop thinking about her, so I made a decision to reach out to her. She answered, sounding real upbeat for someone who was in the process of getting a divorce.

"Should I bring over the champagne so we can celebrate or what?" I asked.

"If it pleases you to know, I've already been celebrating. What did you think I was going to do, Teresa? Crawl underneath a rock or die? No, thank you. I promise you I will bounce back from this. Stephen isn't the last man on earth."

"No, he's not, and I'm sure you will bounce back quickly. You should because you never really cared much for Stephen anyway. I hate to be cruel at a time like this, but I am so glad the marriage is finally coming to an end. It was years wasted. I haven't a clue what you or Stephen was thinking when it pertains to love, and I'm not even sure if he really loves Michelle. But time will surely tell. There are things about her that concern me too, but at least—"

"Teresa, I really don't care to hear about Michelle. I also don't want to discuss how I define love and since you're so glad our marriage is finally over, I'll send you some wine for you to celebrate. One good thing about this whole thing is I don't have to deal with you any longer. Consider this as goodbye and please lose my number."

She had the nerve to hang up on me. I started to call her back and really hurt her feelings, but I decided against it. I'd gotten what I ultimately wanted, and I had no reason to be upset about anything else.

Later that day, I picked up Michelle in my silver Mercedes around four in the afternoon. We had plans to go to a new seafood restaurant by her place and she spoke about how delicious it was when she got in the car.

"They have shrimp like this big," she said, showing me the size of it with her hands. "Everything is seasoned to perfection and if you like lobster, get ready."

"Sounds too good to be true. I can't wait and the last time I had some excellent seafood was in 1977."

She laughed and shook her head. "It hasn't been that long, has it? And how can you remember the taste of food from that long ago?"

"I remember everything. I may be old, but my memory is sharp."

We sat silent for a few minutes, and as the bright sun blocked my view a little, I lowered the visor.

"I want to apologize to you for some of the things I've said and done," I said to her. "I just want the best for my son and, sometimes, I go overboard to protect him. As a mother yourself, I'm sure you can understand. Our children mean everything to us and it's so hard to let go, even when that child is president of the United States."

"I know exactly how you feel when it comes to our children. You don't have to explain why you're so overprotective, but all I ask is that you not interfere in regards to my relationship with Stephen. We're already going to have many challenges going forward, and you know the media, whom I work for, is going to shame us in many ways. Regardless, I love him from the bottom of my heart and I'm looking forward to our future. I don't know if he plans to ever remarry, but after my failed marriage, I'm not in a rush to do it all over again."

"What about having kids? Do you want more kids?"

"I don't mind having more kids, but Stephen and I will discuss that when the time comes. He is so amazing, Teresa. So many people in this country don't know how lucky we are to have him as president. He's going to help pass more life-changing legislation and I truly believe he will make his mark in history.

There is something special about having a black president. They sure know how to get things done, against all odds."

I couldn't have agreed with Michelle more. We were almost at the restaurant, but I had to stop and get gas. While I was at the gas station, I used the restroom. I had to open my purse to get my small container of disinfecting wipes and use them, before I handled my business. I also took a few swigs from the bottle of Hennessy in my purse. After I screwed on the cap, I popped a breath mint in my mouth. I then returned to the car where Michelle had cranked up the music and was snapping her fingers to a song.

"Girl, Jill Scott be taking you there, don't she?" I said. I drove off and cranked up the volume some more.

"Yes, Ma'am," Michelle said. "Jill be putting it down. I can't wait to see her in concert next month. I hope Stephen will be able to go with me. He likes her singing too."

Yes, Stephen was a fan for sure, but not like I was. I blurted out the lyrics, and for whatever reason, I could feel my foot getting heavier on the accelerator. I didn't even hear Michelle telling me to slow down, but when she yelled it louder and I slammed on the brakes, it was too late. A truck that was carrying an oversized load swerved around the corner and smashed into my car head on. All I remembered was glass shattering and numbness washing over me. After that, there was loud screaming and I was out of it.

President of the United States
Stephen C. Jefferson

The day before my trip out of the country started off pretty messed up. I was sitting at my desk in the Oval Office when a package was delivered. I opened it, two things were inside. One stack of papers was a request for Dissolution of Marriage. The other was a manuscript titled, *Black President: The World Will Never Be the Same*. A sticky note was attached to it and Raynetta had written the words: *I had to open the doors to my entire experience with you while at the White House. Feel free to read it; it was worth every penny to me.*

I flipped through the manuscript and wasn't too pleased by some of the things I'd read. She'd written different segments and there was no question in my mind that Raynetta had been at this longer than I'd thought. As I continued to read her words, they were definitely true to who I was. She had made herself appear quite innocent, but what people didn't always realize was there were always two or three sides to every story. My heart fell to my stomach when I read about how my mother was being portrayed. She definitely wasn't going to appreciate this. I planned to reach out to Raynetta and see if it was too late for her to give me a chance to read the whole thing and request revisions. The second I picked up the phone to call her, Andrew appeared in the doorway, yelling at me.

"Mr. President, come now! Your mother has been in a car accident! It's pretty serious!"

This time, my heart dropped to the floor. I rushed up from my chair, grabbed my jacket and blew by everyone inside of the White House who questioned what was so urgent. That included Raynetta who grabbed my arm to inquire.

"What's wrong, Stephen?" she asked. "Why are you running?"

"It's my mother. She's been in an accident."

Raynetta said she would gather her things and follow me to the hospital. I was a nervous wreck—thoughts of losing her pained the shit out of me. I sat on the backseat of the Suburban, patting my foot on the floor while wringing my trembling hands together. Andrew sat across from me with his cell phone pressed up to his ear. He was waiting for a doctor to tell him the current condition of my mother.

"I'll wait," he said to someone. "But can you—"

I reached out and snatched the cell phone from his hand. "No, I will not wait!" I yelled. "I am president of the United States and I need to know, right now, the condition of my mother! Tell me now!"

The woman responded in a shaky voice. "Mr. President, she's in critical but stable condition. I prefer that you speak to the doctor who can give you specific details about her condition. I didn't want to give you the wrong information. I apologize for the delay."

I tossed the phone back to Andrew and told him to end the call. At least she was still alive. I felt a little more relieved, until I got to the hospital and saw her lying in a hospital bed with IV's injected in her hands and arms. Her face was riddled with cuts and bruises. Her head was wrapped with a bandage, and the second she saw me standing in the doorway, her eyes filled with tears. She closed them and tears rolled down her face.

"Clear this whole area," Secret Service ordered the entire hospital staff in emergency. "If you can, move some of the other non-life-threatening patients to another floor and halt all visitors on this floor. We don't need this many doctors and nurses in here and those people out there shouldn't be surrounding that door!"

"Mr. President," a woman outside of the door shouted. "Can I have your autograph?"

"Dang, is the president's mother dead? I think she died. Damn!"

"I'm not moving. My father is in another room, and if they're that privileged, they shouldn't even be here. Send them to another hospital."

I ignored all the hoopla and stepped up to my mother with tears in my eyes. "Why did you scare me like this?" I asked while standing beside her bed. "You're going to be okay, right?"

She slowly nodded and swallowed hard. She struggled to open her mouth and when she did, the first words she said to me was, "I'm sorry. I'm so sorry, I never meant to hurt you."

I touched her hand, squeezing it with mine. "What are you apologizing to me for? All I need to know is you're going to be okay. Does anything hurt and is there anything I or one of the doctors can get you?"

She moved her head from side-to-side, signaling no. Tears ran from the corners of her eyes and she kept staring at me. I don't know why I felt like I was going to lose her, so in a panic, I turned to one of the doctors who was behind me, trying to clear the whole area with Secret Service.

"Tell me what's going on with her," I said. "I need to know what happened."

The doctor nudged his head towards the corner of the room, and as I attempted to release my mother's hand, she squeezed it tight, trying to hold on to it.

"I'm not going anywhere," I said to her. "I'm right here and I'll be right back, okay?"

Her tears kept flowing. She opened her dry mouth to speak again. "Forgive me, baby, I am so sorry."

I wasn't so sure what she kept apologizing for, until I started conversing with the doctor.

"Thankfully, and by the grace of God, your mother is going to be okay. She suffered a concussion, broke some bones in her arms and leg and we stitched some of the abrasions on her face. It will be a while before the swelling subsides and she may need to schedule physical therapy. We won't know until everything starts to heal. I still want to run a few more tests on her, just to make sure all of her organs are functioning properly. You don't know how pleased I am to share this news with you, considering what could have happened to her while driving under the influence of alcohol. Her BAC, blood alcohol content, was at .16 percent, which is way too high to drive. That's why she was unable to see a truck coming around the curve and she smashed right into it."

It felt like the doctor had punched me in my stomach and taken the breath out of me. In a flash, my concern turned into anger. She knew better than to be driving with a BAC that high. No words could express how disappointed I was; I'd warned her, time and time again, about drinking too much.

The doctor released a deep sigh and continued to go in on my mother. "She had to know that drinking that much alcohol would cause serious harm. And while she was able to get through this, her passenger wasn't as lucky."

My face twisted; heart started to beat a little bit faster. "Someone else was in the car with her?" I immediately thought about Malik. I'd told her to leave that fool alone, but I guess she couldn't resist him. Those thoughts angered me more. "Male or female?"

"Female. We're in the process of trying to reach her family so they can come to the hospital."

My face was still scrunched; I hadn't a clue who the female passenger could've been because my mother, intentionally, didn't have many friends. Then again, maybe she did and I just didn't know about them.

"What's the woman's name? Is she going to, eventually, be okay? Maybe I can help you get in touch with her family."

The doctor reached in his pocket and pulled out a notepad. He examined what he had written on it. Right then, I heard my mother calling my name. I was upset with her for causing all this trouble, so in the moment, I ignored her and didn't turn around.

"The, uh, woman's name was Michelle. Michelle Peoples, and unfortunately, sir, she didn't make it."

I stood for a moment, believing I was unclear about what he'd said. My whole body was frozen and I couldn't even force my mouth open to speak. All I did was snatch the notepad from the doctor's hand so I could see with my own eyes the name he'd written. Michelle's name was, indeed, on the paper and when my watery eyes gazed at the doctor, he appeared nervous and in shock too.

"Wha . . .What do you mean, did you say?" I stuttered and tried to catch my breath. "Did you say she didn't make it? Didn't make what?"

He appeared afraid to answer me. And before I knew it, I grabbed his collar and pushed him against the wall. "She didn't make what!" I shouted and banged him harder. "Answer my fucking question and tell me where she's at!"

"She's in the last room down the hall, but you can't go in there, sir! You can't—"

I released him—he fell to the floor. I ran so fast out of the room that I didn't even take a split second to look at my mother who kept calling me. Andrew yelled after me too and so did Secret Service.

"Mr. President, stop! Wait, please!" Andrew said. "I'm coming with you!"

"Sir, we still haven't cleared the area! This is an unsafe environment!"

I hurried down the hallway, damn near falling on my ass as I slipped on the wet floor in my leather shoes. And when I reached the last room to the left, I pushed the door open and entered. Lying on a gurney was a badly bruised stiff body with a sheet partially over it. I had nothing left in me as I grabbed the sheet with my tightened fist and slowly pulled it away from the person lying there. It was Michelle. I gasped, and as so many tears proceeded to rain down my face, I just stared at her without a single blink. She wasn't moving, wasn't breathing, there was no smile and I had never seen her eyes closed so tight. It felt like I was in another world. There was a horrible ache in my throat, my legs felt weak and my heart was beating so fast it was about to explode. I blinked fast, and as I was finally able to open my mouth, I started to plead with her to get up.

"Come on, baby," I said sternly. I sucked in a deep breath and leaned over her. "Don't fuck with me like this, please. This is a joke, right? You . . . You and my mother are trying to get me back. I know I've done some horrible shit, but get up for me, please. Don't you dare lay there and leave me like this. This isn't happening and I need you to get up!"

I smacked my tears away and wiped snot that poured over my trembling lips and dripped from my chin. I then wrapped my arms around her, and since she didn't hug me back, I directed her arms over my shoulders and lifted her from the gurney.

"Let's go home," I said, holding her tight. "To your place or back to the Farmhouse, if you want to. We need to get out of here, baby. I . . . I can't leave you here like this. No way, and I need for you to get up."

As I turned with Michelle in my arms, two Secret Service agents stood like mannequins at the door. Andrew was there, too, down on one knee with his head hanging low. The doctor stood closest to me. With fiery eyes and flush cheeks, he was overcome with emotion.

"She . . . She can't go with you, Mr. President, I'm sorry. We did everything we could to save her, but her injuries were too severe. If you know how to reach her family, please do call them. I'm so sorry about this. No words can express how sorry I am for your loss."

Her family, I thought as I closed my eyes. Her children, her mother and father . . . sister whom she was so close with. I was so damn distraught, and as I stepped forward with her still in my arms, the doctor stood in front of me.

"Move out of my way," I said softly. "We need to go. Now, if you don't mind."

Like always, Andrew came to the rescue. He stood and walked up to me.

"You can't take her, Mr. President, but trust me when I tell you she'll be okay. She's already okay and I know she wants you to be okay too. Lay her down and let her stay here for a little while. It'll only be for a short while and then she'll," Andrew paused. He was choked up and couldn't even give me the advice I needed.

"And then what?" I said as I laid her back down on the gurney. I rubbed the side of her face while gazing at her head that was slumped to the side. "What, Andrew?" I asked. "Do . . . Do you think I should give her a kiss? Can I kiss her?"

"Sure, Mr. President. One last kiss and then we need to go."

My tears dripped on the side of her face, and after I kissed her cheek a few times, I stood up straight. I unbuttoned my suit jacket and cocked my tense neck from one side to the other. My heart felt too heavy for my chest, and as I left the room, Secret Service followed. Every single eye in the hospital was on me as I stared straight ahead. So much was a blur to me, and when I entered the room where my mother was at again, I didn't know what to say. I plopped down in a chair right beside her bed, just staring at her. She cried out to me, once again, telling me how sorry she was.

"You have to believe me when I say I never meant for this to happen. Michelle and I were on our way to dinner. We had reconciled our differences and everything. All of a sudden, that truck got in my way. It swerved into my lane and I tried my best to avoid it."

I didn't move. She got no response from me, nor did Raynetta when she came into the room, dabbing her watery eyes with tissue.

"Are you listening to me, Stephen?" my mother asked. "I don't know what you're thinking right now, but say something to—"

She coughed and cried. Sobbed more like it, but in no way was I moved. This was it for me. It was the last straw, and after this, as far as I was concerned, my mother had died in that accident too.

"Stephen," Raynetta said as she stood by the door. "Why don't you go—"

She paused when three police officers entered the room. They looked at me and I quickly stood up. I secured the only button on my suit jacket and released another deep sigh.

"Lock her up," I said to the officers. "She needs to go to jail for manslaughter and I want her arrested right now."

One of the officers reached for his handcuffs. And not in the mood to witness any of this go down, I walked out the door, ignoring Raynetta who had more drama to write in her fucking book. I heard one officer read my mother her rights. She screamed after me.

"Stephen, come back here! Clean this shit up and don't you let them do this to me! I will start snitching and believe me when I say your hands are just as dirty as mine! Even more dirty and don't let me tell them the real truth about General Stiles! I know and I will tell it! Tell it all . . ."

Her voice faded as I walked away, feeling like I was floating on air. So many people were speaking to me, but I couldn't hear a thing. I ordered Secret Service to drive me to Michelle's place, and right after I put the key in the door and opened it, her sweet scent hit me. I looked in the empty living room area and then at the clean kitchen where thawed chicken was on the counter. Couldn't help but to think about her cooking dinner for me at the

Farmhouse, and just for a few seconds, I saw her pretty self standing in front of the sink.

"What are you doing here, Mr. President?" she asked. "You know you should've called?"

As she smiled at me, I proceeded down the hallway. One of the pictures on the wall of her beautiful children was crooked. I straightened it and felt a severe pain in my stomach as I'd thought more about them and their future. I walked further down the hallway and into her bedroom. Stood in the doorway for a moment, gazing at the empty bed that was topped with a thick cream-colored comforter and lots of fluffy pillows.

"Since you're here," I envisioned her saying while on the bed. "Come here. I have something I need to show you. I need to tell you something too."

I went into the room and sat on the bed. All I could think about was the multiple times she'd told me she loved me. Me, yet I was so broken and was afraid to hear it. Had lost my father, my son, my wife, my mother and also Michelle. Maybe this was payback for all the fucked up things I'd done, but there was still a lot of good in me too. I just had to find a way to be better, and after this, I would never be the same. Even I wasn't sure what that meant for the future—for now, I felt like one dead president. I lay back on Michelle's bed, grabbed her pillow, inhaled her scent and cried my motherfucking heart out. This was the side of presidents that not too many people witnessed. It was so rough sometimes, and no matter what we endured, we had to quickly bounce back and carry on with the people's business. Tough to do, but make no mistake about it, it had to be done.

CPSIA information can be obtained
at www.ICGtesting.com
Printed in the USA
LVHW03s1754010918
588886LV00002B/463/P